# No Greater
# Love

# No Greater
# Love

*a novel by*

ROBERT J. SMITH

ISBN: 10: 0991355008
ISBN-13: 978-0-9913550-0-6

Published by Freeze Time Media
Cover design: Di Freeze
Illustration: John Freeze

*Dedicated to my wife and best friend, Barbara.*
*You have been there to encourage me and support me all these years.*

# PROLOGUE

OUT THE TRAIN WINDOW the bottom lands of my home state are quickly slipping past. It has been more than seven years since I viewed these lands. These are scenes that I never expected to see again. I never really wanted to see them again. After I buried my mother on that cold December morning, I promised myself that I would never come back. It was a promise I meant to keep. The last link to my past would be gone. I could just go away and forget what happened. Nothing would ever bring me back. Nothing could. I would never have to think about it again. How simple it would be. My past would be buried and all those agonizing memories put behind me. But, much to my displeasure, some memories never go away. I had tried to run from mine. But I couldn't. I know now I never can. So, I'm coming back, coming back to confront the nightmarish memories that I hoped were buried forever.

I will never forget, as scoop after scoop of dirt rained down on Mama's coffin, how terribly unhappy she had been since Papa's death ten years earlier. No more sadness, I thought then. It must have been a joyful reunion that day when she met Papa in Heaven. Their bodies lay side by side here on this earth, but somewhere, with a smile on their faces, they walked hand in hand beside their Lord. In the back chambers of my memory, I can still hear them. More than once I heard Mama tell Papa that she hoped the Lord would see fit to take her first because she couldn't bear living without him. But that hadn't happened. Double pneumonia had taken him while I was in my last year at the university. That morning, as I continued to watch the dirt covering the wooden casket, I glanced toward the small headstone that bore his name and thought about that night ten years earlier when the phone call from old Doc Smith had summoned me from a sound sleep.

"James, boy," he had said when I finally pulled myself out of bed and made my way down the two flights of stairs to the only phone in the old building that served as a dormitory, "You must come home straight away. Your father is very ill and your mother needs you."

I muttered something and heard the old doctor grunt back from the other end of the line. Then the metallic click echoed across the miles and the line went dead.

~ ~ ~

It was early morning when I slipped past Doctor Smith's horse and buggy and opened the old screen door at the front of the house. A deathly quiet hung in the air in that little front room. The bedroom Mama and Papa had shared for as long as I could remember was toward the back of the house and, as I tiptoed toward the glow from the kerosene lamp that shone through the open doorway, I could hear Mama gently humming one of Papa's favorite songs. She was sitting on a straight chair from the kitchen table. Her back was to me. Her left hand was resting on Papa's chest gripped in that once strong left hand. With her right she was brushing a damp cloth back and forth across his brow. The old doctor was on the other side of the bed. He was holding Papa's other wrist and staring down at the gold plated watch that he carried in the pocket of his trousers. I could see his eyes. They were damp behind the wire-rimmed glasses that rested forward on his nose. He saw me first and I could tell by his expression that the news would not be good.

I nodded and eased up behind Mama. When I placed my hand softly on her shoulder, she looked up through eyes filled with tears. Without speaking, she took my hand and held it to her cheek for a moment before she got up and put her arms around me. We stood there holding each other for several minutes before she released me. She nodded toward her chair and motioned for me to take her place. When I slipped into the chair she put Papa's hand in mine.

"Papa, Jamie is here," she whispered and bent over to kiss his forehead. It had been a long time since she had called me Jamie, and it brought back memories that had been dormant for a very long time. Good memories. But there was no time to focus on those now. I knew Papa was dying and, inside, Mama was dying with him.

It was nearly half a minute before he responded but finally and with much effort his eyes slowly opened. During those few seconds when his eyes were still closed, I studied his once rugged face until my eyes finally fell on his hair. It had always been coal black. No longer. It had begun to turn gray at the temples and there were streaks of gray on top. I hadn't noticed that on my last trip home. And now I wondered what else I had missed. Why do we take for granted the ones we love until it's too late? Now, he looked up into my eyes, managed a weak smile and tried to squeeze my hand. The illness was evident even more. The once powerful grip could only make a slight impression on my fingers. I knew then just how ill he was and why my mother's heart was breaking.

I sat there for hours, holding his hand and speaking softly about things I knew would be pleasant memories for him. Now and then he would smile or open his eyes for a moment, then lapse back into a fitful sleep. Before dark Mama raised the intensity of the lamp and placed it across the room so that it wouldn't shine in his eyes. I'm sure he would never have noticed the glow. His breathing was growing more labored with every breath. I wanted to help him but there was nothing I could do. Mama had moved to the other side of the bed and was holding and kissing Papa's other hand. In her own way she was suffering as much as he was. Shortly after dark he died.

Several hours earlier Doctor Smith had left, promising to be back later. A baby was due about ten miles away and a mother was already in labor. I wanted the old doctor to stay but even as I asked him to, I knew he couldn't. He told me before he left that there was nothing more he could do. I think he was hurting nearly as much as we were. He and Papa had watched a number of people pass from this life. Papa had always been there when he was needed, whether at the death of a friend or the joyful birth of a new baby. Papa's life was about to be spent and somewhere down the old road a new life was about to begin. It was God's plan. As he was about to leave, the old doctor came around the bed and placed his hand on my arm. He bent down and quietly whispered that Papa was in God's hands now. Then he was at Mama's side, whispering something in her ear. A moment later he went to the foot of the bed and stood for a few seconds gazing down at Papa. I think he was saying his own goodbye. A moment later he slipped out and was gone. He hadn't returned when Papa's hand went limp in mine.

When he died, I looked across the bed at Mama and she looked back at me. She knew immediately and great tears welled up in her eyes and began to flow slowly down her cheeks. She bent over and kissed Papa lightly on the cheek, then took her handkerchief and lovingly wiped the perspiration from his forehead. I'll never forget the look on her face. I don't think I've ever seen anyone who looked so lonely. It was a look that never really left her throughout the remainder of her life. And now, seventeen years after Papa's death and seven after hers, I'm on this train rushing headlong back toward those memories that made the two of them so dear to me.

~ ~ ~

From the train window I can see the cotton fields white unto harvest as far as the eye can see. We're in the Delta now, the unbearably hot Delta. It must be a hundred degrees here in the train. My clothes are soaked with sweat through and through. At least in here we can open the windows and feel a breeze even though it's a hot breeze. But out there in the fields it must be five or ten degrees hotter. Some things never change. The cotton pickers are everywhere. I can see the men, women and even children, some that look to be no older than five or six, moving slowly down the long dusty rows, pulling partially-filled bags of cotton behind them. I've found myself wondering in the past if those former slaves or their children are any better off now than they were before they were freed. They're still prisoners of their environment. The only difference is the meager pay they receive, pay that barely provides a meal for the night. Their tattered and soiled clothing only begins to reveal the human tragedy they endure day after day, week after week and year after year.

In the distance, small one and two-room unpainted shacks dot the flat countryside. Some of those shacks house as many as a dozen people. These are men, women and children with only heartbreak for a past and misery for a future. The sight revives old memories. It's strange how a person can feel a cold shudder even in this heat. A short distance away an old gray-haired man straightens his frail body, his hands clutching the small of his back on both sides for support. He stares, it seems, directly at me, and raises a thin arm for a moment. Then he bends back to his labor. It's the very old and very young who pause, the old considering what might have been and the young with thoughts of what might yet be. They've all seen the train before. They will see it thousands of times before they depart this earth. In an hour it will travel farther than most of these people will ever move from the spot where they stand. It isn't despair or frustration or even hatred on their faces, but resignation, a quiet calm acceptance of what life has dealt them. I wonder if it will always be that way. I pray it won't. I pray that someday, someone with a dream of a better life for these people will come along and change all this. Until then it will remain pure misery for these forgotten souls.

Several rows ahead and across the aisle, a small boy, perhaps ten or eleven, is sitting next to his mother. I've noticed him for the last hour wandering up and down the aisle. He stopped at my seat a short time ago, gazed into my eyes momentarily then looked forward toward his mother. In those few seconds before he broke contact, I found myself staring into his eyes. As I did, my mind began to wander back over the years. Something about him reminded me of someone. I'm not sure who. On the surface he seemed to be quite calm and peaceful but I wondered what was going on behind that innocent looking face. Is there a touch of deviltry just below the surface or is my imagination working overtime. As if he knew I was studying him, his head tilts to one side and our eyes meet again. Coal black eyes stare back at me as they had earlier. I've seen eyes like that before. For just a moment he holds my gaze then turns back and moves closer to his mother. Just a boy, my mind reasons. Just like any other boy but the sight of him was enough to make me pause and remember.

Memory can be a good thing or a bad thing, but to me, on this long journey home, it has become a mixture of apprehension and sadness. I still feel the guilt. It invades every thought. Over these last years it has made me what I am, I hope for the better. All I have to do is rest my head against the seat and close my eyes and memories of my own childhood slip back into my mind. Some are cherished. I shall never forget Mama bending over the old wood stove in the kitchen preparing the evening meal. In my mind, I can still hear her humming "The Old Rugged Cross" as she labored. It was her favorite church song and now it's mine. Then there was Papa. Papa, how can I tell you about him? To me, he was as unique as any human being I have ever known. He was as big a man as Mama was small; over six feet, with long black hair on his head and a generous portion on his stout chest. I can't remember a time when he didn't sport a black handlebar mustache. When I was just a small sprout, I was fond of crawling up in his lap and running my fingers along that curl. In those innocent times, before I knew better, I always wondered about that mustache and thought how very funny Papa must have looked as a boy.

Though Papa was firm and gave the impression to those outside our family that he was a stern disciplinarian, he was a gentle man who loved Mama and me in a very special way. Not to say that he didn't discipline me, for he did on many occasions. But I had a great deal of respect for Papa. It was something he achieved, not through authority or fear, but, because those of us who knew him were strengthened and made just a little bit better for having passed his way. Everyone felt that way about Papa. He was the unspoken head of all who respected Godly leadership.

He and Mama made a great combination. She was small and fragile and able to sway this big man with just the flicker of a smile. How different she was from him and yet the same in so many ways. While Papa grew up just ten miles to the west, she grew up several hundred miles to the north in Memphis, Tennessee. Papa always got great pleasure out of referring to her as his dainty little city girl. To this "funnin" as Papa referred to his dry wit, Mama would put her hands solidly on her hips, turn her head slightly to one side so that her long black hair would slide down off her shoulder, pucker her lips and pretend anger. Papa would laugh and Mama, unable to continue the charade, would smile and her flashing black eyes would dance like a flame perched atop a candle. They would generally end up kissing and that would be the end of it.

For all the time I knew them, I never heard them fight. Oh, they disagreed at times. But the respect each had for the other was too intense for the disagreements to end any other way but with a hug or kiss. Many times when Papa heard Mama's point of view, he realized she was right and would bow to her way of thinking. But in the end it would be Papa who decided the question and Mama, whether she agreed or not, always respected his decision. She was a firm believer in the Bible and took as gospel the third chapter of the book of First Timothy where it said the husband was to rule his own house. To Mama there was no gray area in that verse.

Papa would be gone sometimes for a week or more at a time and it was during these times that Mama seemed different. She was sad, almost displaced. As I recall now, it was much the same look that crossed her face when Papa died, only not nearly as intense. When he was away she knew he would be home soon. Being away a lot was expected of a circuit riding Baptist preacher. And Papa was some kind of hell-fire and brimstone man in the pulpit. Sometimes he got so carried away that his face seemed to light up like the very fires of Hell, from which he was so desperately trying to divert us.

As he traveled his circuit to reach different congregations, he rode a big black stallion that he named Satan. He bought Satan as a colt and trained him to be the finest saddle horse known to anyone in the territory. In one of his lighter moments in the pulpit, I remember him telling the congregation that he was striving daily to keep on top of Satan. Not being used to humor from the pulpit, most of the people never understood the irony of Papa's joke. Most assuredly, as long as I knew him, the devil never rose above his heel. Because of his strength and courage and that of two black men that I shall always love and respect, the disaster that came to my life and the life of our small community was much less than what it might have been. Memories....some were good and some were bad. But very few could be worse than those that still haunt me from that miserably hot summer so long ago. Those are the kind of memories that change lives forever. They did mine and I know they did others. Some good things happened because of the circumstances but much more went wrong, very wrong. And because of those things that went so terribly wrong, I shall always be haunted.

# CHAPTER 1

THE SUMMER OF 1899, the eleventh year of my life, started much the same as all the other summers I could remember. My name is James Edward Peterson and on that hot June afternoon several of us boys were making our way home from our last day of school. I was clutching my last grade card tightly. Something special was promised if my grades were good and I was sure Papa and Mama would be proud of the results of my fifth year in school. As we walked down the dusty road, one of the boys slapped me on the arm and yelled "You're it." The game was on and as we ran and laughed we got closer and closer to our houses. Like always, one by one the boys began to drop off until only my best friend, Eddie Carter, and I remained. Eddie and I lived only a stone's throw from each other and were together as much as possible. Now, as school was dismissed for the summer, we looked forward to a time of swimming in the old pond, secret sharing, and all the other activities that eleven-year-olds live for. We knew each other very well and I could tell whenever something was bothering Eddie, and he knew me the same way. As boys were then, and are to this day, we were apt to find many interesting ways to get ourselves into hot water. And now that we were alone, Eddie caught my arm and pulled me to a stop.

"Jamie, can you meet me down by the old oak tree at the end of the road in a few minutes?"

"Why?" I asked and bent over to examine a small rip in the right knee of my new overalls. It had happened while we were wrestling during the morning recess and I knew then I would be very lucky if I wasn't punished. New overalls didn't happen very often and I knew as well as anyone that I was expected to make them last as long as possible. Mama would be upset. Then I remembered the grade card and smiled, hoping she would make allowances.

"Can't tell ya now," Eddie was saying. "It's somethin' special though, somethin' you ain't gonna wanta miss. You comin'?"

I tried to smooth out the damaged overall knee so it wouldn't show right away and nodded. The rip was still visible. "I reckon, less'n Mama has me some chore to do."

Eddie looked around anxiously, as if someone was spying on us just to learn what special secret he was hiding. "Well, if'n she don't, you be there. You hear?"

"Yeah." I answered and Eddie moved off toward his house. By the time I was halfway home, I had already forgotten about Eddie's secret, whatever it might be. My mind was on the grade card still clutched in my hand. I ran through the gate and up on the porch, fully expecting to find Mama waiting anxiously for my arrival. She wasn't in the front living room.

"Mama," I shouted, "I'm home. Come and see my grade card." She didn't answer. I searched the little four-room house, checking the kitchen last. I finally saw her out the back kitchen door. She was down on her hands and knees digging in the garden, some hundred steps behind the house. I pushed open the door and ran out on the porch and down the plank steps.

"Mama, look at my card and read the note Miss Crowe sent with it."

She got up and brushed the black hair back from her eyes. As she did, I glanced toward the pen where Satan normally was. He was gone. Papa was not home. Only he rode Satan.

"Quickly, James. Let me see what you have." As her eyes studied the card, I noticed a flicker of a smile appear then broaden. "Oh, my! This is good. You have made this day special. And your father will be very pleased, very pleased indeed." She handed the card back to me and opened the folded note. As she did, I glanced down at the rip in the right knee of my overalls and was happy to see that it was hardly visible. Still, I wanted to be sure that she didn't see it just yet so I turned my right knee away from her just enough so that she would be looking at the side of my leg.

I watched as she read the note and my chest filled with pride at the sight of her smile. She was nodding her head as she read and evidently in very good spirits about everything. I thought that this might be the right time for her to see the rip, but I didn't turn so she could see it. I would wait. I didn't want to destroy the moment. When she finished, she put her arm around my shoulder and kissed me on the forehead.

"This is very good, James. Miss Crowe says you've done very well and that we should be proud of you. And I am. Your father will be too."

I looked toward Satan's pen and then the barn another fifty steps to the west. "Where is Papa?" I knew he wasn't scheduled to make the circuit for another two weeks and my mind was on the special reward that he had promised. Mama must have suspected as much, for she laughed and ran her hand through my hair in that special way of hers.

"He'll be back by supper time and I think there might be something special for such a good report."

But I was impatient. "Where is he?"

"Visiting Mr. Plyler. He's been sick and Papa was concerned about him. He'll be home soon. Go put the card and note away and we'll give him a nice surprise when he gets here."

"Yes, Mama," I said and started toward the house. Then I remembered Eddie and his secret. "Mama," I said turning back toward her, "can I go and see Eddie for a little while?"

She glanced up, brushing the hair back over her shoulder. "I suppose, but you must come home shortly. Supper will be on the table soon and your father will be upset if he has to chase you down like he had to last night. You don't want him to be upset with you, not on this special day."

"No, Mama. I won't be long, I promise." I turned back toward the house and started to run when she spoke again.

"And, James, please don't be roughhousing. We don't want that rip in your overalls to get any bigger than it already is. I'll need to stitch it after supper."

This stopped me in my tracks and I turned back toward her. Just the glint of a smile covered her face as she looked into my eyes. I dropped my gaze to the rip, no more evident than it had been a few moments before. When I looked back up the smile was still there. I could only nod and whisper.

"Yes, Mama. I'll be careful."

She only nodded her head and dropped back to her knees, digging once more in the black garden dirt. I watched for a few moments, then slowly turned and made my way back to the house. In the kitchen I dropped the card and note on the table and ran out the front door. I headed down the dusty road toward the old oak tree, suddenly anxious to find out what dark secret Eddie could not tell me just yet. I was sure it was some mischief he had planned for the summer. Papa had told me that mischief was Eddie's middle name and I should be very wary of following him too closely. On a number of occasions I found that to be true but Eddie's mischief could be interesting at times. He never seemed to be satisfied with normal games. Some deviltry was always involved. And sometimes it could be mean-spirited. Only last Halloween Eddie had talked me into slipping down to where several black families lived along the river. One particular family had an outhouse on the riverbank and on that particular evening it was Eddie's idea of a high old time to turn their outhouse over into the river. Only after the deed was done and all manner of yelling and cursing was heard from the inside of the slowly sinking outhouse did we realize that the building was occupied at the time.

And while the occupant was able to escape, it became a matter of much discussion in our small community. While we both acted as if it was a terrible deed, Eddie could not stop laughing when we were alone. I felt very guilty and swore never to follow Eddie's lead again. Another incident occurred just last month when Eddie and another boy, Pete Brady, caught a dog and cat, tied their tails to the opposite ends of a ten foot rope and let them down out in the woods. To hear Eddie tell the story, the next few minutes were only rivaled by the outhouse incident. This last deed made me even more wary of Eddie's pranks. My half-hearted scolding only made him laugh more. Now, I found myself running past his house, knowing all the while that I would probably regret it. And regret it I did.

~ ~ ~

The old oak tree was about five hundred steps from my own home and about half that far from Eddie's. It stood at the edge of a dirt road that ran past both our houses. No other dwellings were nearby and because of this we went there to play quite often. Eddie heard me coming and as I drew near, he poked his head around the tree and I saw that sly grin appear on his face. To this day I wish I had turned and run for home, but I didn't. He motioned me around to the other side, out of sight of our houses, which stood on the outskirts of our little community.

"Whatcha got?" I whispered warily, with just a touch of excitement.

Eddie patted his overall pocket and brushed the blond hair out of his eyes. It was Eddie's nature to kid anyone he could and now he seemed to be relishing the idea of letting me wait until he was ready to reveal his secret. He had shed his shirt and shoes and was busy twisting the big toe of his left foot in the thick dust at the base of the tree. He seemed to be spelling my name out in the dust and, at the same time, trying my patience. Again I asked him what was so important but he only grinned and ignored me. When he was satisfied that he had aggravated me enough, he glanced around the tree toward my house and his. I was losing patience and about to tell him so when he put a dirty finger up to his lips to quiet my inquisitive tongue. I turned away hoping to make him think I had lost interest in his secret.

"Just hush, Jamie boy, and I'll tell ya."

"I ain't got long, Eddie. Papa'll be home most any time and Mama said I should hurry back before...."

Eddie put a finger to his lips again and reached into the overall pocket he had patted a few moments earlier. When he pulled his hand out, there were two thin pieces of wrinkled, soiled paper that must have been white and smooth at one time.

"Here," he said and handed one of the rumpled pieces of paper to me. His hand went deep into the overall pocket again and he drew out a small dirty white bag with a drawstring pulled tight. A bright smile lit his face as he held it up toward me and winked. Then, as if he thought someone might be spying on him, he again looked around the tree and up the dirt road in the direction of our houses. Satisfied that no one was about, he turned back and grinned that devilish grin of his.

"Know what them are?" As he spoke, he let his body slide slowly down the tree until he was sitting in the dust with his back against the trunk.

I dropped to my knees facing him and stuck the paper out toward him. Already, it was beginning to feel hot in my hands. "I ain't dumb, Eddie Carter. Them's the makins you got there. I seen old Mr. Fitch rollin' them down at your Pa's store lotsa times." I shoved the paper at him again, right up against his chest. He only grinned as he took it back.

"Where'd you git um?" As he had moments before, now I stole a glance around the tree to see if anyone could hear us talking. I was beginning to feel guilty and I had done nothing wrong. At least, I hadn't yet.

Eddie dropped his head for a moment, and his face brightened. "I sneaked them when Pa was in the storeroom yestidy. But it ain't stealin' cause Pa told me that the store and everything in it would be mine one of these here days."

"Yeh, but it ain't yours yet."

Eddie wasn't listening to me now. He had opened the bag of tobacco and begun to pour some of the brown fragments onto one of the papers. Then, as if he heard something, he stopped and searched the bushes first to the right and then the left. His eyes moved back and forth until he was satisfied we were alone. Then he concentrated again on the tobacco he was spreading on the paper. Though, like me, he had watched many of his Pa's customers doing it in the past, he still was clumsy and spilled most of the tobacco on the ground before he had the paper covered. "Pete Brady told me his Pa let him take a coupla puffs a time back. Said it was real tasty." When he finished filling the paper to his satisfaction, he slid his tongue along the edge. Some of the mixture came off in his mouth and he made a sour face and spit in the dirt between his legs. What he wasn't able to spit out, he wiped off his tongue with the back of his dusty hand. He poked the empty paper toward me again. "This un's yours."

"Unh unh. Papa would skin me alive. He don't hold with no tobacco. Says it's the devil's weed. I ain't wantin' it." I got up from my knees and moved away from Eddie. "Sides, you said Pete said it was tasty. Ain't likely seein' the face you just made."

He dropped the other cigarette paper in his lap and stuck the roughly manufactured cigarette in his mouth. "I surely didn't want to be a believin' it about you, but I reckon it weren't no lie." He reached over to a rock and struck a match that had suddenly appeared in his hand. Now, as he stuck the lighted match to the end of the cigarette, he pretended to ignore me. Finally, he leaned back against the tree trunk, took a draw on the cigarette and acted as if it were the greatest thing in the world. "Never thought old Pete was right about you," he muttered.

"What you talkin' about?" I repeated the question and moved slightly closer to Eddie.

He was grinning broadly and blowing smoke out as he had seen others do at his Pa's store. My anger had led me into the trap. "Pete Brady....he said you was a sissy. Said you didn't have no backbone. I told him he was crazy. I said you ain't no sissy, but......"

Eddie shrugged his shoulders and let his words trail off before poking the cigarette back into his mouth. He took a long puff, took it out of his mouth, blew smoke and shrugged his shoulders again. "Didn't want to believe it, but....." Again, he stopped in mid-sentence.

I wanted to hit him square on his nose. Deep down I knew what he was doing. Instead, I reached for the paper in his lap. "Gimme that."

But he clamped his hand over the single paper. "What about your Pa. He'll tan your hide if'n he finds out you been smokin."

The sight of Papa and his strap appeared in my mind, a strap he always said he used because he loved me. To that notion, my back end took exception.

Before I could change my mind, Eddie shoved the paper and the bag toward me. "He ain't gonna catch you, Jamie, cause we're gonna be real careful." He took a big puff and leaned his head back against the oak tree. "Boy, oh boy. Ain't that good," he whispered and blew out another puff of smoke. As he did, he pointed toward the paper and bag and nodded impatiently. "Want me to help ya?"

"Don't need no help. I seen it done, too." I opened the bag of tobacco and with the paper in my left hand, I began pouring it slowly on the thin tissue. Old Mr. Fitch, with gnarled hands was able to do it and I knew I could too. When I was sure I had the right amount on the paper, I rolled it together and licked the open edge. As it had with Eddie, some of the foul ingredients came away with my tongue. Just like Eddie's, my face screwed up from the taste. It was nearly as bad as some of the medicine Mama gave me during the winter.

"That's foul tastin' stuff," I said and spit on the ground. I looked from one side of the road to the other. The bushes looked ominous. Was someone in there watching everything we were doing? Had Eddie set me up? Was Pete Brady watching? I froze for a moment, listening and watching. Nothing was there, nothing but my own imagination, my own fear. I looked at Eddie and saw the glint in his eyes. He had me and we both knew it.

He laughed and glanced to the side of the road. Then, as if dismissing the thought of someone watching, he said. "Yeah, but just you wait till you git a taste of it all lit up."

Hesitantly, I stuck the end in my mouth and Eddie reached over to the rock and struck another match. He held it to my cigarette and I watched the white paper begin to turn black.

"Puff real slow like," he whispered.

I did and all of a sudden I felt the heat flow all the way through the thing. I puffed it slowly once then took it out of my mouth. Somewhere down in my chest a fire had been lit. I tried to say something to Eddie but I could only cough and motion with my hands. It was the most foul tasting thing I ever put in my mouth, worse right then than the castor oil Mama forced down me on the night I spent running between the house and the outhouse. That was the night I was proud that Papa had seen fit to make our outhouse a two-holer. Though, for the life of me, I can't begin to see how he could have foreseen the trouble I was to have. For that night I was in sad shape. My stomach was causing me to give up my supper from both ends at the same time and the second hole came in very handy. If I had been Mama that night, I might have washed my hands of the whole mess. Now, I had managed to get myself into another predicament. It took half a minute or more but my lungs finally began to cool. But the coughing persisted. All the while, my good friend, Eddie was doubled up against the tree laughing.

"Jamie, you ought to see your puss. You look like you swallowed half the swimmin' hole. Ain't never seen nothin' so funny in all my born days." He was having a riotous time at my expense. I should have realized right then that friends don't enjoy seeing friends in distress. I know that now but then I only wanted to prove that I was as good or as bad, in this case, as him.

"It ain't funny. That thing burns somethin' fierce. How come it didn't burn and make you cough like me?" It was all I could do to get the words out and now I noticed the raspy sound my voice had taken on.

Eddie leaned back against the tree and took another puff. "Guess some got the knack and some ain't." He looked pleased with himself, as much for trapping me as he was for showing his superiority in such an adventure. I was to find out he began the foul practice a week earlier and had fared little better than me when Pete introduced him to the filthy habit. "Never you mind, Jamie, boy. We got all summer and I'll learn you all there is to know 'bout it."

To my own amazement, I found the cigarette still lodged between the forefinger and middle finger of my right hand. "I ain't learnin' nothin', cause I ain't smokin' no more." I flicked it to the ground and started to step on it, but Eddie must have suspected my intentions. He pounced on it before I could cover it with my foot.

"Hey, Jamie, boy. Don't waste none. Too many good puffs left." Eddie brushed the dirt off the unlit end and lay it on a root beside him. My announcement that I was finished with smoking didn't seem to faze him.

"Ain't no use tryin' to change my thinkin'," I continued. "Ain't no use a'tall."

He resumed puffing on his own weed and shook his head again. "Guess old Pete was right. Guess you ain't got no spine fer grown up things after all." Eddie shook his head sadly, but there was still the hint of a smile creasing his lips.

I could feel the crimson rising in my face. "I got just as much spine as Pete Brady any ol' day. I can run faster and swim better and I ain't 'fraid of snakes like he is," I protested vigorously. I believe I would have fought Pete right then if he had been there, though I should have known that Eddie was only leading me into a rage that he knew would eventually trap me.

"Ain't me that said it," Eddie protested and raised his hands in a gesture of surrender. "Pete, he said it. But I reckon if you ain't got no stomach for it like me and Pete, you better wait till you grow a bit more."

It was all I could stand. I snatched the cigarette from the tree root and held it for a long moment, looking down at it as if it might explode and take my hand with it. Out of the corner of my eye, I saw Eddie watching me intently. Obviously, he already had a smart remark ready in case I didn't stick the thing in my mouth. This time, as I took a quick drag, I was more prepared for the hot, sour taste. Though it didn't burn as much and I was able to control the cough, the taste still didn't appeal to me. I had just settled down beside Eddie with my back against the tree when I heard the sound of horses hooves in the distance. They were getting louder by the second, definitely coming our way. My first thought was of Papa. It was about the right time for him to be coming home. I jumped up and dropped the cigarette at my feet, stomping it out quickly. Eddie had also heard the sound and was quick to follow my lead. He grabbed the tobacco bag and stuffed it back in his overall pocket. Then, with his right foot, he scooted the two cigarettes up against the tree and covered them with dirt. While he was doing that, I flailed away at the dirt and threw it into the air around us. The dust intermingled with the smoke until it made an adequate camouflage. It was that moment that Papa and Satan appeared around the bend of the dirt road. They were moving at a gallop and would be on us in a few seconds.

Eddie poked me with his elbow. "Let's race to my house." He was off before I could answer.

I looked quickly at the suspicious dust and smoke and nodded, hoping Pa would only think we stirred it up scuffling. Then I was off in pursuit of Eddie. About halfway to his house I heard Satan draw close up behind. I didn't turn and look up at Papa until the big horse drew even.

"What are you boys up to?"

"Nothin', Papa." I returned. I was thankful the sound of my voice was no longer raspy.

"Don't you think it's a little warm to be scuffling and running about in such a manner?"

"Oh, no, Papa. We race a lot. It's fun." At least I wasn't lying. We took great joy in running foot races.

"We like to race, Mr. Preacher," Eddie added sheepishly.

"Hmmm," Papa murmured as he braced himself on his saddle horn and glared down at both of us as if we had smoke coming from our noses. I glanced at Eddie but he seemed no different than ever, maybe a bit whiter than usual. I knew he was just as scared as me. His eyes were averted to his toes where he was playing again in the dirt. "Your mother will be preparing the evening meal," Papa continued without taking his eyes off me. "You best come right along home, James." With that he patted Satan on the right flank. "Come, boy." The big horse responded and moved off down the road toward our house.

I breathed properly for the first time in several minutes and started to follow him when Eddie grabbed my arm. He reached into his overall pocket. I started to pull away from him when he pulled out a piece of hard candy and thrust it toward me. "Here, you want them to smell you? Put this in your mouth and suck on it till it's gone. When you git home, drink lots of water and don't git close to your Ma or Pa till you hafta. Pete said that water covers the smell." Then he reached down and grabbed a handful of dirt and pitched it into the air above both our heads. "That'll help cover the smell." I was to find out much later that Pete Brady didn't know what he was talking about when it came to covering the smell of tobacco.

Innocently, I took the candy and slipped it into my mouth. I didn't have a whole lot of confidence that Eddie knew what he was talking about but he was the only one I could trust at this moment. "How long till I quit smellin'?"

"Dunno," Eddie said with a shrug of his shoulders. "But I ain't goin' home till I gotta."

"We almost got caught. I sure am glad that's over."

Eddie nodded and a serious look came over his face. "Yeah, we gotta be smarter, find a better place to do our smokin', maybe down by the old swamp. Ain't nobody down there much, what with snakes and gators and such."

"I ain't about to do no more smokin'," I protested shaking my head vigorously. But when Eddie gave me that look he always did when he was about to cut me down, I knew I would.

Without another word, I turned and trudged up the road toward home. I went directly to the well behind the house and drank several dippers of water. When I finished I was so water-logged I wondered if I would be able to eat anything at all. Then I made the proper amount of noise to let Mama know I was in the yard. It wasn't long before she came to the back door and called to me.

"Time for supper, James."

"Yes, Mama. I'm coming."

Quickly, I retreated to the well again and gulped down some more water. I could hardly move now. Still, I managed to burst into the kitchen and run through as Mama would expect. I ran to the bedroom to get the card and note, but remembered leaving it in the kitchen. Papa was seated at the table talking to Mama when I came back in. The card and note were not in sight, but Mama, realizing what I was looking for, nodded toward the butter churn at one end of the kitchen cabinet. The card and note were tucked safely under the edge of the churn.

"Papa. I have my grade card and a note from Miss Crowe." I could feel the smile spread across my face as I spoke.

His expression didn't change as he held out his massive hand. "Let me see it, James."

I handed it to him and Mama came over behind him. She rested her hands on his two strong shoulders as he studied the card. She was smiling the way she always did when she was proud of something Papa did or said. But, this time the smile was for me. The escapade of the last hour with Eddie made me feel just a little ashamed but I tried to focus on Papa as he read the note and studied the grade card.

"Well, son, it looks as if you've been studying," Papa said matter-of-factly while looking me straight in the eyes. "Do you think you've done your best?

I hesitated a moment, thinking of all the times I knew I could have done better. Then I crossed my fingers behind my back and told what I considered a very small but necessary fib. "Yes sir, I think I did the best I could."

Papa leveled his gaze at me and studied my face for a moment. It seemed he was looking right into my thoughts. Finally, he said. "There was only one who could do no better, James. For He was perfect already. And that was our Lord." As I dropped my head and studied the dirt between my toes, Papa hesitated. "Remember that there is room for improvement in all of us, James." I sneaked a look up at his face, fearful that I had lost my promised reward. Just a hint of a smile creased Papa's lips as he spoke again. "But I must say this is quite a good report and Miss Crowe seems very pleased with your effort."

I looked up at Mama and the smile was still there. I knew then that all was not lost.

"Ellen, hand me that box in the cabinet," Papa said looking up from the note.

I watched her go to the cabinet and move a stack of dishes to the side. A small black box was hidden toward the back. She handed it to Papa and he passed it on to me. "There are rewards for those who work hard and do what's right." Papa said. "Remember that. Always do what is right," he said again with emphasis.

"Yes, Papa," I said and opened the lid. There, resting on a bed of cotton, was the little black pocketknife, the same one I had seen at Mr. Carter's store several weeks earlier when I was helping Mama with her shopping. I looked up at her, knowing she had told Papa what I had been so interested in that day. She nodded and continued to smile.

I threw my arms around my father and hugged his neck with all my strength. "Thank you, Papa," I whispered into his ear. "Thank you." I felt his arms go around my small body and pull me closer. For several moments we remained there motionless. It was a special feeling, for it was very seldom that Papa showed his love in a physical way. If I wanted a hug, it would be Mama that gave it. Now, I held on as long as possible. Finally, I felt Mama's gentle touch on my shoulder.

"James, go and wash," she said quietly. "Supper will be on the table when you get through. And after we finish, you must take off your overalls so I can mend the hole."

"But, first, James, you must give your mother a hug. This present is from her as well," Papa said. He patted me on the back while releasing his grip. It seemed as if he was just as reluctant to end the moment as I was. When I stepped back and looked at Mama, she was still smiling. I noticed just the trace of dampness in the corners of her eyes. I savored the moment for just a second then gave her a hug and turned and went out on the porch to wash.

# CHAPTER 2

THOSE FIRST FEW WEEKS of summer were great fun. A few days Mama let me sleep as late as I wanted. If not for the heat, I might have spent half of those mornings in bed. It was not unusual to wake up drenched with sweat from the night before. As a consequence sleeping late was very difficult. On some of those oppressively hot days I was out of bed, dressed, and ready for breakfast before Papa. He found that strange. More than once he remarked that just a few short weeks before he had been forced to raise his voice to me when I lingered in the bed trying to get that extra wink of sleep. On those days I had nothing to look forward to except school. Now my days were filled with excitement and adventure. I still had my chores. I couldn't get out of them. But I had made a deal with Papa. If I did them early and did them right, I could take the rest of the day for myself. I considered that a good deal and on the days when I didn't sleep late, I finished most of them by the time Mama had breakfast on the table.

Without exception the boys in our community loved to swim. I was no different. Around the middle of the morning we would gather around the big oak tree down the road from my house and head out for the swimming hole. We were all good swimmers. Even so, the pond was not very deep or very far across so our parents weren't too anxious. I told Mama once that if I went under I could walk out before I drowned. Mama still warned me every time she knew that was where we were heading. The old pond was a secluded place perhaps a half-mile from our community. Very few besides us ever ventured near. Because it was so secluded, we would spend most of the morning just as bare to the skin as old Lem Moseley's bald-head. The only time we had to worry about being seen would be when some lady would venture by picking berries or going from her house to a neighbors. On those occasions we had to bury ourselves in the water until she was out of sight. A time or two one or the other of us boys would be too far from the water when a lady passed by and she would get an even greater shock than we would. Invariably it seemed as if women had nothing to do but aggravate us. I'm sure they happened up on us by accident. But there were others who made it a point to aggravate us. Papa always said that jealousy was a sin. He also said your sins would find you out. We had a real example of that early in the summer.

I found out after the fact that some of the girls were jealous of our swimming hole. They had no place to call their own, no swimming hole where they could bare their own nakedness. It irritated them to such a degree that they decided to teach us a lesson. On one particular morning some of the older girls decided they would work some mischief on us. We had an unwritten law. The pond was off limits to the female sex when we were swimming. The reason was obvious. But there was a flaw. The girls did not respect our law. They had been devising a plan since the first week in June. Once they decided on a day and they were sure we were at the pond, they would slip up to the swimming hole and steal our clothes. Then they would taunt us while we begged them to go away. Our clothes were always hanging on some bushes in plain sight. All the girls thought it was a good plan. While some of them were not anxious to view a bunch of naked boys, all of them thought how great it would be to put us in a panic. On another day with another set of circumstances, their plan might have been perfect. But it was not to be on this day.

They weren't prepared for what they encountered that morning. They didn't know about Tommy Watson and his stomach. Tommy was just a year older and a good fifty pounds heavier than most of us. He had experienced a terrible time with his stomach the night before. Most of the night had been spent with him traveling back and forth between his house and their outhouse. Because of his troubles that night, it was a good thing his father had built the outhouse close to the back door of their house. But the next morning he had gotten up and, feeling somewhat better, eaten a large breakfast. That was a mistake. It turned out that his stomach was not ready for the biscuits and greasy gravy that his mother, Irma, had prepared that morning.

By the time he knew we would be congregating by the old tree to head for the swimming hole, his stomach was queasy and growling quite loud. But Tommy would have it no other way. Without telling his mother he felt bad again, he started toward the door, throwing back over his shoulder where he was headed. His mother tried to persuade him not to go swimming that morning. But all her pleading had gone unheeded and now he was here. He was fine that first hour. Not wanting to aggravate his stomach condition, Tommy slipped slowly into the water and was resting against the cool bank in an effort to calm his growling stomach. The rest of us were splashing about in the water. We were dunking each other and generally roughhousing as we always did in the pond. After a few minutes we got tired of that and scurried out onto the bank, ready to explore other avenues of excitement.

An old oak tree rose right at the side of the pond and last year we had secured a rope to the end of a branch that protruded out over the water. It allowed us to swing out and drop into about six or seven feet of water. Since we were all good swimmers, no one feared the water's depth. On this morning everyone but Tommy had taken two turns on the rope. And though his stomach had settled some, he decided he didn't feel well enough to take a turn. But we were relentless and wouldn't let Tommy off the hook so easily. We began teasing him unmercifully until he finally gave up. I could tell as he climbed up to a point about fifteen or twenty feet above the ground that he was less than excited about the prospect. We pulled the rope over to him and he grasped it in both hands. Even from the ground I could see his face was white. He had never been afraid and I knew he wasn't now. Tommy was sick and all of a sudden I wanted to yell for him not to do it. But about that moment his feet left the oak limb and he swept out over the water as he usually did. Once, twice he made the pass. The third time he let go and, as usual, landed flat on his belly. The sound and Tommy's cry could be heard for half a mile. But the sound was not the problem. It was the jar of landing on his belly. It further irritated the problems of the previous night.

Tommy couldn't get to dry ground soon enough. The last time we saw him he was thrashing through the underbrush in search of a private spot. He found it, or so he thought, some fifty feet downwind from our splashing. In his haste, he had rushed past where our clothes hung and now they were between Tommy and the pond. It was there that he settled down to take care of urgent business. Hunkered down where he was, he was well hidden and comfortable and most probably daydreaming.

I'm sure the girls had heard his outcry. But they were totally unaware of Tommy's dilemma. They had been sneaking through the underbrush, moving slowly in the direction of our clothes. About a hundred feet downwind of the pond, they were crawling along through the high grass being very quiet so we wouldn't know they were about. Our clothes were in plain sight and they had taken a path that would lead directly to them.

Tommy was directly between the girls and the clothes. One girl, Matilda Mooney, a rather large girl who wore glasses and seemed to be the undisputed female leader, was in front with three other girls close behind. They were moving very slowly, trying to keep the bushes from swaying so that we would not suspect anything. When they were about twenty or thirty feet from Tommy, one of the girls tugged on Matilda's shirt and quietly whispered something about strange sounds in the bushes just ahead of them. But, Matilda, whose idea this whole episode had been, only shook her head and continued on. The other girls followed obediently.

Matilda was concerned only with whether the sounds of splashing and laughing were coming from the pond. As long as that noise continued, she thought, they were not being observed. You can understand her consternation when she finally broke through an especially thick barrier of bushes and was confronted with a frightening sight. Her first impression was that she had happened upon a great large chicken in the process of laying an egg. By the time her eyes and mind focused properly on what she was really seeing, the scream that escaped her throat must certainly have been heard all the way back in our community. The other girls were right behind her. They took one quick look, screamed nearly as loud as she did, and lit out full speed for home with Matilda leading the way.

As for the girls, I don't know how long it took for the shock to wear off. Their damage was purely psychological. It wasn't for Tommy. He spent the next fifteen minutes alone in the swimming hole. The girls had scared him as much as the vision of him had scared them and in his haste to exit in the opposite direction, he had taken a spill in the worst of places. His bath finished our swimming for that day and several others. The incident gave us, and I'm sure the girls too, an interesting topic to discuss in those first weeks of summer. Needless to say, the girls did not come close to our swimming hole again and for a long time afterward the two groups gave each other a wide berth wherever they came in contact. I have always thought it would have been very interesting to have been there the next time Tommy and Matilda came face to face. I wish that had been the major incident that summer but it wasn't. Our lives were to be drastically changed in those next few days and all because of something I could have prevented.

~ ~ ~

The smoking had not become a daily habit yet. We did sneak off at various times, either down near the swamp, or in a secret place close to the swimming hole. Sometimes, if Eddie's mother and sister were not home and we felt hurried, we would slip under Eddie's house for a quick smoke. I still hadn't grown to like it as much as Eddie, but as the habit became more frequent, I felt less fearful of the consequences. The addiction to a sinful act was dulling my senses more and more. Once I even suggested that we have a smoke before nightfall. I found myself encouraging Eddie as much as he had me. We were always careful when we smoked, careful to pick a time when our parents were less likely to catch us and we had plenty of time to get the foul smell off our bodies. Now that I think back, we must have looked an awful sight with that ugly thing sticking out of our mouths. Silly little boys trying to blow smoke rings, playing with fire.

Fire, how that word has haunted me since that fateful summer.

# CHAPTER 3

IT WAS ANOTHER ONE of those hot, stifling days, the first Saturday in July when it all began. I got up soon after the sun appeared and, like many other days that summer, finished most of my chores before Mama had breakfast on the table. The night had been miserable. Not a breath of air was moving and I was just glad to be able to get out of my bed. I remember that Myrtle only gave a quarter bucket of milk that morning no matter how much I coaxed her. She was feeling the heat just as we were. For the last month Papa had been threatening to get rid of her if she didn't start producing more. But he was as fond of her as Mama and I were so he continued to put off what he said must be done. That particular morning, for some unknown reason, Mama was more cheerful than usual despite the heat.

She smiled as I came in the back door and motioned for me to put the milk bucket on the cabinet. "And how was Myrtle this morning, James?"

I held out the bucket and frowned. "If she don't do no better soon, I'm feared Papa might sell her or somethin'." To me Myrtle was part of the family and I couldn't stand the thought of getting rid of her.

Mama took the bucket and set it on the cabinet. "Afraid, James, not feared."

"Ma'am?"

"You said you were feared Papa might sell Myrtle."

"Yes, Ma'am, I am feared he might."

"James, feared is not the proper word. The proper word is afraid. You're afraid Papa might sell her."

"Oh," I said and scratched my head. "Ain't that what I said?"

Mama laughed and ruffled my hair a bit. "Papa knows what must be done. He is always looking out for what is best for you and me. Still, I'm sure he will discuss anything as important as selling Myrtle with us before he does so."

"Mama, if Myrtle don't keep producin' maybe we could keep her and get another cow for the milk."

"My gracious, at the extravagance," Mama said. "Do you think your Papa is made out of money? A good milk cow might cost ten or twelve dollars. And it costs a lot of money to feed a cow that isn't producing."

I nodded knowing all the while that sooner or later the inevitable would happen. Myrtle would be gone and some new cow would take her place. The thought made me sad.

I shook it off quickly. "Mama, I'm done with my chores. Can I go play with Eddie?"

"I suppose. But you must be on time for the noon meal. I don't want you going all day without something in your stomach."

"Yes, ma'am," I said and ran out the back door and down the trail towards Eddie's. It was as hot a day as I could remember. Before we would even get started playing, we would be drenched with sweat. So I was sure it would be the swimming hole for us. We spent the entire morning there, only getting out at noon to eat. Our intentions were to head back for the swimming hole after we ate, but instead we changed our minds, or should I say Eddie changed our minds, and decided to go down to Mr. Carter's general store and watch some of the men play checkers. I didn't know too much about the game myself, but I did enjoy seeing one or the other players making those long jumps. And then there were the stories about the old days the men would tell. I especially enjoyed hearing stories about the war between the North and South.

Old Lige Sanders was the one that nearly always won the checker games. He had a long white beard and must have been nearly eighty.

Lige was bent at the waist and walked with a pronounced limp. A cannon shell during a Civil War battle had landed too close. It was said that he nearly died. As a result he had a crooked hand-made cane that he used to get around. Years before someone had made him a set of wooden false teeth and now and then he would take them out and put them on the table next to the checkerboard. I was not a witness, but on one occasion he got so excited after making a double jump that he pounded the table so hard his teeth bounced off and landed in a barrel of pickles. I'm not so sure who was the most disturbed about the incident—Mr. Carter, who swore that he would have to empty the whole barrel of pickles or poor Mr. Sanders who had to fish his teeth out of the briny mess. In any case it was a long time before Mr. Sanders took his teeth out again. And I don't think Mr. Carter ever cleaned out the pickle barrel. I didn't eat any pickles for a long time after that happened.

On this Saturday the game was well in progress by the time Eddie and I arrived at the store. Five or six men were gathered around the table and, as usual, Lige was the center of activity. As we came in, Eddie let the screen door slam a little harder than normal—he had a tendency to draw attention to himself—and all eyes turned our way. The looks on their faces told us we were not the most welcome of spectators. Even Eddie's father frowned when he saw us. I paused and would have left quickly, but Eddie grabbed my shirt and pulled me toward the board game. We went around the counter where he climbed up and let his legs dangle over so he could get a better view over the men's shoulders. I looked from Eddie, to the men hovered around the game, to the old screen door at the front of the store. I wanted to go back to the swimming hole but Eddie was having none of that. When I hesitated, he motioned for me to join him and, with all eyes staring in my direction, I put the cool water out of my mind and pulled myself up on the counter beside Eddie.

Mr. Carter was leering at me. The man scared me. For some reason he didn't like me. I knew it was wrong but I felt the same about him. He wasn't a big man, only about five and a half feet with the same color blond hair that Eddie had. He was quite a bit older than Mrs. Carter, maybe fifteen years or so. His face was dark with a ruddy complexion. Sometime, many years ago, someone had left his mark on that face. A two-inch scar stretched from his right ear to the base of his jawbone. He was getting up in years and age had begun to hide the scar. But you could still see that he had been in some kind of brawl. Like old Lige, the story he told Eddie was that he had received the injury in the War Between the States. But the man didn't seem the type to participate in anything that had a cause. His accent wasn't Arkansas, or Mississippi, or Louisiana. It had a strange twang.

Once, when Eddie and I happened to be in the store, a perfume drummer from up North stopped to peddle his wares to Mr. Carter. Their voices sounded much the same. And to top it, they hit it off like long lost cousins once Eddie's father found out the other man was from somewhere in New York State. It was then that I realized that Eddie's father must be a Yankee. That led to other thoughts about which side the man had fought on if he had fought at all. I still had doubts about that. Though I considered him a potentially violent man, I wondered about his bravery and I didn't for one minute trust him. He was still leering at me as these thoughts wound through my mind that afternoon. Then, all of a sudden his eyes left me and darted toward the front of the store. He pointed his finger in that direction and growled under his breath. I could barely hear the words.

"Niggers, ya can't depend on none of them."

Mr. Carter was glaring through the glass at Jesse Culbreath. The big man was hurrying across the street, his old straw hat bouncing atop his head as he lumbered toward the store. Jesse was a gentle man, probably about thirty. And even though he had no formal education, he was a proud man. As I would learn later, he was also an intelligent and caring person. For a long time he had been walking three miles to the store every afternoon and three miles back to his small community. He earned ten cents cleaning up around the store. It seemed like a very meager amount to me, but to Jesse, who had nothing, it must have seemed like a great deal of money. As he opened the old screen door, I looked quickly at Eddie's father. Trouble was brewing. It was all over the man's face and I was not anxious to witness what was about to take place.

"Let's go back to the swimming hole, Eddie," I whispered and jumped off the counter.

But Eddie had other ideas. He could see what was about to happen and an almost evil smile crossed his face in anticipation. He grabbed my shoulder and shook his head without taking his eyes off his father.

"Wait a bit, Jamie." He whispered only loud enough for me to hear. "I want to see what Pa is gonna do. Maybe he'll whip the nigger." Eddie pulled his knees up under his chin and hugged them tight to his chest. "We're gonna have some real fun now."

Carter had worked his way around the checker game and met Jesse as he came through the door. "Boy, where you been? You know how late you are? You was due here five minutes ago."

"Yes, Suh." Jesse was about to say something else, but when Mr. Carter continued his tirade Jesse just stood looking down at the much smaller man.

"I ain't payin' you good money to come in whenever you git good and ready. I want you here when I tell you. You ain't gittin' but a nickel today cause you ain't gonna be here full time. You got that, boy? And I expect this place to be clean when you leave. You understand, boy?"

Carter was standing in front of Jesse, hands placed firmly on his hips, yelling up into the man's face. For all the sputtering and yelling you would have thought that Jesse had stolen all of the money or taken a rock and thrown it through the window at the front of the store. Instead he had only been a few minutes late. As loud and boisterous as Carter had gotten, Jesse remained passive. There seemed to be no fear in him and I think that's what really made Eddie's father all the angrier. He couldn't scare Jesse. Finally, when the tirade was finished and Floyd Carter was catching his breath, Jesse brushed by him and started for the rear of the store.

That made Carter all the more furious and he followed Jesse toward the back of storage room . He was right in front of me when he caught the black man. With one sweep of his hand he reached up and knocked the straw hat from Jesse's head.

"Ain't I told you before to take off that dirty hat in this store. You know better than to come in here with that stinkin' thing on."

I caught a movement of Jesse's big right hand as the fingers curled and the hand became a massive club. Fire sparkled in his eyes and I expected him to bring that big fist up and across Mr. Carter's jaw. My eyes shifted to the other men in the store to see if they had noticed it too. But they were still laughing heartily, enjoying the entertainment as was Eddie. I expected disaster, but just as quickly as Jesse had doubled his fist, the tension in his lower arm and wrist relaxed and his fingers slowly uncurled. I don't think anyone else in the store realized how close Jesse had come to losing his temper. Jesse knew what would happen if he hit the fuming storekeeper. Instead, he just stooped and picked up the old straw hat, dusted it off and looked back at Eddie's father.

"Shore am glad you ain't damaged my hat none, Mr. Carter, Suh," Jesse said with just a touch of sarcasm in his voice. "Been a wearin' this old hat for nigh onto fifteen years." Jesse leveled a gaze at Mr. Carter. "Like an old friend, this here hat is. Hate like all git out for it to be mussed up."

The tone took Carter by surprise and he stepped back from Jesse for a moment. "You got a lot of sass in you, boy. What you need is a good strappin' and I just might give it to you if you ain't careful of that mouth."

I expected Jesse to reach down, pick the man up and fling him half way across the store. He could have and probably should have. But, Jesse did something strange, something a black man wouldn't be expected to do at this time or in this place. He smiled and quietly said, "Ain't no use for you to work up such a sweat on me. Wouldn't be none too healthy for you or me in this heat." It was a subtle threat and I think Carter realized it, though he did not pursue the confrontation any further.

With that said, Jesse walked past Mr. Carter, picked up his broom and began to sweep as if nothing had happened. For a minute Carter seemed too stunned to speak. I think that it scared him for he only watched the big black man as he began sweeping toward the back of the store. Jesse had delivered a strong warning and at that time Carter was not prepared to deal with it. The warning stunned everyone, maybe me more than anyone. Black men did not speak to white men in that way. I didn't know then that it was just the beginning of what would be an eventful summer. An eventful summer is really an understatement. The trouble that began that day was much more devastating than anyone could ever imagine. Mr. Carter would not forget that incident and the perceived threat from Jesse. Trouble was just over the horizon and what would happen very soon would inflame our entire community. We would soon find out how one man's hatred could be meted out on another human being.

When the fun, as Eddie referred to it, was over we headed home. "Boy, Pa sure told old Jesse off," Eddie said. "You ever see anybody so scairt as that nigger?"

I picked up a rock and threw it toward an old pine tree a few feet away. "Didn't look too scared to me."

This brought a long sigh and a look of disgust from Eddie. "Aw, c'mon, Jamie. You know they's always been scairt of white folks."

"I ain't so sure 'bout that."

Eddie looked at me as if I were crazy. "Sure they are, Jamie. Pa says they ain't got the gumption of a rabbit."

"Why you hate black folks so much, Eddie?"

I guess the question startled him, for he stopped in the middle of the road and scratched his head for several seconds. Finally, he shrugged his shoulders. "They's black ain't they. I guess that's why."

His answer made me furious. "That's dumb, Eddie Carter, just plain dumb. I ain't never heard nothin' so dumb in my whole life. My Pa says God made black folks just like he made us white folks. God loves them just like he loves us." With that I turned and started off down the road, leaving Eddie standing there with his mouth wide open. In a moment I heard his feet pounding the ground behind me.

"Jamie, wait up," Eddie called and caught my arm. "Ain't no need gittin' riled up over old Jesse. He ain't worth it." Then, as if nothing had happened, he patted his overall pocket and grinned that sly grin that always meant trouble. "You comin' over before dark. I slipped some more fixins while no one was watchin'."

I shrugged my shoulders and poked my hands down deep into my overall pockets. "Maybe." I wanted to say no, but I didn't and I knew that I would be at Eddie's before dark.

# CHAPTER 4

PAPA WAS SITTING AT the kitchen table reading his Bible when I came in the back door. Even though I had nothing to do with what happened to Jesse, I still felt guilty just from being there. That made it hard to meet Papa's eyes when he looked up from the Bible. Instead, I looked quickly toward Mama. She was bending over the stove stirring something in one of her big black pots.

"James," Mama said. "Go wash your hands. Supper will be ready soon."

"Yes, Mama."

Then she turned to Papa. "Efren, you had better go with your son. As the good book says 'Go thou and do likewise'." She grinned that quick grin I had seen so often, the grin that always seemed to captivate Papa.

He looked at her for several seconds before following me out to the back porch. As it always was, a large pan of clear water was sitting on the old washstand beside the top step. As we washed, the water turned gray, then black and I wondered. What had Papa done to get so dirty today? Then I realized. Papa had stopped washing and the water was still turning dark as I continued to clean. When I looked up, he was studying me intently and the memory of Jesse and what had happened that day returned to my thoughts. I dropped my eyes back to the dingy water and continued to rub, not really cleaning now, but just trying to keep from meeting his eyes. I looked past Papa and fixed my gaze on Satan, nibbling quietly at the hay that Papa had pitched into his corral. The big horse seemed to know that I was watching. He raised his head and peered in my direction then returned to his nibbling. I was troubled. I still needed an answer to the question that had haunted my thoughts most of the afternoon.

"Papa," I blurted out suddenly, "why do some white people hate black folks?" I hesitated a moment to let him absorb the question. "I think Mr. Carter hates Jesse terrible bad."

When I looked into his face, it seemed he was reading my innermost thoughts. After a moment he wiped his hands with a towel and dropped it next to the washbasin. His eyes remained on me for several seconds before he turned and stared off across our yard, past Mama's garden to where Satan now stood with his head draped across the fence. The horse was staring toward us as he pawed the earth beneath his hooves. It seemed that he was also waiting for an answer to my question. When Papa looked back at me, I felt like his eyes were looking right through me. It was as if he knew everything that had happened that day and was measuring my responsibility in the entire matter. I wanted to shrink inside myself. But, when he finally spoke, his voice was as soft and gentle as I ever heard. It was the voice he generally reserved only for Mama.

"Son, that's a hard question." He put his arm around my shoulders and led me toward the back steps. We moved down a couple of steps and Papa sat down with his elbows resting on his knees. I sat beside him for several minutes. He had grown very quiet. When I finally looked into his eyes again, I saw that faraway look he got when he was concerned. He must have felt my stare, for in a second his arm tightened around my shoulder and he shook his head sadly.

"Hatred is a terrible thing, son. It eats at a man. Sometimes it eats at him so bad that it makes him downright mean." He stopped for a minute as if to gather his thoughts. "And sometimes it isn't hatred at all. A lot of bad things have happened to our black brothers over the years. Most of it is our fault. Many times they were treated no better than we might treat our livestock. That can create a terrible guilt for the person responsible for that kind of action. Sometimes that guilt comes across like hatred. Guilt can make us mean."

"Is that why Mr. Carter is mean to Jesse?"

He studied my face for what seemed an eternity before he spoke again.

"Maybe," he said and nodded toward the barn.

"Do you remember how we got Myrtle?"

"Yes, sir," I said after a moment. "You bought her from Mr. Holland."

"That's right. And forty years ago, if I was a mind to, I could have bought a black man just like Jesse from Mr. Holland. He owned Jesse's Papa and Mama."

"Mr. Holland," I squealed in disbelief. "He owned Jesse's folks?"

"Mr. Holland," Papa affirmed with a nod.

I sat there looking out toward the woods several hundred yards away, my mind confused by this new knowledge about Mr. Holland. Finally, I looked up at Papa. "It weren't right, Papa. It weren't right for one man to own another. Was it, Papa?"

"No," Papa said quietly, "it wasn't right. And that's why some white folks mistreat the black man now. They feel guilty for all those days of slavery that folks like Jesse had to endure. But instead of trying to make it right for all the bad things, some try to cover their shame by continuing to insist on their superiority. They're the ones we should pity. Jesse and his people don't want our pity. They only want a chance to make their own way." Papa stopped for a moment and squeezed my shoulder. "Do you understand, James?"

"I think so, Papa." But I really wasn't sure if I did or not. I found it inconceivable that one man could own another.

Just then the back screen door opened. "Supper, boys," Mama called out.

Inside, we waited until Mama sat down, then Papa and I followed suit. After Papa blessed the food, Mama asked.

"You two seemed to be deep in serious conversation out on the porch. Anything I should know about?"

I looked up as Papa spoke.

"I've given the boy some things to think about. He must sort the right and wrong out in his own mind. He'll be a man soon and the way he treats his fellow man is important."

It was all he said. Satisfied, Mama nodded and we began to eat. The rule in our house was that the dinner table was not a place for idle conversation. It was not that no conversation took place at all, but only important conversation and then short and to the point. Though Papa was the dominant force in our family, it was Mama that set the tone during the meal. We never commenced before her nor would we ever start a meal until thanks was given for the blessings God had bestowed on us. Only when Mama finished and pushed her plate away, was I allowed to ask to be excused. I'm sure Papa would not have punished me if I had ever forgotten, but I chose not to find out.

I sat silently picking at my food, intent on my thoughts. A mental picture of Jesse, towering above Mr. Carter, kept reappearing in my mind. In my own limited imagination, I kept expecting that big hand of Jesse's to reach out and knock Eddie's father to the floor. But it didn't happen in my mind or in reality. Had the little white man prevailed? Why, I asked myself?

Why is it that way? It wasn't that way at school. No one fooled with big Bill Harrison. But then he was white as was everyone else in my school.

From where I sat at the table, I could see out the back door and out to where Myrtle was nibbling peacefully at the dry grass and weeds. It was hard to imagine owning a man like we did Myrtle or Satan. It wasn't right. It just wasn't right.

Mama's gentle hand touched my arm and I jumped. "James, your supper won't be fit to eat if you don't get to it."

"Yes, Mama. I'm sorry."

She was just finishing as I shoveled the last spoonful of beans into my mouth. Papa had pushed his plate back a few moments before and sat gazing across the table toward her. A faint smile flickered across his lips. I'm sure she felt his eyes, for as often happened, she looked up and smiled. There was a great amount of love in our home. Mama and Papa found time for each other and they found time for me. That is a feeling of warmth and security I will never forget. Mama brushed a wisp of hair from her forehead and pushed her own plate away. "Would you like to be excused, James?"

I nodded.

"You may go and play a while. But mind you come when I call."

"Yes, Mama. I will."

~ ~ ~

I hurried out the kitchen door and down the back trail to Eddie's house. The sun was still high in the sky and somewhere in the distance I could hear a hound yowling, probably hot on the trail of some scurrying animal. I wondered how it could be so full of energy this late in the day. And yet, here I was off for another hour of fun. It was a straight shot to Eddie's house by the back trail. Weeds were knee deep on each side of the old beaten-down path. In spots the trail was only two feet wide.

Two summers earlier I had run up on a rattler, sunning in the middle of the trail. Since then I had been much more cautious. On that occasion, with the rattler, it had been a standoff. The snake refused to move and I was too scared to pass him in the deep grass. We probably confronted each other for half a minute before he finally quit clicking his tail and slithered off into the weeds. I'm sure I aged twice over during the confrontation. The sound of his rattle is still clear in my mind. I've seen many snakes since but only one other time in such close quarters as that day. But I suppose my snake stories aren't as bad as what happened to Mama and Papa.

During the first year they were married, they slept with a snake under the mattress. They found out the next morning when Mama heard something in the bed. When she pulled the covers back and lifted the mattress the snake slid out. Papa said he was a hundred feet from the house when he heard Mama scream. She must have put the fear in the snake, for Mama made Papa tear the house apart but he never found hide nor hair of the reptile.

For a long time after that, Mama had a habit of searching the bed until she was certain her unwelcome visitor was nowhere in the vicinity. In the same manner it was a year before I could travel the back trail without thinking about my snake encounter.

Now, as I came closer to Eddie's house, I found him sitting on the bottom step, screwing his toe, as was his habit, in the dust. He was squinting his eyes and puckering his lips. His concentration was so intense on the movement of his big toe and what he was creating with it, that he didn't know I was close by until I spoke.

"Whatcha doin'?"

He jumped when I spoke. If his hands hadn't been supporting him on the step, he would have landed in the dirt.

"Hey, Jamie," he frowned as he righted himself on the step. "I ain't too fond of bein' slipped up on like that."

I giggled and sat down on the step beside him. "I didn't aim to scare you."

I watched as he slid his toe around in the soft dirt for several more seconds until he seemed satisfied with whatever he was doodling. Then, as if it hadn't been at all important, he brushed it out with one sweep of his bare foot and leaned back with his elbows propped on the second step.

"What you wanta do?" He asked. From the look in his eyes I knew he already had something in mind.

Even though I thought I knew the answer in advance, I asked the question anyway. "Dunno. You got any ideas?"

Eddie turned and stared toward his back door for a moment. Finally, he patted his pocket and whispered. "Got some makins. Want to go down by the old oak and have a smoke?"

"Naw, it's too much in the open. Someone'll catch us." I hoped that would end his idea at least for today but it didn't.

"How 'bout the swamp then. Ain't nobody gonna catch us down there. Least ways no one important."

"We ain't got time to go down there. Mama'll be callin' me soon and she'll be mad if I don't hear her. Let's do somethin' else today."

Eddie seemed exasperated with me, but I really don't think he heard my suggestion about doing something else for he got up and slipped into the house. After a few minutes he came out, crooked his finger and motioned me around to the side of the house.

"Ma's not feelin' well. She's asleep in her room. Sally's playin' in her room," he whispered. Eddie bent over and peered under the house for several seconds. "Let's slide under here and light up." The glint in his eyes said he was not about to be put off. He would have his smoke, no matter what I said.

Still I tried to find a reason to persuade him that it wasn't a good idea. "What about your Pa? He could catch us."

"He ain't home. Gone back to the store. Probably won't be back till dark. Probably be liquored up when he does get back."

Finally, I shrugged my shoulders and gave a half grin. Eddie was already crawling under the house as I looked around quickly to be sure no one was watching. I ducked my head when I was satisfied and followed to where Eddie already sat, pulling the cigarette makings out of his pocket. Where we were the crawl space was about three feet high. A little farther on it got lower and in places was only a foot high. We were only ten feet from the outer wall and thankfully there were no walls down to the ground anywhere around his house so we were able to see if any unwelcome varmints had crawled under before us. Also, we could see if someone was to happen up.

Eddie was separating the cigarette papers when I dropped on my backside next to him. By now, even I had become an expert, or so I thought at the time, in the art of rolling and smoking a cigarette. As the summer had rolled on and we hadn't been caught, we were both beginning to feel a little invincible. Even so I still felt shame when I thought about Papa and Mama and what they would think if they ever caught me. In the back of my mind, I knew it was inevitable. They would catch me. But the more I smoked, the less it seemed to bother me. It had taken several episodes of smoking, but I finally stopped coughing every time I took a puff. I was quite proud of that.

Eddie found an old rotten board under the house and was tapping the ashes from his smoke on that. Something tickled him and he giggled out loud.

"What's funny?" I whispered.

"Old Jesse. My Pa sure told him what for," Eddie said. He laughed again, a little too loud I thought. "Want to go down to the store tomorrow and see if'n Pa gets riled at him again? We might even be able to egg it on."

I was disgusted at Eddie's attitude. "No. I ain't wantin' to see Jesse get into trouble. Leave him alone, Eddie."

"Aw, come on. He ain't nothin to get all het up over." Then he looked at me suspiciously and asked. "You ain't no nigger lover are you?"

"No," I said defensively and was immediately ashamed of myself.

Eddie was already blowing a ring of smoke out of his mouth. He was proud of himself and the smirk on his face proved it. There were times when I wished I had the courage to take that smirk off. But Eddie was my friend and you don't cross your friends if you want to keep them so I bit my tongue and said nothing else.

"Why you always takin' up for old Jesse if'n you ain't, Jamie?" The look on Eddie's face said that I was trying to protect someone who was his target. The look said back away Jamie or you'll be my target just like Jesse.

I drew back realizing I could be treading on uncertain ground. "I ain't takin' up for him." I watched him put his cigarette back between his lips before I continued. His eyes were studying me closely. "I just ain't got no reason to down-talk him none. He ain't done nothin' to me."

Eddie continued to study my face. Finally, he grinned and shook his head. "Boy, Jamie, don't you know that them kind was put here on this earth to serve white folks. That little war didn't change nothin'. They's still supposed to serve us. My Pa told me that a long time ago. Didn't your Pa tell you?"

I was about to tell him what Papa said when I heard Mama's voice. "James. James, it's time to come home."

The voice came from a long way off, but it still startled me. It was as if Mama was right there under the house with us. I quickly dropped my cigarette and mashed it under my foot. By the time I finished covering the dead ashes with dirt I was still shaking. When I looked over at Eddie, he was grinning.

"Give ya a fright, Jamie?" He handed me a piece of candy and I stuck it in my mouth. I had no faith that it would hide the cigarette smell, but so far I felt I had been able to avoid Mama and Papa until the stench of tobacco had worn off. Still, I knew that one day they would catch me if I didn't quit the filthy habit first. I was determined to do it.

"I gotta go." I whispered. "You comin'?"

He held his half smoked cigarette up and blew a ring of smoke from his mouth directly into my face. Thinking back, I wonder now what made me think Eddie was my friend. He seemed to enjoy my discomfort. "Naw, not till I'm finished. Ain't no use wastin' a good smoke. But you run along, Jamie. Don't want you to git in a heap of trouble."

I watched him squatting in the semi-darkness with his back propped against a crooked rock pillar that helped support the little house. He was just a small blond-haired eleven-year-old boy that thought he knew everything and I guess I was a lot like him. I often picture him in my mind just like he was that July evening, sitting there smiling, blowing those smoke rings, and pretending to enjoy every moment. Maybe he did but I know now that much of it was for show.

Finally, I turned and crawled out from under the house. The air seemed much fresher now and as I hurried down the back path toward my house, the summer sun was beginning to dip down just above our roof. In the distance I could see Papa drawing water from the old well.

# CHAPTER 5

PAPA LOOKED UP AS I approached and motioned to the water bucket when he saw me. "Drink of cool fresh water, James?"

I nodded and walked toward the well, being careful to stay on the far side from Papa. He took a long drink and handed the dipper across to me. It was especially good this night and I drank two large dippers before handing it back to Papa.

"You were thirsty, boy. See that you're careful this night," he cautioned and winked. He knew how I hated to get up in the middle of the night and trek down the path to our old outhouse. More than once one or the other of us had found unwelcome varmints lurking close to the door in the dark.

I thrust that thought out of my mind and nodded to Papa as he started toward the house with the water bucket. It was time to go in but I still didn't want to get too close to Mama or Papa, so I hesitated in the yard and acted as if I was interested in watching one of the chickens scratching in the dirt. After a few minutes I wandered over to where Myrtle was nibbling the stub of a bush. I brushed my hand across her back and patted her rump. She raised her head and looked at me with inquisitive eyes before she returned to her nibbling. I got tired of killing time and decided to take a chance and go in. As I started toward the house I saw Jesse coming down the road. He was on his way home from cleaning the Carter store. I watched as he passed in front of our house and moved on down the road toward Eddie's. He was moving slowly, his head down and his eyes staring blankly at the dusty ground. A moment later he was hidden from my view by a stand of trees that stretched from our house to Eddie's. I tarried in the yard for several more minutes, the events at the Carter's store weighing heavily on my mind. I was deep in thought until I realized Mama was calling me.

"James, do you not hear me? I said sit down on the steps and wash those dirty feet. You will not crawl into bed like you did last night. It looked like a pig was in there with you."

She handed me a fresh pan of water, along with soap and a towel, and pointed toward the top step. "And wash your face and hands and behind your ears. And, mind you James, wash your hands and face before you wash your feet. It works out much better that way."

I nodded and said half under my breath. "Yes, Mama." Really, I was happy for the extra time. Maybe the tobacco smell would be completely gone by the time I finished.

The water was a dirty gray by the time I finished and left the pan on the washstand next to the door. Mama must have been watching, for she came to the screen and looked down at me. Her hands were pressed to her hips and she seemed to be suppressing a smile.

"Is there a special reason for saving that water, James?"

"No, Ma'am. 'Cept I thought Papa might need to wash later."

"I'm sure your Papa will want a clean pan of water. What I see in that pan would not get him very clean, now would it?"

I looked at the pan of gray water then back to her. "No, Ma'am, I guess not." As always her reasoning seemed correct.

"Then why don't you empty the dirty water, rinse the pan good and fetch him some clean water from the well." She winked at me then. "And you're right about Papa needing to clean up before bedtime. I think he would probably appreciate your thoughtfulness in providing him a clean pan of water."

Without a word, I took the pan and gave the dirty water a heave off the porch. The sun had disappeared in the west and dusk was just beginning to settle when I placed the pan of clean water on the little stand beside the steps. I had opened the screen door and was halfway across the kitchen when I heard the loud yell that will haunt me until I die.

"Fire! Fire! The Carter house is on fire!" I recognized the voice immediately. It was coming from the road in front of our house. It was old man Meecham. His house was across the road and some two hundred feet up a narrow dirt trail. From our porch we could barely see his house because of the trees and high weeds. But from the Carter's you could see the Meecham place with no trouble. I retraced my steps toward the back door when I heard another scream from the direction of the Carters'. Because of the distance the scream was not very loud, but it was a woman's scream and I knew it had to be Mrs. Carter. As I hurried out the back, I heard Papa slam the front screen door and run across the front porch. I'm not sure how she did it but somehow Mama was already half way up the back path by the time I jumped off the back porch. As I looked toward the East, I could see the flames leaping through the roof on the near side of Eddie's house. My heart was in my throat as I ran along the path, a path I had very carefully negotiated a short time before. At this moment I had no thought of the snakes I feared so deeply. I could only think of Eddie and Sally and Mrs. Carter and pray they were safe.

I caught up to Mama as she broke into the clearing just behind the Carter house. Several men were already running up the road, buckets in hand. Momentarily, there would be a bucket brigade. When I saw the extent of the fire, which had spread throughout the entire house, I knew it was useless. From the expression on the men's faces, I knew they were thinking the same thing. But it didn't stop them. They began drawing water from the well and throwing it onto the blaze. Papa, Mr. Meecham who must have been seventy, Bill Hargis, Sam Logan, and young Haywood Tollison, who had graduated from school a month earlier, were working feverishly to put out the fire. I tried to fall into line and help, but Sam Logan pushed me aside rather unceremoniously and I retreated, with my feelings slightly bruised, to stand next to Mama. But that was only for a moment. Mama was searching frantically for Mrs. Carter and the children. One moment she was there and the next she was heading around the burning house with me in hot pursuit. We found Mrs. Carter, Eddie and Sally out next to the road. Several other women were already gathering around her trying to help. Little Sally was lying prone on the ground and Mrs. Carter was down on her knees working feverishly over the little girl. Eddie was standing at Sally's feet looking down on his little sister. He looked like a whipped dog.

Mama dropped to her knees beside Sarah Carter and threw an arm around the woman's shoulders.

"Sarah, what happened? What's wrong with Sally? Has she been burned?"

Sarah didn't speak for a moment and when she finally did it was between sobs. "She was in her room," she sobbed, "and I couldn't get to her. I had a hard time getting to her," she repeated. "And....." Sarah's voice cracked with emotion. On the ground Sally still had not moved. Amanda Meecham was on her knees next to the little girl's head, dabbing and rubbing softly with a wet towel. Every now and then she would stop and bend to the girl's chest and listen intently to her heart. Sarah was trying to talk again. "And by the time I got her out of the window there was so much smoke that I..." Sarah Carter raised her hands in a gesture of helplessness.

Mama was massaging the distraught woman's back trying to calm her. "Shh, now, Sarah. Shh. Sally's going to be all right." Mama looked around to all the women. "Has anyone gone for Doctor Smith?"

Mrs. Meecham looked up and nodded. "Carter went to find him soon as we pulled them outta the winder."

I walked slowly around Sally, but I couldn't see any burns. She was lying on her back and I wondered if that was where she had been burned. If it was, I thought, she ought to be rolled over. I looked from Mama to Mrs. Carter, then to Mrs. Meecham who was still rubbing the cloth over Sally's forehead. At the time I didn't know about the devastating effects that smoke inhalation could have on the human body. I learned later that if Sally died it would be from smoke in her lungs and not from the flames that really never touched her.

Eddie retreated from Sally and the women and I wandered over to where he was standing next to a small oak tree at the edge of his yard. It was at that moment that the outer west wall of the house fell away revealing what was left of the front room and Sally's bedroom. Nothing could be saved now. The men, once scurrying about in an effort to save the house, seemed to be resigned to the fact that it was a hopeless case. Even Papa, who always seemed a bundle of energy, had knelt down on the ground and was shaking his head in the direction of the blaze. Only Haywood Tollison was still throwing water toward the fire with any energy. Papa caught the young man's eye and motioned toward him. Haywood nodded and dropped down on the ground beside Papa. I felt Eddie's arm brush against mine and as it did, I heard him groan. When I glanced his way he was trembling. His eyes were wide and frightened and I suddenly felt terribly sorry for him. But when I reached out to put my arm around him as I had seen Mama do with Mrs. Carter, he pulled back and stuffed his hands in his pockets. Then, without a word, he turned and ran back to where Sally lay. I could understand how he felt. He was worried about Sally and rightly so.

Just then a wagon pulled up in the road and I saw Doctor Smith leap out and run toward the knot of women. Mr. Carter was in the seat beside him and he quickly followed the doctor to where his daughter lay. The women parted and the old man dropped to his knees next to Sally and placed his black bag at his side. He pressed his ear to Sally's chest and kept it there for several seconds. Finally, he started to turn her onto her stomach. As he began to move her, Sally spit up a great mouthful of corruption. The sight sickened me and I turned and ran back toward where Papa sat. My own stomach seemed to be rising into my throat and my chest was heaving. I couldn't look at the sight for a few minutes. When I did, I saw them pick Sally up and carry her to the wagon where they lay her on a blanket that suddenly appeared. Doc got up onto the seat, with Mrs. Carter and Mrs. Meecham in the back with the girl. There seemed to be great relief among the women. Sally was awake and, out of my earshot, Doc Smith had announced that he thought she would be all right. He was taking her to his house to make sure she progressed properly. And off down the road they went.

When Eddie appeared by my side a few minutes later he seemed much calmer. I could understand his distress. Sally's condition and the loss of their house were enough to trouble anyone. His eyes seemed to be going from me to the group of men and women that were gathered around his father. He wanted to say something to me but he was holding back. The look in his eyes a few moments before seemed to be anger. Now, they seemed to register fear. He seemed scared and I didn't know why. Suddenly, his eyes shifted back to the house.

It was almost gone now. Only one outside wall and two inside walls still stood. As I watched all three crumbled and fell with a loud crash. A moment later the floor caved in right where we had been less than an hour before. I put my hand on Eddie's arm and shook my head.

"Sure am glad you got out before that happened." I pointed to the spot we had crouched only a short time before.

"It weren't my fault." The fear on Eddie's face was transferred to his voice. His eyes were wide and pleading as he spoke.

"Course it weren't," I answered.

"I seen old Jesse just before it happened," Eddie stammered. He was staring directly in my eyes. I realized later that he was testing me.

"I did, too," I answered. Then I asked. "What's Jesse got to do with anythin'?"

Eddie wasn't looking at me now. His eyes shifted back to the small group of people still gathered around his father. By the faraway expression in his eyes, I knew some thought was racing through Eddie's head. After a moment, he turned back to me and shook my arm hard.

"You musta seen him. He come right by your place jist before the fire. You musta seen him."

I pulled my arm loose. "I said I seen him, but what does Jesse have to do with anythin'?"

He turned toward the remnants of his house and waved his arm wildly. "Don'tcha see, Jamie? He done this. I seen him foolin' round over there by the house. Then in a minute it was on fire. He done it cause of what Pa did to him. He done it, I swear."

I was stunned. Jesse had been mistreated, but to burn down someone's house. I couldn't believe that. Surely he was too smart to do anything so dumb.

For a long time, we stood silently watching as the fire continued destroying what was left of the foundation. Eddie's accusation was rolling around in my head and I didn't know what to say to him. Surely he was mistaken. He had to be. After a moment I glanced at him from the corner of my eye. A slight smile crossed his lips. It stayed for a few seconds then was gone. It was then that Mama came up behind us and put an arm around each of our shoulders.

"Eddie, you are to stay with us tonight. Your father and mother will be staying at the doctor's house with Sally."

Eddie looked up into Mama's face. "Will Sally be all right?"

She smiled and squeezed his shoulder slightly. "Yes, of course she will. By morning she'll be herself again. Now, don't you worry. They're just keeping her there overnight as a precaution." She put a hand on our backs and gently moved us toward the road. "Come along, boys. It's getting late and you need to be in bed soon. Everything will look much better in the morning."

"Where's Pa?" Eddie asked.

"He's already gone to check on Sally. You'll see him first thing in the morning."

"I need to tell him somethin'."

"It'll have to wait, Eddie. You'll see him in the morning."

Mama started off for the road with Eddie and me trailing along behind. The men, including Papa, were throwing water on the rubble that now lay smoldering in the early night air. I heard Papa talking to Sam Logan and Haywood Tollison about staying with the house through the night so that no grass fires would start. They agreed and the men continued their job.

Eddie and I followed Mama down the road in silence. I couldn't get what Eddie said about Jesse out of my mind. Was he going to tell his father that Jesse started the fire? Is that why he wanted to talk to him now? I couldn't believe Eddie would do that. And I most certainly didn't believe Jesse would start the fire. What could have possessed Eddie to make such an accusation.

When we got home, Mama filled a pan of water for each of us and told us to wash good and get ready for bed. Remembering that I had already gone through this process, I was about to protest. When I saw Mama's face, I thought better of it and went out on the porch to clean myself all over again. Eddie remained strangely silent all this time and when we went into my room to get into bed, he grabbed me by the arm and put his finger to his lips to be sure I didn't speak.

"Jamie," he whispered looking anxiously toward the closed door. "You ain't never gonna tell nobody about what we been doin', are you?" He was pleading and for a moment, I truly felt sorry for him. For that moment only, I felt he was repenting from his cigarette habit. And if he was, I would surely do the same.

"Whatcha mean?"

"The fixins I been bringin' home. You ain't gonna tell um we been smokin'." This time it was more of a statement than a question.

"No, I ain't. You think I'm crazy?"

He seemed relieved for he smiled and turned toward the bed. "I ain't never gonna smoke again. I swear I ain't," he said with finality. I was to find out very soon why he was so adamant.

We undressed to our underwear and crawled into bed. In a moment I heard Mama knock on the door. "Are you boys under the covers yet?"

"Yes, Mama."

She came in and bent over to kiss me on the cheek. "Now you go right to sleep. This has been a long hard day. Shut those eyes."

"Yes, Mama."

She went around to the other side of the bed and sat down beside Eddie. "Are you all right, Eddie? Anything you want before you go to sleep?"

Eddie shook his head. "No."

Mama ran her hand through Eddie's hair for a moment. "Don't you worry about anything. Sally's going to be fine. You'll see. In no time everything will be back to normal. I'm sure the men will put you back in a house in no time." Mama bent over and kissed Eddie lightly on the forehead. "Sleep now. Tomorrow's a new day." Then she got up, went to the door and stood there in the lamplight from the living room smiling down at us. A moment later she closed the door and left us in semi-darkness.

As soon as she was out of earshot, Eddie rolled over toward me and grabbed my arm tightly. "Jamie, you gotta swear somethin'," he whispered.

I turned toward him and pulled my arm loose from his grip. "What you mean?"

"You gotta swear. Swear to me, you hear."

"Swear what? What you talkin' about, Eddie?"

I must have spoken too loud for Mama's voice sounded from just the other side of the door. "I hear someone talking in there. You boys go to sleep."

For a minute, neither of us spoke. Then, after a while, I whispered. "What you talkin' about?"

Eddie was just as quiet when he answered me. But there was desperation in his voice. "You gotta swear you'll never tell no one we been smokin', specially under the house. Swear it, Jamie." He slipped quietly out of bed before I could answer and returned a moment later with the little Bible Papa and Mama had given me for my last birthday. I kept it on a table next to the door. "Swear it on this book your Pa puts such stock in." He laid the Bible next to my right hand and stood there in the half light staring down at me.

"Get back in bed before Mama hears us," I whispered.

He was not to be put off. "Not till you swear it on that book."

I was beginning to worry now. Mama would surely hear us if this kept up.

"All right, I swear," I whispered and rested my hand on the Bible. "But I already promised I wouldn't tell nobody."

He crawled into bed and pressed my hand firmly to the Bible. "You swearin' by God that you won't tell nobody?"

"I swear."

"Swear that if you do tell, God'll strike you dead on the spot. You swear that?"

I hesitated. That was a pretty serious swear. Finally, I answered. "Yes."

Eddie relaxed his pressure on my hand and I was about to slip from under the covers and return the book to my dresser when he grabbed my hand and pressed it firmly against the Bible again.

"Jamie, you ain't to never tell no one we was under the house today." Again, even though he was whispering I could hear and feel his desperation. "You gotta swear that, too. Swear it by God."

"I do."

"Say the words, Jamie."

"Whatcha talkin' about?"

"Say you swear it by God. Say I swear it by God and hope he'll strike me dead if'n I don't keep my swear."

"Eddie, that's dumb."

"Say it," Eddie insisted and this time his voice got a little louder than before.

He realized he had been too loud and in unison we both stopped and listened intently. We could hear Mama moving around in the next room, but she apparently hadn't heard us. She was humming as she went about whatever she was doing. It was the melody to the "Old Rugged Cross."

After maybe two minutes, Eddie whispered. "Please, Jamie. Just say the words."

I let out a deep breath and in the darkness I said the words Eddie so desperately wanted me to say. It was the beginning of our short-lived conspiracy, a conspiracy of silence that would nearly destroy all of us.

"I swear by God that I will never tell anyone that we been smokin' under Eddie's house or that we been smokin' anywhere."

Eddie interrupted me. "Or God'll strike you dead."

"Or if I do God should strike me dead," I continued. When I finished, I felt Eddie's hand release the pressure from mine. "You satisfied, Eddie?"

He lay there for several minutes before he spoke again. I felt my eyes getting heavy and when he spoke I was only half awake.

"Jamie, boy, me and you gotta tell Pa about Jesse."

"Tell him what," I said half under my breath. I was nearly asleep now.

"We gotta tell him about Jesse settin' fire to the house."

My eyes sprang open immediately and I sat straight up in bed. To my dismay, the creaking bed sang its own song in the darkness. Mama quit humming in the other room and I could see a shadow appear under the door as she moved close to listen. I dropped my head back on the bed and we both fell silent. After a few moments, the shadow disappeared and Mama began humming again. This time the tune was one I had heard over and over again in church, but I couldn't put my finger on the name.

Now, I quietly sat straight up in bed and looked down at Eddie's face. In the moonlight I could barely make out his expression. What I saw was a look that was altogether different than it had been a few minutes before. The smile that I noticed earlier was there again. Eddie had made his decision and, from the look on his face, I knew it couldn't be good.

"I ain't got nothin' to tell your Pa. I didn't see Jesse do nothin'."

"But don't you see, Jamie. You seen him just before dark comin' down the road. He come right by your house headin' towards mine."

"That don't mean nothin'. He comes by every day after he leaves your Pa's store."

"He done it, Jamie. You just tell Pa you seen him. Tell him you seen him jist before dark. I'll tell him everything else that happened." He lay there looking up at me. A cloud had moved between us and the moon and for a few seconds I couldn't see the expression on his face. But I could imagine the smile. "Promise me, Jamie. Just tell Pa that you seen Jesse jist before the fire. That's all. Tell him that. Promise you will, Jamie. Promise."

"I seen him just before the fire. But, I never seen him start it," I insisted.

"That's enough, Jamie. I seen the rest."

Eddie turned over away from me and I sat there looking at his back for a long time. Finally, I lay back and stared up at the ceiling. There was no way I could bring myself to believe Jesse was responsible for the fire. No way. I lay there thinking back to the events of the day, what had happened at the store, about Jesse coming along the road just a little before the fire and how Eddie claimed that he started the fire that nearly killed Sally. Still, I couldn't believe it. I couldn't bring myself to believe that even Eddie with all his hatred of Jesse and his people would blame him if it were not true. I started running other possibilities through my mind of what might have happened. Maybe Mrs. Carter had accidentally set it when she was cooking. That was a possibility. No one else had a fire going. It must have come from Mrs. Carter's cook stove. But nothing was said about it.

Then it hit me and all of a sudden I knew what must have happened. I knew why Eddie must have been so anxious to make me swear that I saw Jesse. I could still see Eddie, his back propped against that rock post under his house, the smoke filtering out of his lips and the cigarette between his fingers. I could even see the old piece of rotting wood he had dropped the burning cigarette on. Had he forgotten to put it out before he crawled out from under the house?

I rolled over and started to tap his shoulder. His heavy breathing stopped me. I'm not sure how long I lay there staring at his back. It must have been at least an hour. When I finally did sleep, it wasn't restful and I dreamed of the fire and Papa and, of course, Eddie and the cigarette. But what caused me to wake up in a cold sweat in the middle of the night was not any of that. It was the vision of myself, a cigarette sticking out of my mouth, as I watched the Carter house going up in flames all around me. The nightmare made me deathly ill.

# CHAPTER 6

SUNDAY WAS USUALLY A day I looked forward to. But it was different on this hot July morning. I was troubled in mind and in spirit. No. Troubled wasn't exactly right. I was in agony about what to do. Mama would knock on the door any minute and tell us it was time to get ready for church. I was sure of the truth now or I thought I was. Eddie had not put out his cigarette. He knew he was at fault. And now I had promised not to say anything. I felt like a trapped rat, torn between doing what was right and keeping my promise to Eddie. It would be everything I could do to brave my way through the day. So I lay there afraid to move, knowing we had only minutes before it was time to get up. Either Eddie would wake up or Mama would come in to wake both of us up. And I knew what would happen when Eddie woke up. He would tell his lie about Jesse. There had to be a way of stopping him without getting myself into trouble. But I couldn't see how. If I let him blame the fire on Jesse, I would be as guilty as he was. And if I crossed Eddie he might even find a way to make it look like I was the one who left the burning cigarette. There was no way I could escape the consequences of my sin. Lying there in bed, with Eddie sleeping peacefully beside me, I made my decision. We could not lie about Jesse. I was convinced he had not started the fire, no matter what Eddie said. But how could I convince Eddie to tell the truth? He wasn't a bad person, I reasoned. When he thought about it, he would come to the same conclusion I had. I decided that when he woke up, I would tell him what we had to do. We would go to Papa and Mama and tell them about our smoking and what had happened the day before. It would mean a trip to the woodshed for me but it was worth it. It was the right thing to do. I glanced toward Eddie, confident that we would do the right thing. If I had only known what the day had in store, I would have jumped out of bed and blurted out the truth without delay, no matter what the consequences and no matter what I swore before God and Eddie. But I didn't. And because of my inaction the tragedy was set in motion.

Some of what happened during the next few days comes from my own memory but a lot of it, Papa and others who were involved told me after everything was over. Many minor details are still hazy, but what really happened and why it happened are all too clear. I pray that some day God will give me some measure of peace. But until then, I will have to live with the memories as I have been for the more than twenty years since it happened.

That morning was no different than the ones before it. Very little air was stirring and I found myself lying in a pool of my own sweat. Because of the confrontation that I knew would come when Eddie woke up, I was in no hurry to stir him. So I slipped from bed as quickly and quietly as possible and tiptoed to the window. The sun was low in the eastern sky and I knew it was earlier than I had originally thought. No sounds came from the kitchen and I guessed Mama was either still in bed, which was very unlikely, or being very quiet. On Sunday she was usually up shortly after daybreak and I was surprised that I could hear no activity anywhere in the house. Papa would certainly be up though. His sermon for the morning would be getting a thorough going over as it did every Sunday morning. Then, after breakfast, he would go on to the church. Mama and I would generally follow later.

I opened the bedroom door slowly and listened more carefully. It was very quiet in the house. Eddie hadn't moved so I closed the door and tiptoed through the front room toward the porch. The door was open and as I reached to push the screen open, Papa cleared his throat. I must have made some sound because he heard me.

"That you, James?"

I stuck my head through the half open door. "Yes, sir."

"Come outside, son."

"I ain't got nothin' on but my underpants."

"What are you doing up so early?"

I shrugged my shoulders and answered with a part truth. "It was too hot to sleep, Papa."

"It is that, boy."

"Where's Mama?"

Papa was rocking slowly in the big rocking chair he had made several years earlier. He had his Bible and a handful of papers in his lap.

"Gone over to Doc Smith's to see how Sally is faring this morning. She'll be back soon." He looked up and studied my face for a moment. "You don't look good, son. Are you feeling poorly?"

If you only knew, I thought. If you only knew. But I only shook my head. I was not about to tell what I suspected without Eddie and me coming to an agreement about Jesse. I still felt a loyalty to my friend. Although, looking back now, I surely don't see why.

"No, sir. I just couldn't sleep. It was so terrible hot."

He nodded and squinted up toward the sun in the eastern sky. "The Lord will provide us with a cooling rain when it's necessary. Until then we must assume that what comes our way is for the best." He looked toward me as if waiting for a response.

I nodded at his wisdom and answered truthfully. "I wish it weren't so hot. I could sleep better if there was a wind."

"We must not question God's perfect will."

"Yes, sir."

He resumed his studying and I closed the door and slipped back into the bedroom. Eddie was lying in a fetal position in the middle of the bed, still asleep. I had to talk to him when he woke up and I wondered if now wasn't the time while Mama was gone and Papa was engrossed in his study of the Word. But I dismissed that. The bedroom was too close to the front porch and Papa might hear us. We needed a private spot away from everyone. I had to be persuasive and that might take more than whispers. So I continued to be quiet and hope that Eddie didn't wake up and blurt out something we both might regret. I was already formulating in my own mind what I had to say to Eddie, what it would take to keep him from telling his lie. Once told, it would also become my lie, no matter what I did to dissuade him. I didn't look forward to this, what I would say or what Eddie would say in return. But the lie had to be stopped. It would take some convincing but Eddie would come around. He had to. I felt guilty in more ways than one. I made the mistake of smoking and now I had made a promise to God and Eddie and was about to break it the next day. God and Papa would surely mete out a terrible punishment for someone like me. But I was more afraid of Papa's punishment than I was of what God had in store for me. The thought of a trip to the woodshed caused me to shudder all the way down to my feet.

Eddie slept on as I dressed. Outside I could hear the birds chirping. They were happy and I wished I could share their feelings. The only consolation I could feel right now was that Eddie had a habit of sleeping late. The longer he slept, the longer it would be before we confessed. As I slipped out of the bedroom, he turned over on his back and let out a snort. I expected him to open his eyes but he turned back on his side and slept on.

My chores continued on Sunday just like any other day. The only difference was that I had to finish them before we left for church. On this morning I got a good start and I was finished with everything by the time Mama got back from Doc Smith's. She was in the kitchen preparing breakfast when I brought Myrtle's milk in.

"Good morning, James. You're up early. Finished your chores already, I see."

"I couldn't sleep. It was powerful hot."

Mama looked up from her cooking with that concerned look a mother has for one who doesn't seem quite right. She held the back of her hand to my forehead and frowned.

"You're flushed. Are you ill?"

I drew back. First Papa, now Mama. Both could read me like

a book. "No. I feel fine." It came out before I thought about it. I suddenly wished I had moaned some and gotten a little sympathy. It might have helped when Eddie got up and we told what had really happened yesterday. Then I remembered the chill tonic and castor oil in the medicine cabinet and realized I had made the right decision.

She continued to study my face, her hand pressed against my forehead. "Are you quite sure? You feel very warm."

"I'm fine, Mama." I wanted to tell her everything right then but I couldn't. Not without Eddie by my side to take his share of the blame.

After a moment she took her hand away, seemingly satisfied and went back to her cooking. Then over her shoulder she said.

"You'll need to wake Eddie up. He's to eat breakfast here and go to church with us."

"Is Sally going to be okay?" I asked.

Mama nodded and smiled toward me. "She's going to be fine. She woke up early this morning in good spirits. Doctor Smith is going to take care of her today. Eddie's father and mother are going to clean out the storage room in the back of their store and they'll be staying there until the community can come together and build them another house. We're going over to their store after church and help them in their cleaning." Mama shook her head sadly. "This has been a terrible shock for Sarah. Everything they had is gone." She wiped her hands on the old apron she made out of a flour sack and continued. "They very nearly lost Sally, too." She hesitated a moment. "Strange about that fire. Sarah swears that the embers in her stove were dead. Oh, well." She looked my way. "James, go wake up Eddie. Breakfast will be ready soon and Papa has set two pans of fresh well water on the porch for you to wash."

As I expected, Eddie didn't mention a word about Jesse during breakfast. When we finished, Mama excused us from the table with an admonition not to get ourselves dirty before church and we went out into the back yard. We walked down toward where Myrtle was munching on some dry grass. I decided now was as good a time as any to talk.

"I been thinkin' about what you said last night"

"What?" Eddie asked.

"I looked toward the house to be sure no one was listening. "You know," I said. "You know."

Eddie was doing what he was good at, playing dumb. Instead of answering me, he just walked over and patted Myrtle on the backside. She looked up questioningly and slapped him playfully with her tail. Then she went back to her munching.

"Come on," I snapped, tired of his putting me off. It always seemed to please him if he frustrated me. "What you said about Jesse. We can't tell nobody he done it. You ain't really goin' to, are you?"

Still he played dumb with a fake surprised look on his face. "Oh, you mean that no count nigger that done burned down our house," he blurted loud enough that I was afraid Mama would hear.

"Shh," I said and held a finger up to my lips. "Not so loud. Mama will hear you. And sides, you shouldn't call him by that name."

"What name?"

"You know."

"You mean nigger?" Eddie said with a grin. "That's what he is. A nigger."

"He ain't. Papa says that's no proper way to call black folks."

"Can't help what your pa says. They's still niggers."

I shook my head. Arguing with Eddie was a lost cause.

"Besides, ain't no use a worryin' 'bout what we're about to tell on him. Probably ain't no use worryin' 'bout that no good nigger ever again. When Pa catches him, he'll string him up to the first tree he comes to and everybody'll be the better for it." His eyes held mine for several seconds without wavering. It was then I knew. Eddie was really going to do it. He was going to accuse Jesse no matter what I said.

"It ain't true," I blurted out a little louder than I meant to. "It ain't true," I said again, this time with more control of my voice.

"Who says it ain't?"

"I say."

"You wasn't there and I was."

I swallowed hard and plunged ahead. "I know why you made me swear about smokin'. You didn't put out your smoke, did you? I bet you didn't," I said firmly. It was purely a guess because I really wasn't there. There was nothing I could swear to about the fire. But in my own mind I was sure about what had happened. And now I needed to be strong. I needed to face Eddie with conviction if I wanted to turn his thinking around. He needed to be convinced that I knew he had started the fire. But I had to be careful not to put too much pressure on him and turn him completely against me. He could put all of the blame on me if I aggravated him too much.

"You didn't mean to, Eddie. Anyhow," I continued, "you wouldn't git into too much trouble if you told them the truth." I was still bluffing but this took him by surprise and he moved threateningly toward me. His face had gone white and he grabbed my arm roughly. Eddie was as angry as I'd ever seen him.

"I never done it. You hear. Pa would beat me dead." I could feel his fingers digging into my flesh and when I tried to pull loose he only gripped me more tightly. "You ain't gonna tell no one we was smokin', are you?" His voice had taken on a tone I had never heard before. And right now I was more afraid of Eddie than of his lie. "Remember, you swore. You swore if you said anythin' that you hoped God would strike you dead. He would, too." The threat was there and I now feared if God didn't strike me dead, Eddie might.

I thought about it for several moments. God was mighty powerful and might just do what I feared most. Papa had always preached a hellfire and brimstone God. But he also said that God was a loving God. And right now I didn't know who to fear the most. Then I looked into Eddie's eyes. He was here, his face only inches from mine. Right now I was more afraid of him than even God. Everything had backfired on me. Now it seemed I not only made Eddie more resolute in his plans but also alienated him. I melted in Eddie's rough grip.

"I ain't gonna tell nothin'. I don't want Papa and Mama to

know I been smokin' either," I said sheepishly.

Eddie smiled and released my arm. "Sides," he whispered in that conspiratorial voice he kept hidden away, "who could say it was my smoke or yours that set the fire a goin'. Coulda' been yours just as much as mine. I could tell folks it was you that didn't stamp out them ashes."

I was taken back. Now Eddie was doing exactly what I thought he might. He had two scapegoats, Jesse and me. The protest that came out of my mouth was not only genuine, it was pleading. "I put my smoke out. You know I did. You seen me stamp it out with my foot and cover it with dirt. You seen it." I could feel the tears beginning to well up in my eyes.

Eddie had me down and he meant to grind me with his heel. The sneer on his face said I got you and I won't let you up. "Then you better go along with what I say or I'll tell everyone it was your smoke that did it. It'll be your word agin mine and who's to say what they'll believe."

With that, Eddie turned and walked quickly toward the house. I could only gape at his back as he moved away.

# CHAPTER 7

I DIDN'T HEAR MUCH of what Papa said in his sermon that morning. After living through the worst night of my life, this was quickly becoming the worst day in my life to that time. I didn't know it then, but things were about to become worse, much worse. All the while Papa was preaching, Eddie sat beside me with that smug look on his face. Right then I think I hated him. And maybe he hated me too. The only thing I was sure of was that he was confident that I wouldn't say anything. He knew I was afraid of what he might tell, and he knew I was afraid of what Papa and Mama might do if they thought I was guilty. And then, of course, there was God. What was He going to do to me? I never thought to stop and think. God already knew what I was guilty of. He would punish me accordingly whether Papa and Mama ever knew about it or not. I was surrounded by my own sin and I didn't know what to do. But one thing was for sure. Eddie was confident that I wouldn't cross him and, at that moment, so was I.

I must have fidgeted a lot during the service. Mama nudged me with her elbow at least a dozen times before I finally settled down and tried to listen to what Papa was saying. Finally, my eyes just began to rove around the small building. We called it our church but it wasn't really a church. Some of the men had converted an old feed store into the church when old Mr. Burke died. The feed store had not been profitable since Eddie's father started selling feed at his general store; and when Mr. Burke died, his widow sold all the merchandise for little or nothing. She had been excited when she was approached with the idea of making her building into a church.

This morning she was sitting just two rows behind us, fanning the flies away in the heat. Several of the men had built a dozen flat benches without backs for the congregation. They were lined up facing what had been the back of the store. I picked up more than one splinter from those benches over the years. Papa had built a small platform to stand on when he preached and also a pulpit to stand behind. The rough hand-carved letters on the front of the pulpit read "In Loving Memory." An old potbellied stove stood to the right of Papa's pulpit between the forward benches and the front wall. Two windows graced each side of the building. They were installed after the building became a church. The one toward the front and close to the stove was stuck tight and wouldn't budge. The other three would raise about half a foot and allowed some measure of air on our hotter days. They were opened on this morning and, as a result, the flies were especially thick. As a congregation we fluctuated between twenty-five and thirty-five. If Papa's sermon was unusually strong on one Sunday, it dwindled to twenty-five or less the next time we met. It seemed it was always the men who chose to miss after a particularly strong sermon. Mama said Papa was stepping on toes. I wasn't sure what she meant for a long time. But I do know that the intensity of Papa's hellfire and brimstone sermons certainly affected our small congregation.

As I sat looking up toward Papa that morning, his mouth was opening and closing like a rapid-fire rifle. Now and then his fist would bounce off the pulpit so hard that even I, with my mind on other matters, flinched. He was yelling about something and I was catching a word only now and then. Eddie was on my mind and I knew the inevitable was drawing closer and closer. I knew he was just waiting until he could get to his father. Every muscle in my body was drawn tight. Several times I had to physically unclench my fists, and now the muscles in my forearms were tired from the strain of the last few hours. Relaxing was not an option. Only moments later my fists would be clenched again and I would have to go through the process of forcing them to unclench. Even the muscles in my legs were beginning to ache. I thought if I could tune Papa in I might be able to forget my troubles for a few minutes. But it didn't work. I couldn't put the fire or Eddie out of my mind. Again I tried to focus on what Papa was saying.

"….was a terrible tragedy. These folks will need all our prayers and our physical help as they..."

I realized he was talking about the Carter family. I glanced toward Eddie. He was smiling broadly; seemingly he was taking in everything Papa was saying. All around the church people were looking toward Eddie as if he was some kind of hero. He was the center of attention and, as if he suddenly realized the serious-ness of the moment, the smile disappeared and his face took on an expression of anguish that I'm sure he felt was more fitting for the occasion. It was certainly an expression that I had never seen on Eddie's face.

Two rows behind, I heard the widow Burke gasp and whisper something about that poor boy and his mother and sister. Her remark was totally unexpected. Everyone knew she was no lover of the Carter family. After Mr. Burke died, she had sworn up and down that Floyd Carter was to blame. She didn't blame him directly, for Burke had died of a heart attack. But she had claimed that Carter's decision to go into business against her husband eventu-ally led to his premature death. It was an accusation made during her grief and I'm sure she wished many times that she could have taken the remark back. So, her sympathy affected the congregation more than anyone else could have. And for just a moment, even I felt sorry for Eddie. But that lasted only long enough for me to remember what he was about to do. Any sympathy that passed through my mind quickly turned to disgust. Not only disgust for Eddie but disgust for my own cowardice. I turned away to stare out the stuck window behind the stove. I'm not sure how long

I had been staring when Mama squeezed my shoulder and I realized that Papa had everyone standing for closing prayer.

When he finished, I pushed past Eddie and hurried up the aisle toward the door. As I started out, I turned expecting Eddie to be right behind me. To my relief, he was engulfed in Elmira

Higgins' arms. The old woman had never married and it seemed she was always looking for some unexpected person to shower with affection. On more than one occasion, I had been that person. I was glad it was Eddie this time even though he didn't deserve it. She was planting a dry parched kiss on his forehead. Eddie looked embarrassed. I could tell he wanted to escape those pudgy arms as soon as possible. But there was more to come. While Miss Higgins was drooling all over him, Ned Wheatley was patting him on the back and telling him how sorry he was about the fire and how he would be more than glad to help rebuild their house. Just call on him, I heard Ned say. Several others, including the widow Burke, were waiting their turn at Eddie. More kisses and more promises of help would be forthcoming. The sight disgusted me even more. Not the sight of the people who wanted to help, but the sight of Eddie, lavishing in the pity and being treated like a hero when he was about to take us all down a terrible path. I left the church with a knot in my stomach and waited in the shade of a huge magnolia tree a few feet from the front door of the church.

One by one the people finally filed out and made their way through the woods or down the dusty road toward their own houses. Finally, only Papa, Mama, and Eddie remained inside. When Mama and Eddie came out a few minutes later, she had her arm around him. He saw me and said something to Mama. She took her arm from his shoulder and he ran over to where I stood beneath the tree.

"Your Ma fixed a basket of vittles and we're all goin' over to Pa's store and eat. Ya'll are comin' to help clean the old back room. Me and you can take a short cut through the woods."

I didn't want to take a shortcut through the woods. All I wanted to do was go home and hide under my bed until all the trouble was over. I was already aware of the afternoon's agenda and dreaded it. Mama had come up behind Eddie now. The basket with the food was in her right hand. I hoped she had heard what Eddie said and would say I must stay with them. Instead she prompted, "James, you can go along with Eddie. Papa has a few things to finish in the church and we'll be along directly. Tell Sarah we're bringing lunch."

It wasn't what I wanted to hear and I protested mildly. "We could wait and walk along with you and Papa and I could carry the basket." It was an offer I hoped she wouldn't refuse.

"Nonsense," Mama answered. "You boys go ahead. We'll be close behind."

So ahead we went. I had hoped to postpone the inevitable and it hadn't worked. There was really no special reason to except, that maybe Eddie might change his mind if he thought about the consequences a little while longer. I found out soon after we left the church that there was no way he would change his mind. Eddie was set with his story even to the details of where Jesse was actually supposed to have set the fire. According to the story Eddie had concocted, Jesse had crawled up under the house where we were smoking. It was there that Eddie would swear he saw Jesse start the fire. He was obsessed with the lie. And when he repeated his story, he acted as if he really believed it. The lie was suddenly the truth in his own mind and not a fabrication at all. It caused me to wonder for a while. But I knew it was a lie. And I also realized I would keep my mouth shut. The thought made me sick to my stomach, knowing I didn't have the courage to challenge Eddie's story.

When we came in sight of the grocery store, Eddie broke into a jog. I had to nearly run flat out to keep up with him. Sweat was running down my back, soaking my underclothes. My shirt was clinging to my back and I was uncomfortable in more ways than one. When we climbed the steps to the store, I looked back for Papa and Mama. They were nowhere in sight. We had moved much faster through the woods than I had wanted to. They might not get here for several more minutes. I wasn't sure at that moment whether that was good or bad. While I was still looking back for Papa and Mama, I heard the front door of the store open and bang shut. Eddie was inside, but when I reached for the door, Eddie pushed it open instead.

"Come on, Jamie," Eddie said. He was standing just inside the door. The smile was gone and he was eyeing me intently. I knew he was wondering just how I would react when he told his story.

If he backed out now, he felt I would think of him as a coward. I wouldn't have. As much as I was disgusted with him and myself, I probably would have hugged his neck even though I knew what was in store for me when the real truth came out.

We walked back along the main aisle, between the counter and cracker barrel, past the barrel of pickles Lige Sanders' teeth had corrupted. The sound of sweeping was coming from the back room. Through the open door I could see Mrs. Carter moving her broom back and forth, stirring great clouds of dust with each stroke. At least a hundred small boxes were stacked against the inside wall. I wondered, as I stood watching the dust swirling around, how the four of them could ever live here. The room was only slightly larger than the front room of our own house. A smaller storage room adjoined the larger room. It was about half as big as this room.

"Ma, where's Pa?"

She jerked a thumb over her shoulder. "Out back tendin' to a bunch of trash." She eyed me without a word, then turned back to Eddie. Her eyes were swollen and I could tell she had been crying a lot. "What're you two about?"

"I gotta tell Pa somethin', somethin' real important."

"You're gonna help us this day, Eddie. There's a lot of fixin' we gotta do. You hear me, boy?"

"I aim to, Ma, but I gotta talk to Pa first. Somethin' I gotta tell him about the fire." Eddie looked at me with that follow-my-lead look and went through the door into the little room and out a back door to where Mr. Carter was piling a bunch of empty boxes on a charred spot of dirt.

"Pa."

Floyd Carter glanced over his shoulder toward Eddie and, without answering, kept on working.

"Pa."

Carter snapped another look at his son. "Yeah, boy. Whatcha want? You know I got work for you to do. You shoulda been here all mornin'."

Eddie seemed to hesitate for a moment. My heart skipped a beat, hoping he would just ask his father what he wanted him to do. Instead, Eddie dug his hands deep into his pocket, swallowed hard, and with his mouth drawn tight he glanced once more at me and continued.

"It's about the fire, Pa. I gotta tell you what I saw last night."

"Don't bother me, boy. I got a heap of work to do. Go in and tell your Ma to give you another broom so's you can clean out the little room."

Eddie seemed to waver then. He looked at me, I think, for courage to continue. But I had no desire to provide him with anything and he knew that. He pulled his hands out of his pockets, clenched his fists and started over again.

"Pa." He reached up and tugged at his father's flapping shirt-tail. I think it probably took Eddie a lot of courage to do that because even I knew that Floyd would not take kindly to that. "Pa, you gotta listen to me. I seen how the fire got started. I seen who done it."

Floyd froze for a moment. Then he turned, shot an irritated glance toward me, and finally glared into Eddie's eyes. The color evaporated from Eddie's face. He stammered now when he tried to speak and I wondered if he wanted to take it all back. But it was too late. He had said the words that I feared and there was no taking it back.

Floyd eyed his son for several seconds. "What you sayin', boy? What'd you say you seen?"

Eddie froze and dug his hands back into his pockets. I think he wanted to just melt into the ground. I could tell he wanted to stop right then. But he couldn't.

"Answer me, boy."

I was afraid Mr. Carter was going to strike out at Eddie, but before he could, Eddie turned and pointed an accusing finger in my direction. "He seen it too. Me and Jamie. We seen it all. Ain't that right, Jamie?"

"What?"

Mr. Carter turned his attention to me now. I was right where I didn't want to be, in the middle of something that I knew hadn't happened, at least not in the way Eddie was about to tell it. All I saw was Jesse walking down the road toward Eddie's just minutes before the fire started. "I ain't seen nothin," I stammered.

"You seen him right before it happened," Eddie insisted. "You said you seen him. Tell Pa."

My heart was in my throat. I didn't know what to say. I could only tell what I had seen. "I just seen him walkin' down the road twards your house. I didn't see nothin' else."

Floyd reached out, grabbed Eddie by both shoulders and began to shake him. "I ain't likin' what I'm a hearin'. You hear me? Now spit out what you seen." Floyd stopped shaking Eddie after a moment and just stood gripping him by his shoulders and glaring at his frightened son. Carter's knuckles were white from the grip and the look on his face was terrible.

Eddie blurted it out again. He was caught in his own lie and in his own mind he had to finish it. He was not about to back away now. He couldn't and he knew it. Floyd was ready to hurt someone and Eddie didn't want it to be him.

"I seen Jesse, honest. He done set fire to our house. Crawled right in under the floor, he did, under the kitchen. He done it, Pa, cause you was gonna whip him. He wanted to burn us all up."

I gritted my teeth and shut my eyes tight. If I didn't see it, maybe it would go away. But it didn't go away; and when I opened my eyes and relaxed my teeth I saw the red rising in Mr. Carter's face.

"Why didn't you tell me this last night, boy?" Then the man gripped Eddie's shoulders even more firmly. "You sure you're tellin' me true?"

The fingers gripping Eddie's shoulders were digging deep into the flesh. I could see Eddie wincing from the pressure. He only nodded at first. Then he responded. "Honest, Pa. That's what I done seen."

Floyd looked at me and I thought for a moment those hands would find their way to my throat. "You, boy. What'd you see?"

I only shook my head as Eddie gave me a pleading look. My mouth didn't have any saliva in it by then, and I don't think my voice could have been heard.

"I asked what you seen, Preacher's boy?"

Papa, where are you is all I could think right then. I was shaking and my body felt strangely cold. Words didn't want to come out of my mouth but when they did it seemed like they were coming from miles away. "I seen Jesse walkin' down the road towards your house. That's all I seen. Honest."

Floyd Carter was measuring me with his eyes and all I could do was drop my head and study the brown smudge that occupied the right knee of my overalls.

"When'd you see him and don't lie, boy? I don't like no liars," Floyd growled. He was looking squarely at me. He had released his grip on Eddie and taken a step in my direction.

"Late," I managed as I moved back away from the man.

"Jist before the fire, right, Jamie. It was jist before the fire. Tell Pa." Eddie pleaded.

"How 'bout that?" Floyd persisted. "You seen that low down Nigger just afore the fire?"

"I guess." I never felt so low in my entire life. I wanted to shout out what I suspected but I was terrified. Where were Papa and Mama? Why weren't they here?

Floyd roared. "Boy, you're a pussy footin' around the question. Now you answer me straight. Was it close on afore the fire?"

I was shaking when I answered. "Yes, Sir." It was the truth.

"And that's all you seen."

"Yes, sir." With every ounce of strength I was trying to avoid Floyd's eyes. He was towering over me now, his hot, putrid breath blasting down into my face.

"Ain't no nigger a goin' to get away with torchin' a white man's house." He pushed past us and headed toward the back door of the store.

Eddie and I exchanged glances, my friend rubbing first one shoulder and then the other. At the moment, I felt no sympathy for him. And I was also ashamed of myself. I could have put a stop to the whole thing. But I didn't. Now I watched Eddie's father disappear into the store.

A few moments later we heard loud shouting coming from the back room. Eddie and I crept up to the back door and listened intently. What we heard sent shivers up and down my back. Eddie's feelings were a mystery to me. I'm not sure what he wanted right then. If it was confrontation, that had now been set in motion. If it was death, that was also a strong possibility. But, whatever, the seed had been planted and now we, and I say we, because I did nothing to stop it, we were about to reap what the two of us had sown. I can still remember Mrs. Carter's pleas and her husband's rebuke that fateful morning.

"Floyd, not with a gun! You must not!" Her voice was cracking as she pleaded with her husband.

"You go about your cleanin', woman. This is man's business and I'll tend to it in whatever way that's needed."

"I won't let you," Sarah Carter cried.

"You ain't stoppin' me from what's gonna be done. Now let go of the gun or I'll take my hand to you."

Over the noise I heard the front door of the store open and shut. Papa and Mama were finally there. That thought scared me now. I knew how Papa would react. Surely there would be a confrontation between him and Mr. Carter. The thought sent a cold shiver down my spine.

Eddie and I slipped into the little room just in time to see Floyd wrench the gun from his wife's hands and stalk toward the front of the store. Mrs. Carter was standing in the middle of the storage room. Her arms were folded across her chest with her fists clenched. Tears were streaming down her face as she stared after her husband. The broom she had been using was lying beside her feet.

From where we stood, we could see past her into the store. Floyd stood square in front of Papa. Mama was to the side where Papa had moved her when he saw the gun. The shotgun in Floyd's hands was pointed toward the floor. Floyd was telling Papa what we had told him just moments before and what he now planned to do about it. Papa looked over Floyd's shoulder toward Eddie and me. Then he put up his big right hand and placed it firmly in Floyd's chest.

"No!" It was all that Papa said and at that moment I was afraid that Mr. Carter might shoot him. "Let me talk to the boys before you do anything you'll regret."

Instead, he slapped Papa's hand away and shouted. "You ain't stoppin' me, Preacher."

"Man, have you lost your senses. You can't go out and kill a man like that."

I punched Eddie. "We gotta tell."

"Shut up," he snapped. It seemed all Eddie's bravado had returned and his snappy retort caught me by surprise. "Remember, you swore." He looked me up and down intently. Then he attacked my weak spot. "Sides, you want everybody to find out what you was doin under the house? You want them to think you done started the fire?" I wilted under the heat of the moment. The threat was there. He would shift the blame to me if I didn't go along. I certainly didn't want his father to turn the gun on me.

I shuddered and almost called out as Papa reached for the gun. Floyd started to swing it up toward Papa but thought better of it. With his left hand, he reached out and gave Papa a hard shove that sent him reeling back against a stack of cans. As they crashed to the floor, he stalked past Papa and out the door. When Papa regained his balance, he started after Floyd. It was then that Mama appeared from the side and grabbed his arm.

"Efren, don't. He's in a dangerous state of mind. He could shoot you."

Papa shook her hand from his arm and followed Floyd outside. Mr. Carter was thirty paces from the porch when Papa called after him.

"Floyd Carter, there'll not be a man or woman you can turn to if you do this foul deed."

Floyd turned and glared at Papa. "I got friends here abouts

that'll help me, Preacher. I don't expect help from no high and mighty psalm singer." With that he turned and stalked off toward the river.

Papa watched a moment, and came back into the store.

"Where are the boys?" I heard him ask.

I felt a cold shudder knife through my body again. I wanted to hide but I knew there was no place I could. Now both of us had to face Papa.

"Here, Papa," I called out from a few feet behind him.

"What did you boys tell Floyd?"

Mama came around from the other side of the pile of cans and stood at Papa's shoulder. Mrs. Carter was bent over the counter weeping softly.

I swallowed hard. "I didn't tell him nothin', Papa, 'cept that I saw Jesse walkin' along the road towards his house just a while before the fire."

Papa studied me as if he was looking right into the depths of my soul. "That wouldn't set a man off that way. You must have said something else."

"No sir, I didn't say no more."

"James, this is very serious. You must tell Papa everything you know," Mama interjected.

I looked at Eddie. "That's all I told him, honest, Mama. Eddie said he saw it." I was committed now. I didn't actually think I was telling a lie but in my heart I knew what I was doing was just as bad. If I knew Eddie at all, he would admit to the truth only by threat of death. The trap was set and I was caught. Only the truth would stop what was happening. But I was terrified and unprepared to implicate myself yet.

"Eddie, you must tell me everything you saw last night. Tell it just like you told it to your father."

Eddie was much calmer now. He felt he was in control and the words flowed smoothly out of his mouth. Now and then he would glance my way as he brought me into the conspiracy. I know he was watching my reaction to be sure I didn't waver. Unfortunately,

I didn't. When he finished, Papa took him by the shoulders the same way his father had. The only difference was in the manner. There was gentleness in Papa's touch as he knelt in front of Eddie.

"You must be sure, Eddie. This is very serious. People could be hurt, maybe killed. Did it happen exactly the way you told me?"

Eddie glanced at me and nodded, then gave a sheepish, "Yes."

Papa studied Eddie's face for several more seconds, his eyes meeting Eddie's until finally he breathed a heavy sigh and stood up. His big hands still rested on Eddie's shoulders.

"You're sure about this, Eddie? You must tell the truth. Do you understand what can happen?"

"I am tellin' the truth. He done it. I seen him. He done it." There was anger mixed with fear in Eddie's voice as he squealed the words.

Papa stared hard into Eddie's eyes, then turned his attention to me. I could see his pain. Papa knew something wasn't right. As he looked at me, I could see disappointment replace the pain. I wanted to cry out what I suspected but even though I knew that someday the truth would be known, I couldn't. Finally, Papa released Eddie's shoulders and looked toward Mama.

"Ellen, take Sarah and the boys to our house and watch after them. I must hurry now and saddle Satan. We must stop this. But first, I have to warn Jesse and the people in the shantytown." He looked directly at me now. "We will talk when I get home tonight."

Mama was looking at me also when she said. "Efren, please be careful." Then she said it again. "Please be careful." The look on her face was one that I saw only twice — that terrible day and then years later when she sat beside Papa's bed on that last night of his life.

Papa nodded and without another word, turned and hurried out of the store. I will forever wish I had ended the whole matter right there. I could have. I should have but fear does strange things to people. I didn't and terrible things happened for which I can never forgive myself.

# CHAPTER 8

PAPA KNEW HE HAD time to get to the shantytown before Mr. Carter. The direction Floyd took when he left the store led northeast toward the river and not to the shantytown where Jesse lived. Close to a hundred of Jesse's people, many of them relatives, lived in the dozen or so rundown shacks that lay just a short distance from the swamp. Unpainted and about to rot under their feet, they refused to move. They had no money and no way to buy the supplies to repair the old shanties, but they maintained them as well as they could.

Many of the people were born in the one and two room shacks where they still lived. A few were in their late forties and older. If they were older than forty they were probably born into slavery. It was the only life they had known before the war. Though the days of slavery were gone, they still worked the land as best they could. It was land they were given when the war ended, and they lived on it much as their parents and grandparents before them. The land was theirs, and they had the freedom to work it as they pleased.

They were a close-knit people, led by an old woman called Granny Ruby. Some around our small community wondered if she hadn't been there as long as the land. Of course, everyone knew different. She was well into her eighties, small and squat with gray hair and a face that was all wrinkles. Her voice was raspy and low and she spoke with some effort. An old corncob pipe was nearly always protruding out of one corner of her mouth. In my infrequent meetings with the old woman I never saw the pipe lit. Granny was the unspoken head of all that lived in the shantytown. And she was probably the hardest worker of all her people. You could still see her every day trudging along the trail toward our community to do the washing and house cleaning for one of the several white families she still worked for. When she wasn't working, she would be rocking back and forth on her front porch enjoying her pipe. She was tireless. An old landowner gave the land to Granny's people because of her. She had been a slave in the landowner's house and it was said that he had a soft spot in his heart for Granny Ruby because of her loyalty to his family during the worst of the war. She was not only the leader, she was also the law in the shantytown. Any disturbance between her people was settled on Granny's porch with her decision being sacred. Even with all his anger, Floyd would not challenge her, especially alone. And though no one in Granny's world would admit it, it was well known that there was more than one gun in the possession of some of her neighbors.

Papa felt like he knew where Floyd was going and it wasn't to the shantytown. He would later, but Papa knew he wouldn't go there alone. The storekeeper had friends that would do anything for the right price. Papa was most concerned about the four Billings' brothers. They lived along the river several miles from the store. No meaner bunch could be found anywhere within a hundred miles. They were just old enough to remember when black people were slaves, and they grew up resenting the fact that these people were no longer shackled as they once were. They made no bones about hating anything connected to the North. Even though none of them were aware of Lincoln when he was president, they still hated him for everything he had stood for. They blamed their own unfortunate situation on him.

On this day Papa had a very good idea where Floyd was heading. And he knew what would happen if Floyd persuaded the brothers to go after Jesse. People could very well die, innocent people. It was there Floyd would most likely be going for help. And if he knew the four brothers, for a price they would be more than happy to help. They were always itching for a fight and only needed a cause to hang their hats on. This could be that cause.

Once he was saddled, Satan galloped out of the yard as if he knew the urgency of the mission as well as Papa did. The trail to the shantytown led across our back pasture and through a dense stand of woods that was nearly too weedy and briar-covered for a man on horseback.

Papa and I had come here the winter before to hunt rabbits. It was the first time he allowed me to fire the shotgun. Before he handed me the gun that snowy morning he told me to brace for the kick that would come when I pulled the trigger. I listened with excitement but dismissed the admonishment about the kick. My eyes were already searching the thin white layer of snow that fell the night before. We no sooner settled into a small gully behind some bushes before the first rabbit appeared. Like Papa said, the rabbits would be plentiful and they were that day. I was trembling with excitement as I pulled the shotgun up. Papa had instructed me on how to sight down the barrel. I did, or thought I did just as he told me, and pulled the trigger. A small limb five feet off the ground tore loose and fell beside the frightened animal. I found myself on my backside, watching as the rabbit disappeared in the snow-covered brush. All I could think of then was my bruised pride and the terrible ache in my shoulder. Papa reached down and lifted me to my feet, taking the shotgun as he did. I thought my shoulder must be broken; but when I complained to Papa, he only shook his head and assured me it was no more than a bruise. I was disappointed that he gave me no more sympathy as he trudged farther through the brush looking for more rabbits.

Papa didn't laugh at my first miserable shooting exhibition, and I was thankful for that. Later he put his arm around me and assured me that his first experience with a weapon could have been much more painful. In his haste to kill his first rabbit, he had pulled the trigger before raising the gun and missed his own feet by just inches. It was nearly a year before his papa, my grandfather, let him near another gun. I carried that picture in my mind for a long time and took comfort when Papa turned the shotgun over to me the next time.

~ ~ ~

Now, as Papa rode through these same woods, I'm sure he wasn't thinking about our rabbit hunt. More than once the trail narrowed, and he stopped and pulled the thorn bushes back away from his Sunday coat. Mama had just finished sewing a patch on the right elbow. The coat would require more work after this venture. About halfway to the shantytown Satan came upon a rattler. But thoroughbred that he was, he came to a quick stop and stood stock still. He and Papa had encountered rattlers on more than one occasion. The snake was a good ten feet ahead and coiled with his head pointed toward them. Papa reached back and patted the big horse on the rump.

"Good boy." Both Papa and Satan watched the snake as it continued its distinctive rattle. "Back up, Satan. Back up, boy." Papa pulled back on both reins, and the horse took half a dozen steps backward. There was a small clearing to the left and Papa pulled gently on the left rein and patted Satan on his rear. "Let's go this way, big fella. We'll leave that gentleman to his own pleasures." As they passed some twenty feet to the left of the snake, Papa glanced toward it, saw it uncoil and continue on down the path.

It was early afternoon when Papa came in sight of the scattered houses that made up the little shantytown. It lay across a clearing in another stand of woods. A narrow trail led through the trees separating the old houses from each other. Eight shacks were on the right side of the trail and ten more were on the left. At the far end and barely visible through the foliage was the shack where Granny Ruby lived alone. That's where he was headed.

He nudged Satan, and they moved out into the clearing. Off to the left and perhaps a mile away was the border of the swamp. He hadn't been in there, but those who had said you didn't want to go there. And he was not eager to ignore their advice.

By the time he was halfway across the clearing, he could see people coming out of their shacks and pointing his way. He knew most of them and they were always friendly when he encountered them in his own community. He wasn't sure how they would react to him here where they lived. This was their home and very few white people had ventured into the shanty- town in the past. They were already congregating in front of one of the shacks. He counted ten. They were in front of the third shack on the left. He knew them all by sight and many by name. They came and went back in the white community, always minding their own business, always speaking when you spoke to them. He rode past these ten, his eyes searching for Jesse as he did so. He was not among them. But the dogs were, yelping at Satan's heels until even the normally stable thoroughbred became skittish. Now, with the yowling of the hounds and other noise, more people were beginning to come out of the shacks to see what was going on.

"Easy, boy." Papa patted the horse on the neck and it seemed to calm him a little.

Granny Ruby appeared about halfway up the path to her shack and stood studying him as he moved closer to her. She was looking suspiciously at Papa as he reined up in front of her. Her right jaw was bulging and instead of the corncob pipe, the putrid stench of tobacco was in the air. The corners of her mouth were moist and brown.

"Granny Ruby," Papa said.

"Preacher," the old woman returned.

Papa sat tall in the saddle and looked around at the people closing in around him. Jesse was still nowhere in sight. He looked back at Granny not wanting to dismount until invited.

"Granny, I'm looking for Jesse?"

Granny spit a mouthful of brown liquid toward the ground and wiped the back of her hand across her mouth. "What for you wantin' to see him, preacher man?" The suspicious look of a few moments before was evident in her tone.

Papa looked toward the people again. "Can we talk somewhere,

Granny?" He motioned with his head toward her shack.

Granny waved her arms back and forth to take in the whole assemblage that surrounded him. "These here's my people and they's Jesse's folks too. You tells me, you tells them," she said and let go with another stream of tobacco juice toward Satan's feet.

A baby cried out and Papa turned to see a young girl of about twenty, her tattered blouse open to the waist baring her partially covered breasts. The naked baby in her arms had lost its hold and was searching hungrily for its meal. The girl caught the small head that was bobbing back and forth and maneuvered it back into position. The crying stopped.

Papa turned back to the old woman. "Granny, there was a fire last night. Floyd Carter's house was destroyed."

"We heerd."

Papa knew then why the people seemed to be on edge when he rode in. "I need to speak to Jesse about the fire."

Granny searched the crowd and without looking back to Papa asked, "What that boy got to do with no fire noway?"

Papa hesitated, trying to choose his words carefully. "Jesse was seen close by shortly before the fire." He could hear mumbling and feel the people stirring all around him.

Someone moved against Satan's flank and the animal moved slightly. Any friendliness these people might have felt earlier was no longer evident.

Granny Ruby jerked her eyes up toward Papa. "Preacher, we always took a likin' to you. You and your missus done treated us right. We ain't likely to fergit that. But what you're a jawin' now don't sound none too friendly to me. You needs to spell out what you're a meanin'."

Papa felt Satan move under him again and looked around. A large, muscular man he had seen before but didn't know by name moved close. The rest of the crowd was pushing against him, causing Satan to fight for his balance.

Papa patted the horse gently on the right side of his neck. "Whoa, Satan. Whoa, boy."

Granny waved her arms at the people, gesturing toward Papa as she did. "All you, git back away. You hear me. Git back away from that animal."

As if one, they moved slowly back away from Satan and the horse settled down.

"Land sakes. A body can't talk to a neighbor now a days without some busybody buttin' in. This here's a God man and a friend. You all knows that. Ain't that right, Preacher? You is a friend, ain't you?" She turned her gaze from the man standing close to Satan's right flank back to Papa as she asked the question.

Papa recognized the tone. Just a hint of sarcasm was directed at him. It wasn't a threat, but it was as close as you could get without actually being one.

"I think you know who I am, Granny," Papa said calmly. "And I think you know I'm your friend."

"What you want with Jesse then?"

Papa put both hands on the saddle horn and sat straight up in the leather saddle. "I need to ask Jesse if he saw anything last night when he passed the Carter's house after work." Papa paused for a moment trying to decide how to continue. He was treading in dangerous territory and he didn't want to add fuel to the fire that could be brewing. "Granny, someone saw Jesse around the Carter house just before the fire. I need to talk to him and get his side of the story."

Granny spit a stream of tobacco and stared hard at Papa. "Say it straight out, Preacher. What you gittin' at?"

Papa tried to make himself even more straight in the saddle. "Granny, someone said Jesse may have set it. I don't believe that but I need to talk to him and head off any trouble."

This set all the people to buzzing. The girl with the baby must have moved suddenly because the infant started screaming and, without looking, Papa guessed it was searching for its' meal again. In all the excitement, Granny Ruby never batted an eye.

"All of you, keep them mouths shet." She looked at Papa and spit again, this time directly on Satan's hooves. "I thought you was a gittin' to that. Who done told that lie?"

Papa shook his head, unwilling to divulge Eddie's name to this crowd. "Granny, there's likely to be trouble. Carter has some dangerous friends. If they catch Jesse alone, they most likely will resort to violence. You know as well as I do, that we can't let that happen."

"I knows that boy. He ain't no house burner. Done gone and got hisself a woman and a new youngun. He ain't likely to do no ruination to that." Granny waved her arm toward the girl with the baby.

Papa remembered. Jesse had told him about the child two months earlier. He nodded. "I feel same as you, Granny. I know Jesse would never do anything like this. But this could get out of hand. Let me talk to him, maybe take him over to the sheriff in Sumpter until Floyd cools down. He'll be safe there. Sheriff over there's a good man."

The man at Satan's right flank swore softly but Papa ignored him. He would do nothing without Granny's okay, and Papa was convinced she wouldn't do anything foolish.

Granny Ruby shook her head. "Ain't fer me or you to decide. Jesse, he the one to do that."

Papa felt someone bump Satan's right rear. "We ain't turnin' Jesse over to no white sheriff." The man had moved up close to Papa's right leg and was leering up into his face.

Papa was about to say something but it was Granny who spoke first. "John, you git back now and you hush that trap. Hear me?" She moved to that side of the horse and was standing toe to toe with the man she called John.

The man hesitated, looking first at Granny then back to Papa. Finally, unwillingly, he moved back away from Papa and Satan.

Granny looked up at Papa now. "You ride that black animal outta here, Preacher. You git on home. We gonna find Jesse and we gonna find out fer sure what done happened if'n he knows. But, whatever, we sticks together and what he say gonna go a tolerable way with us. If'n he 'cides to go with you to the law, then go he can. That bein' the case we'll send one of the younguns to fetch you. Ain't no Floyd Carter gonna take him. We'll do what we needs to do to see to that. If'n you see Carter, you say so to him."

Papa leaned over the saddle horn. "The last time I saw Floyd he was headed toward the river and the Billings place. You know what they're like. He may be trying to buy their services to help him catch Jesse. Keep an eye out, Granny."

Granny nodded. "We done dealt with them four Billings afore." She reached up and patted Satan just above his nostrils. "We appreciates you a comin' here, Preacher. Ain't many who would." She glanced at the man who had made the threatening gestures a few minutes before. "We all does."

Papa held Granny Ruby's eyes for several seconds before he sighed and said. "You'll know where to find me if I'm needed."

Granny nodded and without another word wheeled around and headed back up the path toward her house. Papa watched a moment, pulled on Satan's right rein and turned the horse back up the path toward the clearing they crossed only a few minutes before. As he did, John and the rest of the people made a path for him. Still, their eyes remained on him as he moved along the narrow trail they provided. Even though he was there to help, the tension was heavy in the air. He could see the suspicion, anger and in a few cases the hatred brought on by generations of deprivation. They had known him for years, knew what he stood for and yet they still didn't trust him completely. He had been the messenger of bad news. And while he felt that he understood their feelings, he wondered if any white person ever could without walking in their shoes.

# CHAPTER 9

GRANNY RUBY STOPPED SHORT of her porch and watched Papa's back until Satan crossed the open stretch and disappeared from sight. Then she picked up a limb and ambled up to John, the man that had shown hostility toward Papa. She raised her arm and brought it down hard against the man's shoulder.

"John Andrews, your mama done raised a fool. That preacher man ain't our enemy. He done come to warn Jesse, not kill him."

John didn't flinch at the limb. "He white, Granny. He got no use for us no more'n them other whites does and we ain't got no use for them." John looked around for support but found no one willing to buck the old woman.

"Fool," she said and spit a stream of tobacco juice to the side. "God done put somethin' in that knot on yore shoulders and he aims for you to put it to some kind of use. If'n you was to do some foul deed to that white preacher..." She hesitated and spit at John's feet. "Wouldn't be airy a place none of us could hide," she snapped, wiping the brown juice from the corners of her mouth with the back of her hand.

John straightened his shoulders. "Ain't none of us..." He looked around before continuing. "I ain't standin' by and seein' Jesse strung up for somethin' he ain't done." He looked around again, this time to make his commitment. "Makes no never mind to me whether Jesse done it or not. If'n he did, then he had good cause and they ain't gonna hang him."

"That's a fool jabberin'. First place, if'n you knowed Jesse like you claims, you'd know he never done no such thing." Granny turned away from John and her eyes were searching the crowd now. John was momentarily forgotten. Finally, she spotted who she was looking for.

"Ezra."

"Yes um." A tall skinny boy of about seventeen stepped out from behind the girl with the baby. He wore no shoes or shirt. Beads of perspiration were flowing freely down his chest and the waist of his homemade britches was moist with the sticky sweat. He didn't say anything else as he approached Granny.

"You know where Jesse be?"

"Yes um."

"Lizabeth," the old woman said. "You go and fix your man enough vittles to last him two days and give um to Ezra. Leave the youngun with your mama and git. Time's a wastin'."

The girl pulled the child away from her uncovered breast and handed it to an older woman standing close by. Startled by this strange turn of events, the infant let out a loud wail and immediately began digging its mouth into the older woman's dress. Unable to find satisfaction, the baby began screaming again. The old woman finally moved away through the crowd and settled into an old rocking chair on a porch at the far end of the trail.

"Ezra, soon as you gits them vittles you come see me. You hear what I'm sayin', boy?" Without waiting for an answer, Granny turned and made for her own shack.

Ten minutes passed before she appeared back on her porch. She was carrying a brown paper bag. Inside was a knife and her last plug of tobacco. Ezra and the girl were coming up the path toward her. The girl still had a cloth sack in her arms.

"You fix enough fer two days, girl?"

"Yesum," the girl grunted.

"Good. Hand it to this here boy." She looked at Ezra. "Let's go. The sun'll be goin' down dreckly." She put her hand in the middle of Ezra's back and motioned. "Hurry now."

Ezra nodded and started off toward the river. Granny followed and the girl started after them.

Granny stopped suddenly. "Where you goin', girl?"

"To my man."

"No, you ain't. You git back to your place and tend to that youngun. He ain't finished his eatin'." Granny motioned her away. "We'll take care of that man of your'n."

Without any argument, the girl stopped in her tracks and watched as the two of them disappeared around Granny's shack. Then she made her way down the path toward where her mother sat rocking a crying baby.

~ ~ ~

With Granny Ruby following close on Ezra's heels, the two of them made their way through the woods, heading west toward the river. The young man set a hard pace, but Granny, despite her age, kept up. All the years of hard work had made the little woman tough. She called on that toughness now as they fought through the dense undergrowth for more than two miles. After an hour, Ezra paused and they listened.

"Ain't fur now, Granny. I can hear the water a beatin' and a splashin'."

"Git on with you," Granny said and gave him a gentle push.

They broke out of the woods about fifty yards from the river and Ezra stopped and looked both ways along the bank. No one was in sight. Granny's eyes were searching too. But the old woman's vision was fading and most of the scene in the distance was a blur.

"Well, boy, where he be?"

Ezra shook his head and extended his arm, crooking his elbow so that the forearm turned back toward his head. The long fingers flopped down in his hair and he began scratching. After a moment he shrugged his shoulders.

"Ain't here."

Granny didn't hesitate. She reached out and slapped him hard on the arm. "I sees that, boy. Be a thinkin'. You comes fishin' with him regular like. Where else he likely to be?"

Ezra thought a moment and a smile appeared. "Bout a half mile up river he say the catfish comes into the shallows a lot. Sometimes he catches um by hand." He pointed north along the river and started in that direction.

But Granny grabbed his arm and spewed out another mouthful of tobacco juice. She looked both ways along the river, wondering as she did if Jesse might have started back by the path to the shantytown. In their haste to reach this spot, they hadn't used the regular path, for it wound around through the woods and took another half hour to travel. But they had come this far, and they must make sure he wasn't still at the river before they searched elsewhere. Somewhere behind them they could hear a hound bark and Granny turned, wondering if it might be Floyd Carter. She watched and listened, but there was no other sound, only the rushing water as it boiled over the rocks and shoals. Finally, she pointed north up the river.

"Git movin', boy. We gots to hurry."

They walked for perhaps ten minutes before Ezra stopped and pointed to a knoll about a hundred yards ahead.

"Right yonder, on tuther side of the rise. The waters slides in there and don't run mean like out here," he said as he motioned toward the rushing water.

Granny took the lead now, moving faster than Ezra. The ground was hard from lack of rain. Normally, the ground this close to the river would have been soft and slushy. Rain had not fallen for more than three weeks and even though the waters were still moving lustily, the river was down. This was a spot where it always seemed more violent than in other stretches. Granny reached the knoll and scurried right up. At the top she stopped and surveyed what she could see of the area. Ezra was standing next to her panting for breath.

"There, Granny, there he be." He was pointing to a spot about two hundred yards away. Jesse was standing knee deep and motionless in the middle of a quiet pool of water. His hands were outstretched in front of him and he was peering intently down into the clear water. While they watched, his hands moved like lightning and he pulled a small fish out and pitched it quickly toward the bank. Ezra saw it but it was only a blur to Granny. Everything at that distance was a blur to Granny. But she did hear Ezra's low whistle.

"What is it, boy?"

"Jesse, he done moved so fast that fish never knowed he was about till he was caught and throwed on the bank."

"Never you mind that," Granny said and started down the hill toward Jesse. By the time they reached him, he was out of the water and dropping that fish and two others into a small tow-sack with five more. Jesse was about to step back into the pool when he caught sight of Ezra and Granny. He paused and raised a hand in their direction as they approached.

He was dripping to the waist. His overalls were ragged around his ankles and just above his right knee there was a hole about half the size of an apple. The only thing covering his upper body was the overall straps crisscrossing his chest and back and lapping over his shoulders. His feet were shoeless. As Granny and Ezra drew close, Jesse picked up the sack and held it toward them. A wide grin spread across his face as the two hurried up.

"Granny, Ezra. I done had me a good day. Good vittles fer a heap of folks."

"Ain't no time fer that, Jesse. We gots news and it ain't good." Granny motioned toward Jesse's worn out shoes on the ground and the tattered shirt beside them. "Git yer belongings and let's git where no eyes can see us."

"My woman and youngun..." Jesse's first concern was his wife and new baby.

"Ain't that," Granny said. "Git them things and let's be a goin'."

"What then?" Jesse insisted. His smile had turned to puzzlement as he looked first at Ezra then back to Granny. She didn't stop for an explanation but proceeded to gather Jesse's shirt and shoes and start for the woods. Both men watched her until she turned around.

"You two do what I tells you and do it now. You hear?"

They both began to move then, but Jesse grabbed Ezra's arm as they did.

"I ain't understandin'," he shot at Ezra. The statement demanded an answer.

Ezra looked about as if he was afraid someone might hear. Ahead, Granny was beating a path toward cover.

"The fire at the Carter place. You heerd about that?"

Jesse nodded. They were halfway to the covering of the trees. Somewhere in the distance a dog let out a mournful yell. To Ezra, it sounded like the same animal he and Granny heard twenty minutes earlier. He stopped and Jesse stopped with him. Granny kept moving in front of them. The dog was much closer than before. Ezra looked around suspiciously, his eyes searching up and down the riverbank. He was clearly afraid.

Jesse could see and feel his friend's fear. "Ezra, what you mean 'bout the fire?"

But Ezra wasn't ready to talk. He continued to look in the direction of the dog's cry, seemingly afraid to move any further. Finally, he turned and fixed his eyes on Jesse. "They done say you set that fire. That Carter feller is out a lookin' to string you up."

Jesse didn't move. He just stood there staring into Ezra's face. Ezra turned his attention back to the riverbank. It was clear that he wished he was anywhere but here right now. From the tree line Granny finally broke the silence. She had heard the dog again but doubted it belonged to Carter or the Billings' brothers. Still, there was no reason to take a chance. The sight of Ezra and Jesse, standing calmly in the middle of the clearing, angered her. What would she have to do to get these two men to move into the shadows? She knew Jesse. He was fearless and in his own way one of the most intelligent men she knew, black or white. Getting him to hide would be a chore. Keeping him alive until he could prove he was innocent might be impossible. And here he was exposing himself to anyone that might be about.

"Jesse, Ezra, git yerself out of sight. Ain't no tellin' who might be chasin' them dogs."

Jesse moved, but not out of fear. He had great respect for Granny. She was wise even beyond her years. He would listen to what she had to say.

"There a place here bouts that we can have our say without nobody seein'?" Granny asked, looking up into Jesse's face.

Jesse thought a moment. "An old rock ledge over that a way. I go there to nap sometimes. Ain't easy to see a body when they slide up under it."

Granny nodded. "Lead out."

Jesse did with Granny behind him and Ezra bringing up the rear. The younger man kept looking behind as if something or someone was following. Within five minutes they were out of sight under the ledge. Granny was satisfied that no one could approach unnoticed.

Now she faced Jesse and he could see the concern on her wrinkled face. The dress she wore was torn and tattered from her journey through the undergrowth and there were several scratches where the thorns had grabbed her arms and ripped the flesh. But she ignored them and faced Jesse.

"Boy, you in a heap a trouble. Ezra done told you about the fire."

"I knowed last night," Jesse replied.

Granny looked at Ezra. The younger man was listening intently. "Boy, you go yonder and look and listen." She motioned to Ezra. "If'n you hear anything or see anybody, you come and give us warning. Hear?"

Ezra nodded and moved off a few steps to watch the approach to the ledge.

Granny turned back to Jesse. "They's a sayin' you done set that fire. What you say to that?"

"Who say that?" Jesse blurted.

"Don't know, but the preacher, he done brought word. Said Floyd Carter was out to kill you. You understand. Some of them white folks is goin' to be after you. Like as not, it'll be them Billings trash and Carter." She stopped and studied Jesse carefully. "I told the preacher that you didn't do no such. Tell me I was right, boy."

Jesse shook his head vehemently. "I never done no such thing, Granny."

"I believes you. But that Carter ain't a goin' to. If'n he finds you, he ain't about to ask no questions. He's likely to lynch you on the spot or maybe shoot you like a dog, whichever he has a mind to do. And the preacher thinks he done gone to git that crazy Billings bunch."

"I ain't scairt of Carter or them Billings."

Granny spit another mouthful of brown tobacco and eyed Jesse angrily. His courage could get him killed, and she needed to shock him into doing something to protect himself until the truth was known.

"You ain't no fool, Jesse. Ezra, maybe, but you ain't." She shot a look toward the younger man. At the sound of his name he looked around sheepishly. When he saw Granny looking his way, he turned his head and looked back to his job. But the words bit deep. Without another glance toward the younger man, Granny turned her attention back to Jesse.

"They ain't a goin' to give you no chance. Now the preacher, he done said he would take you over to Sumpter to the sheriff. Said you'd be safe there till this got settled. I told him that we takes care of our own. But what you got to say? This here is your mess. You want to go with the preacher to Sumpter or no?"

Jesse straightened his shoulders and glared down into Granny's face. "You wantin' me to give myself up?" He shook his head before she could answer. "I ain't done nothin' and I ain't givin' up to no sheriff." He shook his head again. "You best git that thinkin' outa your head, Granny. I ain't givin' up."

"That be my thinkin' all along," Granny said and picked up the sack of food Ezra had set on the ground. "Didn't think you had no mind to do that. Here's two day vittles Lizabeth done fixed you. You put on these shoes and shirt." She handed Jesse's clothes to him and stepped back. "I done a heap of thinkin' on the way over here and I'm a believing' the swamp be your best place to hide. What you think bout that? Ain't many likely to come lookin' fer you in there." But Granny found it hard to believe her own words. If Carter offered them enough, the Billings brothers would follow Jesse anywhere, especially if it meant killing a black man.

Jesse sat down on the ground and began pulling on the old worn out shoes. "I ain't wantin' to hide, Granny. I ain't done nothin'." Without strings the old shoes fit loosely around Jesse's feet. "But, if'n I was hankerin' to hide, the swamp would be the best spot."

Granny placed her hands on her hips and looked up in the young man's face. "Boy, some of them white folks ain't carin' if'n you did or if'n you didn't start that fire. They's gonna string you up first and worry 'bout what really happened later. Now, you do what I tells you. Go to that old alligator hole you done telled everybody about. If'n I remembers kreckly, you said there's a clearin' close by on Alligator Island. Ain't too safe a place I reckon but there ain't many whites that'll come lookin' in there. You just be careful them gators don't do what Carter and the Billings aim to do."

Jesse stood up and pulled his arms through the holes in the soiled shirt. "I been on the island a heap of times, Granny. Never thought I'd be hidin' there," Jesse muttered.

Granny nodded and pulled a knife and a few matches out of the small sack. "Take this. You gonna need protectin' from more'n one kind of varmint." She pulled a plug of tobacco out of the sack. "This chew is the onliest one I got. I'll send more." She hesitated. "I'll send one of the boys in with more vittles 'fore you needs more. You stay hid till this thing gits settled. Hear me, boy?"

Jesse stuck the knife in the rope belt holding up his pants and dropped the tobacco in his pocket. "I ain't likin' this, Granny. I ain't never run from nothin'."

"Ain't never been nothin' like this happened to you afore," she said. "You wants to live to see that youngun grow up, you best do what I says."

Jesse nodded but the frown on his face told Granny he might

not follow her lead for long. "I gonna do it fer now, Granny." He turned to Ezra. "You git Granny home." It wasn't a request but an order to the young man.

Ezra nodded and backed away toward the direction they would have to take. But Granny wasn't through just yet, not until she was sure Jesse was on his way to the swamp.

"Now, you git," Granny ordered. "And take care. You the best we got."

Jesse bent and kissed the old woman on the forehead. She pushed him away and he noticed just a touch of dampness on her cheek. "My woman and youngun...."

"Git," she said. "We gonna take care of them two. You don't need to worry none."

Jesse nodded and turned to Ezra. Without a word, he motioned toward the direction of the shantytown. The younger man understood and whispered. "We goin'." That determined, Jesse started out in the direction of the swamp and disappeared into the dense undergrowth.

Granny and Ezra watched him for several seconds. Somewhere behind them, maybe a half-mile away, a dog yelped again. A moment later a shot rang out and there was silence. Granny let out a sigh of relief. The shot came from the opposite direction that Jesse had disappeared.

"Let's go, Ezra. We got a powerful lot to do."

They made their way out from under the ledge and started for home. Tonight there would have to be a meeting, Granny reasoned in her mind. Plans would need to be made. The next days would not be pleasant. But, then, Granny thought, many days had not been pleasant in the past and they had made it through. They would get through this too.

# CHAPTER 10

AFTER HIS CONFRONTATION WITH Papa, Floyd fully intended to borrow a horse at the Holland plantation and ride straight to the old shantytown. But the farther he went the more convinced he was that it was a bad idea. He certainly had no use for any of the blacks in the shantytown and they had no love for him. Sometime, a year or so earlier, he had been told that there were weapons distributed among the people who resided in those rundown shacks. One man alone in that situation would be suicide and, as angry as he was, he was not ready for that. The more he thought of it, the more convinced he was that several armed men could ride into and out of the shantytown without too much danger. And he knew just the bunch that fit that description. Amos Billings and his three brothers would be more than happy to accompany him. And if one of them didn't ride back out, as long as it wasn't him, well that wasn't anything he needed to worry about. None of the brothers would be a loss if they didn't make it out of the shantytown alive. It would be a good sacrifice to get Jesse and teach all the niggers a lesson. But he had to sell it to the brothers. Amos, the oldest and meanest of the four, would be the one he had to convince. After that the others would fall into line. Amos commented once that he didn't need an excuse to kill those shantytowners as he called them. On other occasions Amos had used more descriptive language. All that Amos needed was a reason. Floyd was about to give him that. He would find out now if Amos was just blowing air or if he really meant what he said.

It was a two-mile walk to Holland's land and, when Floyd reached the fence some quarter of a mile from the main house, he was breathing hard. The weight of the shotgun and the fast pace he set left his face red and his body drenched with sweat. Even his shoes felt as if there was a puddle of water standing in them. He stopped for a moment and rested his hand against the wooden gate. It felt like he touched the bottom side of a hot iron. His hand came away burning. The sensation reminded him of the time he had inadvertently leaned against the old potbellied stove in the store and came away with a badly burned forearm. This time he shook his hand back and forth and the pain slowly subsided. Carefully, now, Floyd lifted the iron latch and let himself onto the property. He shut the gate and started up the dusty road toward the house. A peeling six-foot board fence, that was white at one time, bordered the road on both sides and led right into the main yard. To the left, several acres of flat pasture land stretched to a stand of trees some quarter of a mile away. About thirty horses were running loose behind the fence on that side of the road. On the right, the trees came within several hundred feet of the fence. Floyd had been living in this part of the country only about fifteen years. Early on, someone had told him that Holland had between two and three hundred mounts at one time. That was at the beginning of the war.

A year after the start of the conflict the South bought most of Holland's stock, paying him with Confederate money which he stored away until after the conflict ended. It was worthless now. The old man found himself with limited funds and very little stock. His slaves were gone, his son killed at Bunker Hill and his wife dead from pneumonia six months before Appomattox. Holland was alone. The war had left him devastated. By the time the South surrendered, there seemed to be no reason for him to build the stock back to prewar numbers. No one was left to leave anything to. So he became something of a hermit living alone in the big house. Five years earlier he fell out of the barn loft and broke his leg. It was more than twenty-four hours before Granny Ruby found him and went for the doctor. To add to all his other problems, he was now handicapped and walked slowly and painfully with a cane. Granny Ruby came by two days a week to wash his clothes, clean the house and cook his meals. He made the food last until Granny came again. No one was sure if or how he paid her. Most people felt she did it out of loyalty. If Holland was anything he was good to the former slaves who had worked his land for so many years.

It was nearly a quarter mile from the front gate to the house and from a distance the big colonial mansion looked as grand as it once had, all four columns standing straight and strong, reminding everyone who passed of glorious days; the parties, the hunts, the friends that no longer visited, the gay chatter that no longer echoed through the halls and across the lawn of this once proud plantation. As Floyd drew closer he could see how, like the six-foot fence, the paint was chipping off the once sparkling columns and the bright white walls. Under one of the downstairs windows, a missing board revealed a hole in the outside wall. More than thirty years had passed since the house had felt the stroke of a paintbrush. High up at the pinnacle there was evidence that deterioration was slowly rotting portions of the roof, allowing the rain entrance into the attic of the old house. The grounds were no longer kept, and tangled weeds and grass were growing wild on the once well-groomed lawn. The house had seen much happiness in its day. But that was many years ago. Some time in the past, a narrow path had been cleared from the front porch of the house to the road where Carter now stood.

Floyd walked along the path between the weeds and started up the steps. Wood gave under his feet and he heard a loud crack. Moving quickly he jumped to the next step before the one he was standing on gave way. Somewhere, behind the house, a dog bellowed, then another and in a moment three hounds came chasing around the corner of the house, bawling and yelling at the top of their lungs. Holland was not completely alone.

Floyd stopped on the porch and glared down at them. They were creating a terrible racket and acting as if they would attack at any moment. A noise behind Floyd caused him to turn quickly just in time to see the old man charge out through the screen door.

"You lop-eared, mangy varmints," he yelled. "Git. You hear me. Now git." He took the cane and swung wildly at the animals catching one flush on the side of the head. The dog had advanced halfway up the stairs and was snarling at Floyd. It gave a yelp and fell backward into the other two. The old man swung again, this time missing. For a second it looked as if he would lose his own balance and tumble down the steps into the dogs, but he righted himself and let out with a chorus of foul language. The dogs backed away and looked up at him. It seemed as if they couldn't decide what to do. Then, the one Holland had struck gave one last yelp and took off around the house. He must have been their leader because the other two followed.

Holland turned and leaned heavily on his cane. His white hair was unkempt and there was a dirty-gray stubble on his face that had been there for some time. The front of his shirt was stained brown in several spots where food and tobacco had slipped from the old man's mouth and taken root. His clothes looked as if they were attached to his body. The stench told Floyd that he had not bathed in weeks.

Holland eyed the storekeeper for several seconds before Floyd spoke.

"Holland," Floyd said nodding his head.

"What you want, Carter?" Holland nodded toward the screen door and pulled it open.

"Ain't got no time fer socializing," Floyd said. "Came to borrow one of those nags of your'n."

The old man frowned and motioned toward the open screen door again. "Come in and sit a spell and we'll jaw about it."

"Ain't got time for no jawin'," Floyd spat impatiently.

"Heerd about the fire at your place last night. Right sorry," the old man said. Without pausing he continued. "What you want the animal fer?"

Floyd was growing impatient. He shifted the shotgun to his left hand, cleared his throat, and spat on the steps as he studied the crippled man for several seconds. He knew that Jesse Culbreath's parents had been slaves on this land. He also knew that some of these so-called southern gentlemen still felt a sense of protection for the slaves who had worked their land even though the ties of ownership no longer existed. Floyd wasn't sure how Holland felt about Jesse or any of the others from the shantytown. But he knew the man had given Granny and her people the land they now lived on. Someone had told him Granny had been in charge of the household duties when Mrs. Holland was alive. Sometime after the war ended, she and the rest of the Holland slaves moved out and built the shantytown. As the years passed other former slaves, hearing about the shantytown, had migrated there and Granny and the former Holland slaves welcomed them with open arms. Still, Holland was white, Floyd reasoned, and any decent white man wouldn't stand by and let a nigger burn down a white man's house. Floyd answered Holland's question without too much concern about the old man's feelings.

"Jesse Culbreath set the fire and I aim to hunt him down." Floyd said straightaway.

Holland's glance shifted from Floyd to the shotgun and back to Floyd. The frown on the man's face grew deeper. Holland knew Jesse wouldn't do anything so foolish. But Jesse probably had plenty of reason to hate the storekeeper. He had seen how Carter treated, not only Jesse, but every black person he crossed. And for that reason the old man felt no love for Floyd Carter.

"Hold on now. How you know he did it?"

Floyd shifted his weight from one side to the other. The shotgun was beginning to weigh him down. "My boy done seen him do it."

Holland threw his head back and gave out a short laugh. "Yer boy done seen him do it. I don't put much stock in what that youngun of your'n says. He ain't got the gumption of a jackass."

It was the wrong thing to say to Floyd right then. He shifted his weight back to the balls of his feet, and the barrel of the gun came up to rest in the crook of his left arm. "Ain't nobody askin' you to put stock in nothin'. I come here fer a nag. Now, you gonna make me the loan of one or not?"

Holland leaned forward on his cane, his eyes staring straight into Floyd's. "You ain't give me no good reason to." He paused. "If'n I should, what you gonna do with it?"

"Ain't none of your affair," Floyd snapped. "I'm waitin' fer an answer, Holland."

Asa Holland studied Floyd for several seconds before it came to him. "You gonna ride out to them Billings, ain't you? You got no stomach to go after Jesse alone." He could see the fire rising in Floyd's face but he pushed on. "Them four ain't nothin' but scum. Jesse is more man than all four of them trash. But you gonna sic em on him, ain't you?" He paused to catch his breath but Floyd spoke before he could continue.

"If'n I wanted preachin', I'd of gone and listened to that Psalm singin' neighbor of mine. From you I want a nag. If you ain't gonna make me the loan, I'll just take me one." He turned to step off the porch but Holland painfully shifted his weight to his good leg and hooked the handle of the cane around Floyd's arm. As he did, he jerked hard, pulling the storekeeper toward him.

"You stay away from my horses or I'll..."

Holland never finished the sentence. As Floyd regained his balance, he turned on the man and drove the butt of his shotgun against the old man's forehead just above the right eye. The sound of wood against skin and bone produced a sickening thud. Holland's eyes became glazed and unseeing before the lids drooped heavily and closed. The cane clattered to the porch and Holland fell across it. By the time his body quit twitching, a streak of blood was already beginning to show at a point just below the hairline. It began to puddle under his head and flow slowly through the cracks in the deteriorating porch. Left here in the heat of the day, it would soon stop flowing and become a dry cake around the man's head.

Floyd stared at the prostrate figure for several seconds, then looked quickly around to the open fields. No one was in sight. After a few more seconds of staring at the motionless body, he reached down, took hold of the man under his armpits and pulled him inside the screen door of the house and placed him at the foot of the stairs.

He knelt over the body for several seconds until he was sure that Holland was no longer breathing. Then without another thought about the man, he went outside to catch the horse he came for in the first place. In less than half an hour he had located a saddle, caught one of the mares, and was riding down the front road toward the gate. Behind, he could hear the mournful wails of the dogs as they fought to gain entrance to the house. His last thought before turning his attention to the task at hand was that it was the old man's fault, not his. Holland was responsible for his own death. No one had seen him come or go, Floyd reasoned. They might suspect him, but they would never prove he killed the old man.

# CHAPTER 11

IT WAS A TEN-MILE ride to the bend of the river where the four brothers lived in two old run-down shacks. The river and the shacks were separated by a quarter mile stand of dense trees and underbrush with only a narrow path leading from the shacks to the river. Between the trees and river was a narrow stretch of sandy beach. The shacks were set at the edge of the woods with the back of the buildings facing towards the trees. A fenced pen with three hogs separated the two houses. The fence had been in disrepair for some time and the hogs were free to roam wherever they pleased, at times even entering the houses. The ground in front of the shacks was strewn with all manner of garbage, worn and rusting tools, an old wheel from a long forgotten wagon, a rotted out wooden washtub, several tin plates, and numerous whiskey bottles that had been lying there for years. Half a dozen scrawny hounds of various sizes and descriptions lazed on the porch of the first shack. They were as filthy as their surroundings. An old rocking chair with one arm missing sat on the left side of the porch and two straight chairs in amazingly good condition sat on the other side. A line was stretched from the left-hand post to the center post where three pairs of overalls hung. The only window on the porch had two panes broken. It offered ventilation in the summer as well as the winter.

The front door was open allowing entrance to any and everything that cared to venture inside. The interior of the old shack was no better than the exterior. Clothes were scattered everywhere.

Robert J. Smith

One bed, two chairs, a table and a stove were in the larger of the two rooms. A half-full bottle of whiskey, a partial loaf of bread and two dirty knives lay on the table. Flies were everywhere. The bed covers looked as if they had never been changed and probably hadn't in years. Several telltale yellowish stains were visible on what at one time had been white sheets. Two unmade beds and a chair were in the smaller room. The condition and appearance of the beds were much the same as the one in the big room except the yellow stains were missing.

Three of the brothers, Amos, Pete and Alf, lived in this shack. Amos and Pete shared the smaller room and Alf, who was kicked in the head by a horse when he was only ten, slept in the main room. He had never recovered his senses since that incident.

The other shack was Jim's. Five years earlier he brought a woman home and they moved into the smaller one-room shack. Three months later she slipped away while the brothers were gone to buy provisions. She had tired of Jim, but mostly the brothers had worn on her nerves. Jim made no effort to bring her back. Since then he continued to live alone in the small shack.

The oldest and the unchallenged leader of the four was Amos. At six foot six inches and three hundred pounds, he ruled the roost with very little argument from the other three. A thick black beard covered most of his face, but a wicked scar that stretched from the bottom of his right nostril to the outside of the right eye was still visible. He got it nearly ten years earlier when he was breaking up a fight between Alf and Pete. Alf attacked Pete with a knife because the smaller man was making fun of him. It happened on a morning when Pete noticed that Alf's bed was soaked but not with perspiration. As Amos was pulling them apart, Alf struck out toward Pete with the knife and caught Amos next to his nose, ripping upward, barely missing his brother's right eye. In a rage and bleeding profusely, Amos took the knife away and beat Alf until it was necessary for the unbalanced man to take to his bed for a week. A lesser man than Alf would have died. But even though he had his mental problems, he was still very strong. Not nearly

112

as large as Amos, he was nevertheless much of a man. He stood just over six feet and sported a thick beard like Amos. Unlike the bigger man, his beard should have been a rusty red. But it was filthy from misplaced food particles and his own saliva and as a consequence it had turned a dirty brown. Weighing fifty pounds less than Amos, his weight was distributed more in his shoulders and chest instead of his stomach as Amos' was. His eyes were a deep blue with a wild, searching look about them.

Pete was twenty-five and the youngest of the four, fifteen years younger than Amos and twelve younger than Alf. The woman who bore the four brothers out of wedlock died the same night Pete was born. No one ever knew who Pete's father was. A procession of men passed the old shack over the years and took up residence only to move on soon afterward. Those that knew the mother said she had been quite attractive when she was younger. But the years and the men took their toll on her health and her looks. She died when she was thirty-nine. Her last born, Pete, was clean-shaven and the smarter of the four brothers. The overalls hanging out to dry on the rotting porch were his. He did the cooking and the occasional washing that was done. These chores became his when he was just barely old enough to reach the kitchen stove. No one was sure how he had survived those first few years. But he did and when he was old enough, Amos decided he was responsible for their mother's death so it was up to him to take over her chores. He was the slightest of the brothers, standing just over five foot ten and weighing less than two hundred pounds. As he grew older, it was his intelligence that allowed him to cope with the others. It kept him alive on more than one occasion.

The other brother, Jim, was five years older than Pete and built much like Amos, only to a lesser degree. The most glaring difference in their looks was the hair. Jim had been losing his for several years and sported a bald spot from front to back with thin patches of black above his ears. His stomach, like Amos', hung heavy over the top of his pants. Sometime in the past he was in a fight with one of the brothers and lost four of his upper teeth. He was not a pretty sight when he smiled. But he seldom smiled. There was not much to smile about in the Billings household.

~ ~ ~

It was into this atmosphere that Floyd rode on that late July afternoon. He was soaked in sweat and irritable by the time he came in hailing distance of the two shacks. He had done a considerable amount of thinking since he left Holland dead in his front hall. If he secured their help he would have to pay. He was willing to do that. Eight hundred dollars was all the money Floyd had saved over the years. It was money only he knew about. For years he had been hiding whatever he left over under a loose board in the storage room of his store. He could lift the board and reach down to one of the rock supports. Years ago he had chiseled one of the rocks loose halfway down on the support and placed the money behind the rock. No one had ever been the wiser. While Sarah was cleaning the main room of the store that morning, he had quietly slipped the money out and stuck it in his pocket. He had no idea that he would need it, or part of it, that very day. It was still tucked deep in his overalls pocket. That was what was bothering him now. The Billings brothers were not beyond slitting his throat and lifting the money from his dead body. But if he only showed a small part and promised more, they might be easier to deal with.

Floyd turned the horse around and backtracked several hundred yards into a stand of trees that took him out of sight of the shacks. The four brothers were milling around outside the old shacks. And he was sure they had not seen him. About thirty feet off the trail, he spotted an old hollowed out tree. He wrapped all but fifty dollars in an old rag and tied it with a strip of cloth from his shirt. When he was sure no one was watching, he dropped it into the hollow tree and put a rock on top of the money to further conceal it. Satisfied, he mounted his horse and rode back toward the shacks. This time he rode directly in, pausing a stone's throw from the larger shack. All four brothers had disappeared.

"Hello the house. This here's Floyd Carter. Anybody to home?"

Floyd saw the flash from inside the open door. His horse rared up as the bullet plowed into the ground a few feet to the right of his front hooves. Floyd's heart was pumping wildly as Amos stepped out onto the porch. The older brother was holding the rifle with his right hand, the muzzle resting in the crook of his left arm and pointed directly at Floyd's chest. Alf had moved into the doorway, a tin plate of food in one hand and a hunk of bread in the other. A stupid grin was etched on the younger man's face and Floyd could hear him giggling crazily.

"You know me, Amos. Floyd Carter from the store."

"What you about, Carter?"

Floyd started to dismount.

"Sit steady in that saddle, man. Ain't nobody told you to move."

Floyd was halfway down, but stopped and threw his right leg back over the saddle. Amos moved away from the doorway and slightly to the side. Floyd could barely see the other two brothers sitting inside at the table, seemingly oblivious to him and what was going on outside the house. They did not forsake their meal, knowing Amos could handle any disturbance without their help.

Amos saw the shotgun next to Floyd's right leg, and he motioned to the crazy brother.

"Git that gun, Alf," he barked.

Alf only stared at Amos and muttered, "Hunh?"

The shotgun," Amos snapped and pointed toward Floyd without taking his eyes off the storekeeper. "Git his gun, halfwit."

"Ain't no reason to call me that," Alf protested. He reached toward his head with the hand that held the bread and scratched through the dirty red hair. Loose particles of bread fell off and disappeared into the shaggy mess. His eyes were on Floyd now but it was evident he was trying to focus on what Amos had said to him. "The gun?"

Amos reached over and slapped the plate of food from his hand. It hit the porch with a clatter and several of the dogs fell on it immediately. Alf quickly dropped to his knees, swung wildly at the dogs, and grabbed the plate away from them. But, most of the food had already been engulfed by the hungry hounds, leaving Alf to stare at the remnants of his meal.

Amos had not taken his eyes off Floyd and now, seeing that his brother didn't understand, he motioned toward Floyd.

"Step down, real easy like, with your hands empty and above your head."

Floyd did as he was told. Once he was on the ground, Amos motioned him away from the horse and slipped the shotgun from its resting place next to the saddle.

"Billings, I came here as a friend to make you a proposition. I'm willin' to pay good money if you'll help me do a little job," Floyd said. He pulled the fifty dollars out of his pocket and held it out toward the big man. "There's more where this come from, much more if you'll help me." Amos was watching Alf as he tried to fight the dogs off. Now he shook his head and turned his attention back to the storekeeper. Without moving the rifle barrel from Floyd's chest, Amos snatched the money from his hand. He counted it and stuck it in his pocket.

"I'm a listenin'. That fifty was fer listenin' to the proposition."

Floyd was beginning to have second thoughts. Maybe he had stuck his neck out too far. The other brothers, Jim and Pete, were up from the table at the mention of money and sauntered slowly outside. Pete leaned against the doorframe and Jim settled in the old rocking chair on the right side of the porch. Both were studying Floyd and at the same time glancing toward Alf, who was gulping down the rest of the food the dogs had not gotten.

Floyd had dealt with these four brothers before but always on his own turf. He knew they were wild and bad but he never expected a greeting like this. He would have to be very careful. Fifty dollars might be all they needed to kill him and bury him out here in the bushes. But if he could convince them that he would be willing to pay a lot more, maybe he could win them over.

"Like I was saying, there's more money where that come from," he said.

Amos sat down on the edge of the porch next to the shotgun. "I'm still listenin'. But be a knowin' I got little patience."

Floyd looked from one brother to the other, studying each of them quickly. Jim and Pete had lost interest in him. Amos seemed to be the only one paying any attention to him now. Pete took a seat in an old straight chair by the door and was whittling on a piece of wood about the size of a cigar. Alf was still on his knees, sopping a hunk of bread in what was left of his tin of food. Jim was watching Alf, his face showing his disapproval at his brother's actions. Watching Alf, Floyd felt a surge rise from his stomach to his throat and fought to keep what was in his own stomach down. To choke back the bile, he focused on Amos and the reason he was here.

"You hear what happened to my house?"

"Yep," Amos said.

"You hear how it happened?"

"Naw. Ain't interested."

"That big shantytown nigger, Jesse, he done torched it."

Amos didn't move but only stared at Floyd all the harder. The other three brothers stopped what they were doing and seemed to find more interest in what Floyd was saying.

"So?" Amos said.

Floyd looked around to make sure no one else was close by. "I want him caught and I want him strung up. Ain't no one gonna burn down my house, least wise not one of them."

Amos continued to stare at Floyd as if nothing out of the ordinary had been said. After a moment he coughed up a mouthful of yellow corruption and spit it in the dirt at his feet. From under the porch, one of the dogs crawled out and began sniffing. Amos gave it a hard kick in the ribs and it yelped its way back under the porch.

"How much you willin' to pay?" There was a wicked grin on Amos' face.

"You ain't got no reservations about killin' that good fer nothing?"

Amos shook his head. "None atall. Money's money." He wiped the back of his massive right hand across his nose and flung it toward the ground. "Long as it's enough, I ain't gonna quibble about how I got it." Amos lowered his rifle so that it was pointing toward the ground now.

"He tried to burn me out. Nearly killed my gal. I got a right to take a measure of justice ain't I." Floyd was looking for sympathy now but none came from the brothers.

"How much you got storekeeper?" The question came from Jim this time. He was rocking slowly in the chair, his eyes measuring Floyd carefully. There was no trust on either side of this devil's bargain.

"You got fifty already and there's a hundred and fifty more where that come from." He was looking at Amos, not Jim as he answered. Floyd knew that the older brother would make the final decision. And he knew that Amos would ask for more and he was willing to pay more but not all of his savings. "Is it a deal?"

"What's to keep us from shootin' you and takin the rest right now?" Amos spat.

"Ain't got the rest on me. It's in a safe place."

Alf had moved up behind Amos and was glaring at Floyd, his head nearly resting on Amos' left shoulder. "We could make him tell where the rest is," the crazed man said. He gave out an ominous laugh and nudged Amos in the back.

The older brother ignored him. "Cost you three hundred."

Floyd studied that for a moment. He would still have five hundred. It was more than he wanted to pay. And just maybe it would work out where he didn't have to pay anything. But he didn't want them to know that. Finally, he frowned and nodded.

"Deal. "I'll pay you the other two hundred and fifty when the job's done."

"You ain't been a listenin', Carter. You'll pay another three hundred if'n you want the job done."

"But you already got fifty."

"That was fer listenin'. The three hundred is fer doin'.'"

The frown on Floyd's face was real now. They were going to wipe out more of his savings than he expected. It took years to save the eight hundred. But if he was smart, he wouldn't have to pay it all. He would just have to figure a way.

As if Amos could read his thoughts, he repositioned the gun until it was pointing directly toward Floyd's chest again. "If'n you got any notion of cheatin' us, you better git that thinkin' outa yer head." He didn't need to say more. Floyd got the point.

Pete, still whittling, raised his head and peered at Floyd. "Who'd you say done this?"

"Jesse Culbreath. You know him?" Floyd questioned.

"I know him," Jim answered with a chuckle. "It'll pleasure me to do him in." He hesitated and winked at Pete. "Why, I'd almost do it fer nothin'."

Pete and Alf retreated into the house and Jim got up to follow. Floyd started for the door but Amos pushed the rifle barrel hard into his chest.

"Where you goin'?"

Floyd motioned to the door and opened his mouth. But before he could speak, Amos shook his head and motioned for him to move back.

"Jist cause we goin' to do a job fer you don't mean we gotta hobnob with you." Amos nodded toward the woods where Floyd had hidden the money. "You can bed down out there somewhere."

Floyd pointed at his shotgun. "What about my gun?"

"I'll jist hold that safe till mornin'."

Floyd stared up at Amos for a moment, then retreated to his horse and slipped into the saddle.

"I sleep real light, Carter. Don't git no ideas. I been known to shoot anything that moves anywhere around these here shacks. Member that if'n you git nervous in the night."

The hairs on the back of Floyd's neck were stiff as he turned the horse and rode out.

# CHAPTER 12

THAT SUNDAY AFTERNOON WAS especially long. After Papa left to find Jesse, we didn't stay at the store long. Mrs. Carter was close to hysterics and Mama couldn't quiet her. They completely forgot about cleaning the storage rooms so Mama decided we should all go to our house. Mrs. Carter finally agreed. But she cried the whole way. For once Eddie had very little to say. I looked at him once as we walked along behind Mama and Mrs. Carter, and his face was as white as the chalk dust on the board in Mrs. Crowe's schoolhouse. I was convinced that he was responsible for the fire. Not on purpose, of course, but I thought he unknowingly set it. I was growing more certain all the time. But I knew Eddie was too terrified to admit it. And to be truthful, I was as frightened as he was. The consequences would not be pleasant for either of us. I suppose that's the reason I continued to keep quiet. It was a mistake I will always live with.

We ate our lunch of cornbread and beans very quietly. When we were finished, Mama excused us from the table. Mrs. Carter, overwhelmed by the events of the past two days, was resting on Mama's bed. All through our meal we could hear her sobbing. It was a relief to go outside where I didn't have to listen to the misery that poor woman was bearing. As we came out onto the back porch, we both stopped and stared across the field toward the woods. I knew it was too early for Papa to get back, but I still peered intently in the direction I expected him to come. I looked at Eddie and he looked back. His eyes dropped from mine and I knew he was ashamed and scared. Shame was something I had never associated with Eddie before this day.

Finally, after several minutes of silence, Eddie asked, "Want to go swimmin'?"

"No," I answered and went down the steps into the yard. I hoped he would follow but, instead, he hung there on the porch with his arm draped around the post and his eyes still searching the distant woods. I'm not sure if he was watching for my papa or his.

"What you want to do?" He asked, but his eyes never looked my way.

I don't remember how I answered Eddie's question. Most of that afternoon is a blank. I just remember sitting there on the back steps waiting for Papa and Satan to ride into view. I'm sure we talked about something but never about the fire or my suspicions. I couldn't get my mind off of Jesse and Mr. Carter hunting him with a shotgun. And Papa ... Papa trying to stop it. Papa could get hurt, maybe killed. I shuddered at the possibility. Still, I sat there without confronting Eddie again.

It was late afternoon and the sun was beginning to drop behind the trees to the West when I first got sight of Satan. Six hours had passed and Papa was coming from the Northeast. The shantytown was due east from our house and the direction puzzled me. As he drew near, I got up and walked slowly out into the yard. The strain on his face was clear. The normally straight shoulders were sagging and he looked older than I ever remembered. There was no smile on his face as he handed me the reins and stepped down.

"See to Satan, James. He's had a hard day." Papa reached up and gave the horse a fond pat. "You and Eddie come in as soon as you're finished. We need to talk." He measured us for a moment as if he knew the secret both of us were hiding, then turned and went up the back steps and into the house.

I looked to Eddie, half hoping I could get him to confess and all the while knowing I would be implicated. "Papa don't think Jesse done it."

Eddie ignored me and began pulling the water bucket up from the bottom of the well.

"You hear what I said?"

"I heerd. He done it alright cause I seen him."

As the bucket came out of the well, Eddie set it on the ledge and scooped a handful of water out with his hands and splashed it on his face. Then he dipped out another handful and poured it down his throat.

"Don't do that. Mama says it ain't sanitary."

Eddie laughed. "You don't know what sanitary is."

"I do so. It means you ain't bein' clean. You was playing with Myrtle and she was lickin' your hands."

The Eddie I knew was beginning to show through. He thought no one was going to find out what really happened. I was beginning to think he might be right. The thought frightened me. Still, I didn't think I could do anything because it was his word against mine and I couldn't prove it was his cigarette that caused the fire. And without proof I felt helpless as long as Eddie insisted that it was Jesse.

I took the bucket from the ledge, emptied it and let it down into the well again. Once it was full, I began to pull it back up. "Papa says cleanliness is next to Godliness," I continued.

Eddie shrugged. "So what. My Pa says there ain't no such thing as a God. He says we come from monkeys a long time ago." He paused for a few seconds. "Maybe as long as a thousand, million years ago."

"That ain't so, Eddie," I snapped as I began pulling the saddle off Satan. He was challenging beliefs that I had held sacred for as long as I could remember, and it was beginning to make me angry. "God made us all. We never come from no monkey."

It was then that Mama stepped out onto the back porch. "Boys."

My eyes didn't leave Eddie. And I only noticed then that my fists were doubled. I think Eddie noticed that too and that silly grin crossed his face.

"Boys, do you hear me calling?" Mama's voice seemed subdued, almost as if she was grief stricken.

I answered then. "Yes, Mama. We're coming just as soon as I feed Satan."

For all his laughing and talking, I could tell that Eddie was afraid to go into the house. He might have thought that Papa knew more than he was letting on. I know I was afraid to face Papa. He had a way of looking right through you, and I was sure if anyone could get Eddie to talk, it would be Papa. I was in no hurry to be implicated or for Papa and Mama to find out about the smoking. When I finished with Satan, I turned and faced Eddie.

"You ready?"

"I ain't ready to go in."

I persisted. "We gotta go in. If'n we don't, Papa will come lookin' fer us."

I could see the uneasiness in Eddie's eyes but without another word he nodded and started toward the house. I followed close behind.

Papa was sitting at the kitchen table reading his Bible when we came in. He closed it and motioned for us to sit down. I tried to act normal and noticed that Eddie was making the same effort. His eyes were moving all around the room, stopping everywhere but on Papa. If I looked as jumpy and nervous as Eddie did, I knew Papa would guess the truth if he hadn't already. He sat there looking from one to the other of us until we finally dropped our eyes to stare at our hands, clasped together on the table in front of us. I could feel a chill around my neck while the sweat was soaking my shirt. Still, Papa stared at us until I thought he might never speak. Actually, I think it was less than a minute since we sat down. My heart was pumping and I felt I needed to say something, anything to relieve the tension.

I glanced toward Mama. "What we havin' fer supper, Mama?"

"Cornbread and sweet milk," she said glancing from me to Papa and then to Eddie.

Eddie was still staring at his clasped hands. "You like cornbread and sweet milk, Eddie?" Papa's eyes were burning holes in me and I was beginning to shake.

"I guess," Eddie grunted. I couldn't tell whether he did or didn't and really wasn't concerned about it. I was terribly uncomfortable.

"Boys," Papa finally said, "what you've told this day is of a very serious nature. I'm sure you know that."

I started to speak but the look in Papa's eyes caused me to pause and my eyes dropped to my hands again.

"I've just come from the shantytown where Jesse lives." Papa pushed his Bible to the side and glanced toward Mama. She had her back to us and was slicing cornbread on the cabinet.

I heard a sigh behind me and looked around to see Mrs. Carter leaning against the door frame. Her hair had been taken down from the bun she normally wore and hung in a tangle almost to her waist. Great dark puffs of skin bulged under her red eyes. She was done with the crying but she looked terrible.

Mama saw her there and spoke softly. "Come and sit down, Sarah." She moved around the table and put her arm around Mrs. Carter, but the woman shook her head and bit her bottom lip. She seemed on the verge of crying again.

"No. No, please. I'm fine. Just let me stand here for a moment."

Mama remained with her arm around Mrs. Carter, her face grave and concerned for the woman. Then she reached up and smoothed Mrs. Carter's hair, giving her a small kiss on the cheek as she did.

"Can I get you anything, a drink of water, anything?"

Mrs. Carter smiled and shook her head. "I'm alright now. Please don't let me hinder you."

Mama smiled, gave the woman a quick hug and returned to the cornbread.

All the while, Papa remained silent. I thought he might be hesitant to question us further with Eddie's mama there but I quickly found out he wasn't.

"Eddie," Papa said, "you say that you saw Jesse set the fire."

Eddie nodded sheepishly. He couldn't look Papa in the eye.

"Tell me about it. What did you see? Was he carrying anything with him, anything that might help him start the fire, a bucket perhaps with coal oil, an arm full of twigs, anything?"

Eddie shook his head and looked toward me. Papa's eyes shot in my direction for just a second, then back to Eddie. "I just seen him sneakin' up the side of the house like he was afeared someone might see him. Then he slipped quiet like under the floor. Next thing I knowed, the house was all smoke and fire. I heerd Ma a hollerin' and seen her and Sally git out jist in time. I come to help Ma and when I looked fer the nigger, he had done run off."

Mrs. Carter was sobbing again and Mama went back around to where she stood and put her arm around the distraught woman.

"Sarah, let me take you into the other room. You need to rest."

The woman shook her head and moved out of Mama's grasp. "No, I want to hear this. Please. I'll be all right."

Again Mama moved away from the woman. "If it won't upset you too much."

"Please. I'm fine."

"All right," Mama said and went back to the cabinet again.

Eddie was looking down at his hands, away from Papa's steady gaze. "I seen him do it. I swear he do-done it." He was stammering now and Papa was looking at him with suspicious eyes. Even though he wasn't looking my way, I could feel what was about to come and after just a moment, he turned my way.

"What do you have to say about this, James? Do you know anything we should know?

I gathered all my courage. I could feel Eddie's eyes on me. It was all I could do to keep my eyes focused on Papa's. "I never seen nothin' cept Jesse when he come along the road. Last I seen he was goin' towards Eddie's house. Then I come in. Honest, Papa." I hoped he couldn't see my fingers crossed behind my back. For the most part, what I had said was the truth, just not the whole truth. "I never seen him settin' no fire."

"Was he carrying anything?" Papa asked.

"I didn't take no notice of nothin'."

In his eyes I could see that Papa was questioning the whole business even if he wasn't saying so. "Is that all you can tell me,

James? This is a very serious business." Then Papa looked at both of us. "Are you boys quite sure that everything you've told me is the truth?"

Eddie moved closer to me now and was still trying to avoid Papa's eyes. He managed to look up at Papa and nod. I did the same. With Eddie sitting so close, I couldn't get up the courage to tell Papa what I suspected. And I couldn't prove that Eddie was lying. Eddie was so close now that his elbow was burrowing into my side. "I done told the truth," I said. "That's all I rightly know, Papa."

Papa continued to stare at me. I had never before lied to him. I wasn't really lying now, I thought. In my own misguided way I felt I had to protect Eddie until he was willing to tell all the truth. I think Papa knew that. The look on his face was bitter disappointment. He was hurting, hurting for Mama, for himself, for Jesse, but mostly for me. Papa was afraid for me and maybe even Eddie. He knew what it would be like for us to carry this with us. He was trying his best to get us to own up to our responsibility, while still trying to find a way to help Jesse. I glanced toward Eddie. His eyes had a look of determination and his jaw was set. He was not about to waver now. Papa saw that too. He sighed and stood up.

With one more glance in my direction, he slipped his arm around Mama's tiny waist and drew her to him. He looked very tired now. "I rode by Jim Long's cabin on the way home. He's out passing word to those I missed. We're to have a meeting across the road at the Meecham house just after sundown. Something must be done to avert trouble." Papa looked down at me one more time. Eddie must have thought I was about to say something, for under the table, he quietly took hold of my arm and squeezed it just hard enough to get my attention. I'm sure Papa didn't notice for he turned from me and back to Mama to plant a kiss on her forehead. Then without saying anything else he turned and went out of the house through the front door.

# CHAPTER 13

THE MEETING PAPA CALLED at the Meecham house wasn't the only one that night. Granny Ruby watched until Jesse disappeared toward the swamp before she and Ezra started back to the shantytown. The old woman felt heavy of heart as she followed the young man through the woods. For nearly thirty-five years, since their freedom had been won in the war, they had existed on the small patch of land Mr. Holland gave them. Their life was little if any better than before the war. The only difference was their freedom. They were free to come and go as they pleased. The land was theirs, deeded to them years before. During those years they were able to scratch out an existence. Whites and blacks had very little trouble living together as equals. With very few exceptions most of the white people were satisfied to leave Granny's people alone. In those first years after the war Mr. Holland wielded a strong influence in the small community. That had changed. And Granny feared what might happen if Carter were to catch Jesse. She knew the people respected her authority, but if something happened to Jesse she didn't know if she could control some of the younger ones. This could jeopardize the entire shantytown. But, no matter the risk, she knew they could see this through together. But one thing was certain. They could not allow Jesse to be taken by Carter and his friends. Yes, there would have to be a meeting tonight, Granny Ruby thought.

It was late afternoon before they arrived back in the shanty-town. Granny was relieved to see that activity was going on as usual. Carter had not arrived yet. But he would. She knew it was inevitable. Trouble would be brewing for them, all of them, and she had to find a way to prevent it. And after that they had to find out what really happened at the Carter house. It might be their only chance to stop bloodshed.

"Boy," she said to Ezra, "you passes the word to all the folk, women too. Tell um to bring their younguns along. They'll be a meetin outside my shack just past sundown. You makes sure we got people posted round abouts so's no one can hear what's said. You hear, boy? And keeps your mouth shet 'bout where Jesse done gone. You don't tell nobody. You understand what I jist said, boy?"

"Yes 'um, Granny," Ezra said. "I does understand." With that he started off toward the row of shacks and Granny went up the steps of her own. It was two hours before sundown and she had a lot of thinking to do, thinking and some heavy praying. For that she needed privacy and her corncob pipe.

~ ~ ~

It was the man called John that led the people up the trail that evening. When Granny heard John's steps on the porch, she called out.

"I'm a comin', John." She came out on the porch and sat down in the old rocking chair. For several seconds her eyes moved back and forth across the faces of her people before coming to rest on John and Ezra, standing at the foot of the stairs.

"Is we all here?"

It was Ezra who answered. "Yes um. All ceptin' them we got guardin' round about."

"How many?"

"Six."

"Good. Once the meetin's over, you gather them up and tell um what's done been said and decided on. You go with him, John. You hear?"

Ezra nodded and looked to John who nodded and muttered something inaudible.

Granny stared in his direction. "What you done said, John?"

"Jist sayed okay, Granny, that's all."

Granny stared at him all the harder. Then she turned her attention back to the people. Elizabeth, Jesse's wife, was standing next to John, the baby tucked in the crook of her left arm with its head resting against her shoulder. Granny nodded to the young woman, thankful the child was asleep.

"Don't you worry none, girl. Jesse be safe."

Elizabeth nodded and began to sway back and forth, humming softly in the baby's ear.

It was beginning to get dark as Granny turned her attention back to the rest of the people. She weighed her words carefully before she spoke. Even though these were good people, she knew some were hot heads and John could be the worst of all. She could not let the meeting get out of her control. Her eyes moved back to Elizabeth again.

"Like I said afore, your man is safe, Lizabeth, and we aims to keep him that away." She held the young woman's gaze for several more seconds then looked back to the others. One by one she searched their faces, stopping on John's last.

"You know what done happened over to Floyd Carter's house and what's been said 'bout Jesse." She was talking to all the people but her eyes were still focused on John. Granny stopped and looked toward Ezra. "Boy, you sure we got good people a watchin' after us?"

"Yes um, Granny. Can't even a lizard slip close without a body seein' him."

The only light now was from the lamp inside Granny's shack but she could still see Ezra looking up at her.

"You better be right, boy."

"I is, Granny."

Satisfied, Granny continued. "Like I done said, our Jesse done been accused of settin' fire to the Carter's house. Now he says he ain't done it and I believes him. He ain't no fool. And that's what he'd be if'n he done it." She stopped and let her eyes drift back and forth over the people again before continuing. They were murmuring and nodding their heads at Granny's words. Granny let them talk among themselves for maybe half a minute before she continued. "Now, that man Carter is out a lookin' fer him. It's goin' to be up to the likes of us to see that Carter don't find him."

Granny stopped and gazed into the darkness above the people's head. A breeze was beginning to blow, and she could see the forms of the trees as they began to sway back and forth. The tree frogs were beginning to sing louder now. Their music at any other time would have been pleasant to the ear. But this wasn't that time. This was now and she focused on her business again. Granny lowered her voice as if to make sure that even if someone had managed to slip close to camp, they still wouldn't hear her. "Jesse done took to hidin' till this thing's settled. We goin' to have to keep him supplied with vittles. Ever other day, we gonna make sure he got vittles and good water." These last couple of hours Granny had thought hard about what she would say next. If she could get John on her side she knew she could control the rest of the younger crowd.

"You in charge, John. You in charge of seein' to Jesse's feedin' and waterin'." She let that sink in and saw no hint of rebellion in the man's eyes before she continued. "Ezra, Roy, Andrew and George. You boys goin' to help John. Mind you, now, he be in charge. You hear?" Granny stopped and took several seconds eyeing each young man. "You all knows what done gonna happen if they catches that boy. They gonna tie him to a tree and beat him till he's nigh onto dead. Then they gonna finish what they done started with a rope hangin'. That ain't happenin' while this old woman still got breath. You hear what I'm a sayin'?"

There was more murmuring in the crowd now. Granny noticed Elizabeth shudder, clasp her arms tightly around the baby and begin to rock back and forth. John, standing next to Elizabeth, blurted out, "We gonna have a little hangin' party of our own if'n that happens." He turned to face the group and several of the less vocal men nodded their approval.

"You a fool, John Andrews." The old woman spat in his direction before continuing. "Yore Mama done raised a fool." She picked up a pole sitting next to her door and poked the big man in the chest. John winced and stepped back. "I goin' to tell you jist what you to do and you better open up them ears." She spat another mouthful of tobacco juice at John's feet and glared down into his face. "You ain't doin' nothin', you hear me, nothin' to rile them whites no more than they already is. Ain't no way we can help Jesse if'n we do that." She poked the big man again. "You hear me?" She glanced over his head toward those who had nodded their approval at John's words a few moments earlier. "You all better be a hearin' me."

This time the same ones who had agreed with John nodded in Granny's direction. When her eyes met John's again, she knew trouble could still be brewing from the big man. His eyes were set on her and there was fire in them. Granny lifted the stick above his head as if she would bring it down on him. But he did not give ground. Her plan to get John on her side was not working yet but she had hope the big man would come around.

"What you say, John? I waitin' fer a word. You gonna help us help Jesse or give the whites more reason to string him up? What you say, boy?"

They held each other's gaze for several seconds before John answered. "We gonna do it your way," he said. Then as an afterthought he added, "For now anyways."

Granny spit again, this time not in John's direction. Still, she stared down at him. Finally, she sighed and turned her attention back to the rest of the people.

"That settled, we can git down to the business of vittles." Her eyes roamed the crowd until they stopped on a rather large woman near the back.

"Where Jesse hidin', Granny?" The question came from Elizabeth.

Granny hesitated and looked down at the young woman. "I doesn't want to talk to that right now, girl. You be patient, you hear."

Elizabeth only nodded and began to hum and sway back and forth with the baby still secured in her arms.

Granny watched her for a few seconds and turned back to the others.

"Now, we gots to plan out the next few days and who is to prepare vittles for Jesse." Granny let her eyes wander around the group until they stopped on the big woman again.

"Rose Harris, you is in charge. You git some of the women folk to help you. Plans is to take vittles to Jesse ever other day, but we gots to realize they may be times when we ain't gonna be able to. If'n that happens, we don't want Jesse goin' without. So make sure you sends enough to last at least three days. And remember that Jesse got a powerful big appetite." She looked at Rose for some sign of understanding and the woman nodded.

"Good." Granny leaned the stick back against the wall and looked the people over slowly, starting with John. "I doesn't need to tell none of you to keep yore mouth shet tight. Don't trust nobody. And lands sakes, don't tell none of the whites you works fer. Now, I knows most of them is decent folk but that don't change a whit. You keeps what's been said here to yourself. Don't go trustin' nobody cause they gives you an extra dime now and again." Granny hesitated. "Now git to home and 'member what I done said."

As the crowd turned to go, Granny spoke again.

"John, you and Rose stay. I got somethin' more to say to you." She glanced around the crowd again. "Ezra, you stays, too."

Rose worked her way through the crowd toward the porch. She was wearing a red rag tied around her head with holes just above each ear that allowed tufts of her hair to protrude through. The old black dress was torn just below her right breast and again above the left hip. The tear on her hip looked as if her size had been too much for the material and it had parted from strain and age. Her movement was laborious, partly because of her size and partly because of her age. No one, not even Rose, knew exactly how old she was, but most believed she was well into her seventies.

Granny watched as she negotiated the steps slowly. She pressed her hands on her knees to help her climb. Once she gained the porch, Granny motioned the three of them inside her shack. The single room was lit by one lamp, resting on an old table that leaned to one side where one leg was shorter than the others. Two boxes and one straight chair were the only places to sit except for a narrow bed against the far wall. Granny waved her arm toward the boxes and John and Ezra sat. Rose fell heavily onto the straight chair and spread her legs for stability. Granny settled on the bed and pulled a bucket up in front of her. After a moment she spit into the bucket and wiped the brown saliva off her mouth with the back of her hand. Then she transferred the tobacco juice to the side of her dress with a quick swipe.

"Ezra, you ain't told nobody where Jesse be off to?" It was more of a statement than a question. The tone of Granny's voice made Ezra sit up straight on the box.

"No ma'am, no ma'am. I ain't told nary a soul and I ain't bout to. No ma'am, Granny. I done jist what you told me to do and nothin' more. No ma'am." He shook his head vigorously and looked hurt that Granny would even suggest such a thing.

"Good. That the way I wants to keep it." Granny looked out the door to see if anyone was trying to listen in, then toward the two windows. Satisfied that only the four of them were within earshot she turned to Rose. "What you about to hear, you keep to yerself. You hear me Rose?"

The big woman nodded. "I ain't tellin' nobody nothin'. You knows me, Ruby."

"I knows you, Rose." Granny nodded and turned her attention to John.

"You been in the swamp with Jesse, ain't you?"

John nodded and leaned his elbows on the table. It tilted a bit and the lamp teetered for a moment then settled.

Granny watched for a second. "You two used to go deep and stay for days if'n I recollect. Set the whole bunch of us to frettin' once cause you stayed such a long spell." Granny looked to the windows and door again. "That be right?"

John smiled as if he enjoyed the fact that everyone was worried about him. "We done it all right."

Granny leaned forward, elbows on her knees and spit into the bucket again. "You 'member the place some calls Alligator Hole?"

"I does. A mean place. Ain't safe day or night." His eyes took on a serious glint. "Why you askin' about the hole? You sayin' Jesse be there?"

Granny looked from Rose to Ezra and then back to John. "That's where he be."

Rose took a deep breath, "Umm umm. Ain't nobody likely to follow that boy in there. Ain't too likely he'll be comin' out whole."

John reacted as if he hadn't heard what Rose said. "Ain't likely he gonna come out alive," John said. "I ain't never seen no worse place round abouts. Snakes and gators is thicker in there than flies on the red of a melon."

"I knows," Granny said quietly and sat back in her chair. "But, Jesse didn't seem afeared of them."

John got up and walked toward the door. "He ain't never been afeared of nothin'. But that don't mean he can't be kilt by one of them varmints. You done sent him in to die, old woman." John was defiant again now. His hands became fists and he was glaring at Granny.

"Umm umm," Rose mumbled again, "umm umm."

Ezra just shook his head and dug his hands deep into his overall pockets.

Granny and John glanced toward the other two at the same time then back to each other. She didn't like John hovering over her, leering down at her. "Sit back down, John."

John didn't move.

"I sayed fer you to sit back on that there box." For emphasis she pointed toward the box and wagged her finger up and down. "Sit back down and hears what I gots to say."

Finally, he dropped back to the box and leaned his elbows on the little table. The lamp tilted again, but settled quickly.

Satisfied, Granny continued. "Now, you knows yourself, Jesse ain't got no chance if'n they catch him. In there he do. He been in there more than anybody, even you John. And Jesse is smart. He ain't gonna git kilt. He too smart." She let that settle in before continuing. "Two days from tomorrow's sunup you gonna take his vittles in. You hears that, Rose. You and them women you gonna have helpin' you, you gotta have them vittles ready. Everything that Jesse gonna need to stay alive."

"Umm umm," The big woman said with emphasis, "I hopes we ain't feedin' them gators."

"Hush, woman. You jist git them vittles ready and be sure you don't let your tongue slip bout what's sayed here tonight."

Rose only nodded this time.

Granny turned back to John. "Jesse done told me that Alligator Hole is near onto more than a half day's walk once you get to solid ground. Means you gotta stay the night with Jesse and come back the next day. You got qualms 'bout that?"

John nodded. "I done stayed in the swamp before. But ain't never stayed at the hole."

"I ain't feared to go, Granny." It was Ezra, a grin stretched across his face and his hand raised like a schoolboy asking to be excused from class.

Granny grunted. "You ain't never been to Alligator Hole."

Ezra scratched his head. "No ma'am, but I reckon I can finds it if John tells me where it be."

"You dumb, Ezra. You know that. You dumb as a hog," John growled. "If'n you didn't fall outa the boat and drown, you'd step into the first quicksand pit you comes to." John sneered. "You make good gator meat."

Ezra dropped his head and slumped back on the box. He would not challenge John without his friend, Jesse, to back him up.

Granny shook her head, wishing John would shut up. "All right," she said, "then we meets here in two nights, just after sundown to make final plans. Rose, you have the vittles and water ready. Now all three of you git on home and keep them loose tongues shet up. I gots me a powerful lot of thinkin' to do."

"Umm umm," Rose said rising.

They filed out the door, John first, followed by Rose and then Ezra. Granny watched until they disappeared down the dark path. Then she took out the old corncob pipe, tamped in some tobacco and lit it. She blew out the lamp and went out onto the porch. The sounds of the tree frogs were unmistakable and somewhere close the 'who' of an owl resounded through the humid evening breeze. It was especially warm on this night. The only relief was the breeze drifting in from the direction of the swamp. The swamp, she thought. The swamp and Jesse. "Oh, Lord up there in heaven. Protects that boy during these terrible days," she whispered. "Lord, you knows that he's gonna need all the help he can get."

She stared up at the sky for several minutes until her eyes fell on a special group of stars. When she was a small girl her papa had shown her those stars. He had pointed out the two dippers, one much larger than the other, the bear and another group her grandmother had shown her papa when he was a boy. Her grand-mother had called it the Milky Way as had her papa those many years ago when he had shown her. As she had so many times over the years, Granny let her eyes drift back and forth from one group to another. Finally, she leaned back in her rocker and took a pull on the old pipe only to find the fire had gone out. It didn't matter. The pipe was the least of her worries tonight.

She leaned forward again in the rocker and bowed her head. She felt she needed to talk to the Lord again. "Oh, Lord," she whispered, "You has made all this world. You can do most anything. You done delivered Lazarus. We gots one now that needs deliverin'. Our Jesse done need you now. I asks you to fetch him out of the hand of evil. I asks you to defeat them devilish rascals that wants to do him harm." She remained bowed for several seconds, then, satisfied that she had made her plea as best she could, she leaned back again and resumed rocking. The old pipe, though unlit now, still protruded out of her mouth. For several minutes she continued to rock and then the rocker began to slow down until it stopped completely, her head drooping to her bosom then rising again as she fought the urge to sleep. But the events of the day had been too much and it wasn't long before her eyes closed for good and she dozed, the pipe dropping harmlessly to her lap.

# CHAPTER 14

I SLEPT VERY LITTLE that Sunday night. Eddie kept rolling over to my side until I found myself clinging to the edge of the bed. Every time I pushed him away, he would stay for a few minutes then roll against me again. Finally, I gave up and tried to make the best of it. But it was no use. With the guilt and Eddie's body pressed against me, I couldn't sleep.

It must have been close to midnight when Papa came home from the meeting. Light from the lamp was visible under my door, and I knew Mama had heard him come in and met him in the front room. I slipped out of bed and tiptoed across the room. Papa was talking very quietly, but I could hear a word now and then. There was something about horses, then I heard Mr. Holland's name mentioned. A moment later the light disappeared. Mama and Papa had gone into the kitchen. I couldn't hear them talking so I cracked the door and peeked out. The front room was dark. Now the light was peeking under the door that led into the kitchen. I was about to tiptoe over to that door when I heard a movement by the far wall and remembered Eddie's mother. In the semi-darkness I could barely make her out on a pallet on the floor. Her back was to me but I decided against slipping into the room and stepped back and shut my door quietly.

Eddie was stretched out in the middle of my bed, his arms thrown out to each side until there was very little room left for me. I lay down and drew myself into a small knot, trying to find some spot to get comfortable but again it was no use. His body followed me wherever I went. It must have been two or three in the morning before I finally fell asleep and then only from pure exhaustion. Sleep that night was worse than being awake. The rest of the night I had nightmares about Jesse, the fire, Eddie and his lie, my lie. Sometime before full light I awoke with a jerk and sat straight up in bed. My body was drenched with sweat, and the bed covers felt like someone had not been able to keep their kidneys in check. But that wasn't the case. It was pure sweat. My first thought was of Jesse. Where was he? Was he all right? Eddie had rolled to the other side of the bed but now he was breathing so loud I couldn't sleep. If it wasn't one thing it was another. The first rays of sunlight were just beginning to light up the eastern sky. I slipped out of bed and pulled my clothes on as quietly as possible. Mrs. Carter was sleeping peacefully when I tiptoed through the front room to the kitchen. Mama and Papa's bedroom door was closed and there was no sound coming from their room. It was just barely light enough to see across the meadow to the woods east of the house when I slipped out on the back porch. My mind wandered through those woods to the shantytown and the swamp that lay on the far side. I could only imagine what lived in there.

~ ~ ~

Jesse had suffered much the same kind of night as I had. After leaving Granny and Ezra the afternoon before, he had made his way to the edge of the swamp where several old dugout boats were tied. One was half full of water and the rear end floated barely above the surface. He decided against that one and untied one of the other boats and pushed it out into the murky water. An old flat board lay in the bottom and Jesse used it as a paddle, pulling his way across the open water toward the cypress and magnolia trees on the far side. Once past them he would be hidden in the shadows and undergrowth of the swamp. The boat slid along swiftly over the surface until it disappeared from view in the dense cover of the trees. In here the brightness of the summer sun was transformed into a sort of half-light. Only now and then a shaft of sunlight slipped down past the heavy foliage and entered this dreary world. At first Jesse had to squint hard to make out the trees that rose like silent sentries in front of him. As his eyes became more accustomed to his environment, he was able to pull harder on the makeshift paddle until the old boat began to move swiftly and smoothly through the maze of trees. Here the water was only a few feet deep but the bottom was so uncertain that no one in their right mind was likely to try wading. Jesse knew about the quicksand pits that dotted the swamp and knew that some lay under the water. A person could step out into the murky water and never be heard from.

His mind shook off the thought of danger and focused on the sounds around him. The singing of birds, herons, turkeys, spoonbills, and cormorants resounded in Jesse's ears until it began to sound like one loud continuous ringing that might never stop. It was much cooler now, even comfortable under the canopy of trees. Ahead and off to the left some thirty feet, a huge bald cypress stretched high above the rest of the vegetation. Its hollow knobby knees protruded above the surface of the water, carrying life-giving air to the roots. Jesse marveled at the tree standing so erect and strong after what must have been centuries of growth. The farther he moved into the depths of the swamp, the denser the vegetation became. At times he found it hard to see more than fifty feet ahead. Four years had elapsed since his last trip into the swamp and he wondered if he could still find Alligator Hole. It was easy to get lost in here and dangerous too, he thought, as he spied a moccasin dangling from a low limb off to his right. As he watched, the serpent dropped into the water and swam away in the opposite direction. Nevertheless, Jesse felt a shudder ripple through his body. One bite from one of those and he could be done.

"You leaves me alone and I do you the same turn," he whispered after the fleeing snake.

The dense vegetation was beginning to reach down toward the boat now, and it was here that Jesse knew he had to be extra careful. In here the snakes draped themselves just above the water like the one he had just seen. They blended so well with the foliage that you might not see them until it was too late. For that reason Jesse was especially glad just to make out solid ground some thirty or forty feet in the distance. The rest of the way he would go on foot. He worked his way through the thick limbs until the boat buried its front end in the muddy bog just a few feet short of a small clearing. Jesse stepped out and looked around slowly. There was a noise in the brush a dozen steps away and a young fawn skittered away out of sight. A moment later a doe, about three feet high, jumped out, stared at him for a second before running off after the fawn.

Jesse smiled, "I ain't a goin' to hurt you or your baby none, pretty thing." He looked around solemnly. "But they is those in here that would, so you take care." For a moment he stared toward the spot where they disappeared, then turned and pulled the boat up on the bank. He dragged it across the clearing to a clump of high grass on the far side and hid it from sight. Then he broke a branch from one of the trees and began to wipe out the marks the boat had left. After several minutes he walked back to the bank and looked back and forth across the clearing until he was convinced there was no sign of his being there. Satisfied, he stared up through the trees toward the barely visible sun, put it behind him and struck off in the direction where he remembered Alligator Hole to be. His goal was to get there before dark. If he couldn't reach the hole, he should be able to reach Twin Willows. He would be relatively safe there if he were careful. But moving through the swamp after dark, he thought, could be suicide.

Everything, all the dangers in the swamp, took on new dimensions now. Not only the snakes and alligators, but now there were the many quicksand pits that dotted the soft ground. Once trapped in one, a man had to keep a clear head if he wanted to get out. Old Elias, the first man he had ever accompanied into the swamp, once told him that if ever he stepped into one unknowingly he should throw himself over on his side and try to roll out. The old man had said that a person lying flat would float. To fight and thrash about would only cause you to sink that much faster. But what man could keep his head in that situation? Not many, Jesse thought. Still, he figured the old man could be right. It might be the only way to escape if you were alone. Jesse didn't want to have to find out.

He had been moving steadily and carefully through the brush for nearly an hour when he broke out into a small clearing no more than thirty feet across at the widest point. He looked about a moment to get his bearings. He was about to move across the clearing when something told him not to. What was wrong? He studied the small area carefully and then realized what it was. Nothing was growing in the clearing, no weeds or grass, not even a rock was visible. No sign of vegetation, only fallen leaves from the trees overhead. He reached behind him in the weeds, found a loose rock about the size of his fist and tossed it toward the middle of the clearing. There was a gurgle and a sucking sound and the rock disappeared quickly. The surface of the clearing was as smooth and innocent as it had been a few moments before. Jesse's shoulders sagged as he realized just how close he had come to testing out what Elias had told him. His heart was pounding heavily in his chest now. Still, he had to find a way around the quicksand.

He searched in the underbrush until he found a stout stick. Slowly, he tested the ground around him until he found a narrow ledge of solid footing around the edge of the pit. Using the stick and keeping close to the brush, Jesse worked his way clockwise around the clearing until he was halfway around to the other side. Then he pulled up suddenly. A loud roar or growl off to his left caused him to freeze in his tracks. His mind and ears became even more alert. The first thing that came to mind was an alligator. But the more he thought about it, the more convinced he became that what he was hearing was a bear. The rumor was that bear lived in the swamp. He had never seen one. But legend had it that they were here. Many years before on one of his first treks close to the swamp he had heard the same sound, only then it was much farther away. He was only thirteen then, and his pa had taken him rabbit trapping near the boundary of the swamp. They were baiting one of their traps when they heard the same bone-chilling roar.

Jesse remembered how he jumped and looked around wide-eyed, "What that, Daddy?"

"Hush, boy," the old man had cautioned while pressing his index finger up and down in front of his lips.

Jesse fell silent that morning, but his eyes remained wide open. He turned his head from side to side. Seeing nothing, he tugged at the old man's sleeve.

"Leave be, boy. Leave be," his father whispered. The man gripped the old skinning knife he always carried in a sheath attached to his belt. After several minutes the sounds slowly faded away and his father relaxed and turned his attention back to the trap.

But Jesse wasn't satisfied and he continued to question. "What be that, Daddy?"

The old man didn't look up but continued to work the trap. "Bear, boy. They be big bear in them swamps." It was all the man said, but it was enough to keep Jesse looking over his shoulder the rest of that day. And he was aware of it every time he set foot in the swamp after that.

Now, as he stood poised on the edge of the quicksand pit, those distant memories came back, the sound, same as he and his father had heard those many years before. He listened intently now. But the roar didn't come again and, like his father those many years ago, his attention shifted back to the task at hand, working his way around the quicksand. When he finally reached the opposite side, he turned and pitched the stick back to the center of the pit. It floated.

Jesse was relieved to put the pit behind him. But he knew there were more out there. He became even more cautious now, making sure of each step as he moved through the underbrush. The bear had unnerved him and he wondered if the beast knew he was there, maybe even stalking him now. He stopped at this new thought and studied the vegetation around him. He neither saw nor heard anything out of the ordinary. So he pressed on. After another half hour, he turned and checked for the sun again. It was low now, and he knew that he would have to bed down somewhere short of his goal. Alligator Hole was still another two hours distant, and he knew what could happen if he insisted on making it that far with darkness settling around him. Now his thoughts turned to his alternate destination. Twin Willows was a small clearing on the bank of a stream. He and John had spent the night there about five or six years ago. If he hadn't gotten himself lost, Jesse was sure it had to be near. He looked for something familiar but nothing was like he remembered it. Convinced he was heading in the right direction, he again put the sun over his left shoulder and started to head northeast.

As he turned his right foot caught on something hidden in the grass and he fell heavily on his left side. His first thought was a log, but as he rolled over to see what had tripped him, a chill passed through him. He was face to face with the largest snapping turtle he had ever seen. Or so it seemed at first glance. The powerful jaws were just a couple of feet from his left arm and they were open. It was moving closer and Jesse jerked the arm back quickly and rolled to his feet.

"Man alive. You the biggest, ugliest turtle I done ever seen. If'n I wasn't in such a hurry, you'd make a fine supper."

For several seconds Jesse and the turtle stared at each other. Finally, Jesse backed away. He took one last look at his would-be meal, and hurried off toward the northeast where he hoped he would find the little clearing next to the stream.

It was getting dusky dark when he finally broke out of the heavy undergrowth near the bank of a clear stream. He had just about decided that he was lost and in danger of spending the night in the thick vegetation when he finally broke into the open. Quickly, now, his eyes swept the clearing, then to the stream and the far bank. Relief flooded through him as he saw the willows on the opposite bank. They were just as he remembered them only some-what larger. He had made it. This was the place, the place he and John had named Twin Willows. In this forsaken swamp the name they had given this place sounded innocent and safe but it was far from that. Still, it was better than spending the night in the thick underbrush. Without any unnecessary movement, he studied the clearing carefully. Once he was satisfied that there were no hidden dangers, he set about gathering wood before the darkness completely engulfed him. Within an hour he had a small fire going and settled down beside it. The sounds of night in the swamp were rapidly increasing, blending in with the crackling fire. The birds were still now. A few feet away Jesse recognized the throaty croak of a frog. There was an answering call from across the stream and another farther downstream.

"If'n I wasn't so wore down, Little Toad, me and you would share a meal tonight. Only it wouldn't pleasure you near so much as me."

The woods all around were dark now. Through the trees to the east Jesse could just make out the full moon. He fed the fire one more time and settled his head back on a large chunk of wood. There was a splash down by the stream and he sat bolt upright. The light from the fire illuminated the clearing and half way across the stream. He could see a ring of water moving out from the shore. Snake maybe, he thought. No, he reasoned, not a snake. They slid quietly. Didn't make noise when they entered the water. In the darkness a person could imagine all sorts of things that could be out there. Maybe a gator, he thought. Maybe the frog. He watched for a few seconds but nothing was moving. The ring disappeared and Jesse settled back against the chunk of wood. As he did, he became conscious that his hand had been gripping the handle of the fish knife he had tucked into the rope belt around his waist. Jesse loosened his grip on the knife and managed a chuckle at his own nervousness.

"Git aholt of yourself, Jesse boy. No tellin' how many more nights like this you got till this be done." He paused and his mind flashed to Alligator Hole. "And maybe worse spots to spends them in." He didn't like running and hiding, but he knew he was safer here if Carter came looking for him. Jesse adjusted his head on the wood pillow and stared up at the sky and the stars that were easily visible here from the clearing. Even though there were plenty of trees around there was still a large opening here in the clearing, and he could make out the moon just peeking above the cypress trees to the east. His eyes were beginning to feel very heavy now and he was fighting to keep them open. He knew that sometime he had to sleep and he reasoned in his own mind that he was safer tonight, right here, than he might be for some time to come. He opened his eyes for a moment, checked the fire one last time. Satisfied that it would burn for several hours, he closed his eyes again. His last thoughts were that he would have to wake up soon to make sure the fire continued to burn. In seconds he was asleep, his exhausted body giving in to the pressures he had felt for the last few hours.

~ ~ ~

He wasn't sure what it was that woke him. The first thing he saw when his eyes opened was the moon, full and bright, straight above his head. His first impression was the darkness all around him. Even with the moon illuminating the area, it was still very dark just thirty feet away. The stream was no longer visible. Jesse glanced quickly toward the fire. Only embers remained. He pulled the knife from his belt and poked at the few remaining coals. At the same time he dropped some twigs on the fast dying light. In a moment the blaze was building and he put some larger pieces of wood on the stack. Only then did he relax and study the surrounding area. His mind tried to replay the last few moments and what had caused him to wake up. As tired as he was, he was surprised that he hadn't slept through the night. But he was glad for whatever had awakened him. Anything could have happened with the fire out. His body shuddered at the thought.

"Gots to be more careful," he whispered under his breath. "Gots to train myself to wake up 'fore the fire die."

The only time Jesse had spent the night in the swamp was when he and John had gotten lost several years earlier. Then there was always someone awake and watching for danger. Now it was just him. He settled back against the log again and closed his eyes. The knife was resting on his stomach with his fingers wrapped loosely around the handle. His mind was on the fire blazing lustily near his left shoulder. He wanted to sleep, needed to sleep. Yet he was cautious. A person could stay awake only so long, only so long he thought and again he slept.

# CHAPTER 15

AMOS BILLINGS WOKE BEFORE dawn that Monday morning. His window faced east, but he could see no hint of the rising sun. Still, he knew it was near. He could feel it just as surely as he could hear Alf's loud snoring from the next room. As his eyes adjusted to the darkness, he could make out Pete's form lying across the bed where he had collapsed in a whiskey-induced state the night before. He hadn't moved and Amos grunted in disgust.

"Fool can't hold his liquor," Amos muttered. He rolled over and dropped his feet onto the rough wood floor. A splinter gouged into the soft pad behind the big toe on his right foot, causing him to wince with discomfort. He reached down, scratched around the bottom of his foot until he had found the sticker and pulled it out. In the darkness he began searching the floor for his boots. Once found, he pulled one on his left foot. With the right boot, he reached over and brought it down hard against Pete's bottom.

"Git up, you lazy jackass, and fix some grub."

Pete moaned and rolled onto his back. He was motionless again, his mouth wide open and emitting loud roaring noises. Amos pulled on the right boot, stood up, grabbed Pete's legs and flipped him off the other side of the bed. This time he woke up. Even in the darkness Amos could make out Pete's clenched fists. The smaller man was straining his eyes to make out his attacker.

"Git some grub a workin'," Amos growled and began pulling his pants on over the boots. He turned his back and ignored Pete as the younger man strode around the bed toward him. One leg was off the floor as Amos struggled to pull on his pants. Pete lifted a foot to the other man's buttocks and gave a hard push. Amos flew head first across his bed and landed on his side against the far wall. He came up cursing, but Pete only laughed and strode out of the room. The first rays of the sun were just beginning to streak across the eastern sky.

Pete opened the wood box next to the old stove and swore quietly under his breath. It was Alf's job to keep it full. He hadn't done it the night before. Pete strode across the room and hovered over his brother.

"Fool, git outta that bunk and git me a load of wood."

Alf didn't respond.

"Git up, Idjit," Pete shouted. Alf was laying on his stomach with nothing on but his long underwear. His legs were spread and each arm hung off the bed. He still gave no indication that he heard Pete. His pants, shirt, and boots lay in a pile on the floor beside his right arm.

"You stupid idjit. I said roll out." Taking a page out of Amos' book, Pete picked up one of Alf's boots and brought it down hard on the prostrate man's backside. Alf howled and rolled out of the bunk. There was fire in his eyes when he saw it was Pete. If both hands hadn't suddenly been forced to become very busy, there would have been trouble. But with one rubbing at the pain and the other clutching at the pressure from his kidneys, he burst out the door, tripped over one of the hounds lying at the head of the steps and tumbled head over heels into the dirt at the edge of the porch. While he was rolling to his feet his kidneys began to empty.

"Bring back a load of wood," Pete hollered after him.

"You shouldn't oughta done that, Pete. You shouldn't oughta done that." After a few moments of silence Pete heard Alf's moan. "Now see what you went and made me do. I just put these whites on," Alf whined.

Pete walked to the front door and stared out at his brother. Alf was standing with his arms spread and staring toward Pete in the doorway. The whites as Alf had called them had not been white for weeks. Now they were heavily stained. Pete shook his head in disgust.

"Stinkin' fool, you done had them underpants on fer more'n a month," Pete muttered. He turned and disgustedly threw a pot across the room where it clanked against the far wall. The sound brought Amos into the room.

"Fool, bring in some wood and change them long johns. I seen polecats that's better smellin'," Pete shouted through the open doorway.

"I'm a goin' to knock heads together if'n there ain't a little peace around here, boy."

Pete sneered at Amos. "Go to knockin'. Then you can fix your own grub." He scowled at his older brother. "Jist what you need is to poison yerself."

Amos walked across the room and lifted Pete off the floor. "You talk real careful like. I ain't beyond feedin' you to them gators out in the swamp." He shook Pete violently and pitched him on Alf's bunk. "Now you git the grub a goin' or I'll carve another mouth into that neck of your'n," he growled and drew his forefinger across his own neck in a cutting motion. Amos let that sink in then turned and stalked out the front door.

Alf was standing a few yards from the porch holding the wet underwear away from his body. His back was to Amos and his bottom was shining in the newborn light of day. Amos yanked a set of underwear off the porch line and threw it in the dirt at Alf's feet.

Alf turned, looked down at the underwear, then up quizzically at Amos. "What's them fer?"

"Put um on and git that wood inside so's your brother can cook up some vittles."

Alf held the wet underwear toward Amos. "Ain't no need. These'll be dry in a while. They's still good."

"Pete's right. You stink like a polecat," Amos grunted at him. "Put them dry long johns on and put them smelly ones in the wash tub."

Amos grabbed a bucket and strode past Alf toward the well. As he passed his brother, the stench was nearly too much for even him.

"You're worse than a polecat. You ain't comin in to eat till you been in the pond. Now you tote in a load of wood and then git down to that pond. I ain't never smelt nothin' so foul."

"Aw, Amos. I jist had a dunk a while back. Couldn't have been more'n a week or two.

"Git, boy, git, afore I pitch you down the well. Jist be sure you take in that wood first."

"Aw, Amos. Ain't no sense in another dunkin' so quick," Alf muttered. But he picked up several pieces of wood and walked up the steps into the house. A few minutes later he came out and struck off through the woods toward the pond. He was still buck-naked and all he carried was the grayish white underwear Amos had pitched at his feet.

It was nearly half an hour before he came back in sight of the cabins. He was wearing the clean underwear as he picked his way up the narrow path toward the smell that had caused him to speed up his pace. One thing about Alf functioned perfectly if nothing else did. His sense of smell and his appetite were a match for anyone's. He was still angry at Pete and Amos. They had no call to treat him that way, he thought to himself. Still, he wouldn't challenge Amos. Pete was another matter. Pete, he knew he could handle. The only thing stopping him was his stomach. If he damaged his brother, who would do the cooking?

As he came around the front of the shack, Amos was standing on the porch with his rifle aimed toward the sky. He pulled the trigger once.

"What you doin', Amos?"

Amos turned and glared down at Alf. "You smell any better?"

"You ain't got no call to bad mouth me none," Alf muttered.

Amos stepped off the porch and sniffed hard. "You go all the way to the pond, boy?"

"I shore did. Got clear up to my waist. Nearly got wet all over afore I was done."

Amos sniffed again and looked disbelievingly at Alf. "Might be some better. Even so, ain't no time to dip again. Git in there and light into that grub afore Carter gits here."

Alf nodded and went inside where Jim and Pete were shoveling down the food.

~ ~ ~

Floyd heard the rifle shot just as he was stepping into the stirrups. At first he thought it might be trouble; but when no other shots followed, he dismissed the thought and swung his right leg over the saddle. The ride to the Billings' shack would take only a couple of minutes.

~ ~ ~

Papa got up about an hour after I did that morning. I was out on the back porch, staring aimlessly across the meadow when I heard his step in the kitchen. A moment later he came through the screen door and stood beside me on the porch.

"You're up early, James."

"Yes sir."

"Did you have trouble sleeping?" He dipped his hands in the pan of water and splashed some up in his face. After he toweled off, he stood staring down at me waiting for an answer. I knew he was giving me a chance to tell him more about what he thought I knew. But I continued to evade him.

"Yes sir," I finally answered. "I did. It was terrible hot and Eddie stretched all over the bed. I couldn't find no place to lay that wasn't soakin' wet." My half-truths did not seem to be getting any easier.

"I see," Papa answered. "Nothing else bothering you?" I could hear the disappointment in his voice and I knew he still doubted me. That hurt. I knew it would hurt a lot more when he found out the whole truth. I also knew that was only a matter of time. Still, I put off the inevitable.

"Very serious thing, this fire. Very serious. People could have died. Someone still might if we can't find out what happened." Papa let that sink in for several seconds while I held my breath.

Finally, he sighed and turned and went back into the kitchen. It wasn't just the heat of the day that had me sweating. It was my own cowardice. I knew it and Papa suspected it. He knew something was wrong, very wrong and he felt that I could tell him much more than I had. The thought of disappointing Papa devastated me. Still, I could not bring myself to say more.

~ ~ ~

It was only a half hour later when the wagon pulled up out front. We were just finishing breakfast and Papa wiped his mouth and reached over to squeeze Mama's hand and give her a quick peck on the cheek.

"They're here, Ellen."

"Efren, please be careful. She looked toward the closed door to the front room where Sarah still slept. "That man is not to be trusted," she whispered. "Please take care."

Papa nodded. "I'll be fine. Don't wait meals. I don't know how long I'll be gone."

"Papa," I started, "what....". I couldn't get out anymore.

"Yes, James," he said after I failed to go on.

"Where you goin'?" I finally managed and hated myself because I didn't say more.

"Some of us are going to try and find Jesse before Mr. Carter does." He looked at Mama then back to me. "Is there anything I should know before I go?"

I looked from Papa to Mama then back to Papa. The lump in my throat seemed to be choking me and I couldn't speak. All I could do was shake my head and mutter. "No Sir." I swallowed and looked down to find my hands trembling in my lap.

Mama came around the table, knelt, and put her arm around my shoulder. "Jamie, your father and I love you. Whatever you've done or haven't done isn't important now. If you know more you must tell us. It could save Jesse's life." She hesitated and glanced up at Papa. "It might even save someone else's life. Papa could be putting himself in danger."

After a moment she stood up and rested her hand on my shoulder. My eyes were beginning to fill with tears, and I could feel their eyes staring down at the top of my head. When I looked up, there was a terrible sadness in Mama's eyes.

"We love you, son. No matter what, we always will." She leaned over and kissed me on the forehead.

I couldn't stand the pain I saw in her eyes. My arms slid around her waist and I buried my head in her apron. All of a sudden it all began to pour out of me. "I never done nothin', Mama. I don't really know how the fire started. I just suspicion how." It was Papa who responded.

"Just tell us what you think, son. It's important."

I looked at Mama for support, and she took a damp cloth and wiped away the tears that were beginning to run down my face. Then she knelt and, with her arm firmly around my shoulder, I took a deep breath and began.

"Papa," I said sheepishly and stopped to swallow the lump in my throat, "me and Eddie been doin' somethin' we shouldn't oughta." My eyes dropped to my hands and I paused.

Mama's arm tightened around my shoulder. "Are you talking about the smoking, James? If you are, Papa and I know about that."

I gasped and went limp. The shock was like a hammer blow to my chest. All I could do was mutter. "How?" As I did, I turned my head toward Papa. His eyes were boring into my flesh.

After several seconds of silence he answered. "The odor," he said, "The rotten stench of tobacco has been all over you and your clothes for days."

"James, we had to let you find out for yourself about the smoking. Papa and I knew when you did, you would make the right decision. But, it had to be your decision, not ours. When you said a moment ago you had been doing something wrong, we knew." She hesitated and looked toward Papa who affirmed what she said with a nod, "We both knew you had finally made that decision. Sooner or later good boys make the right decision without being prodded."

I nodded and my eyes dropped to the floor. I couldn't bear to look either of them in the eyes. "I'm sorry," I managed to say, my eyes still staring at the floor. "I know I did wrong."

It was Papa that pressed on. "Now, son, back to the problem at hand. What does your smoking have to do with the fire?"

I looked from one to the other and then back to Papa as I wiped the perspiration from my brow. I must have taken a little too long because Papa leaned forward and spoke sharply.

"Time's a wastin', James. Let's hear it."

"Yes, sir." I swallowed and started. "We was under the house smokin'..."

"What house?" Papa interrupted.

"Eddie's house," I whispered.

"Go on," Papa persisted.

"We was under Eddie's house smokin' a little while before the fire. When Mama called I put out my smoke but Eddie kept on." I stopped and took a deep breath before I continued. "I don't think Eddie put his out good when he finished."

"Why do you say that, James? Did he say he didn't?"

I shook my head. "He didn't say that. He just keeps saying Jesse done it. But he made me promise not to tell about the smokin'. He was real scared about that."

Mama looked at Papa inquisitively. "You think a cigarette may have started the fire?"

"Let's get Eddie up and get to the bottom of this," Papa said firmly. "Ellen, go and wake the boy and his mother."

Mama gave me one last squeeze and hurried toward my bedroom. In less than a minute she was back.

"Eddie's gone, Efren."

Papa got quickly to his feet. "And his mother?"

"She's still asleep on the pallet, poor soul."

Without another word, Papa strode through the little living room and out onto the front porch. Three men were astride horses and another four were in a wagon.

"You men see young Eddie come out in the last few minutes?"

Mr. Meecham nodded. "Yup, came out all in a lather. Seemed to be in a powerful hurry. Took off down that away, he did." The old man pointed a calloused finger in the direction of the ruins of the Carter house. Eddie was nowhere in sight.

"I'll be right with you boys," Papa said and came back in the house. "Eddie must have heard us talking and took off." Papa said in a low voice. "No matter. We must stop Floyd before he does something we'll all be sorry for." Papa gave Mama a kiss and reached down to squeeze my shoulder.

"You did the right thing, James. But we'll have to have a long talk when this is over."

"I know, Papa. I'm sorry. I ain't ever gonna smoke again. Like you said, it's the devil's weed."

"It is that." Papa turned to go and Mama grabbed his arm. "Efren, what about..." She only pointed toward the other room where Mrs. Carter still slept.

"Don't say anything to her yet. We still don't know for sure what happened."

Mama nodded and Papa turned and went out to where Satan was tied. I went to the door and watched him climb into the saddle. The other men all turned, waiting for him to lead out.

"All right, men. We'll ride to Mr. Holland's for mounts like we planned last night. On the way I have new developments I must tell you about. It could change our whole approach to this ordeal." With that Papa raised his arm and motioned for the wagon to lead out.

## CHAPTER 16

RUFUS HAD BEEN IN the tree since an hour before dawn. Now, as the sun began to rise in the eastern sky, he could feel the intense heat radiating on his dark skin. His overalls were wet to such a degree that anyone might think he had experienced an unwanted accident. He wanted to drop out of the tree and go find a cool pond to wash off the smelly perspiration. But he wouldn't. Granny Ruby had sent him here. She trusted him to do a job and he would do it. He would watch and report. Stationed as he was, he could view half a mile in every direction. The shantytown was behind him and the swamp off to his right. Nobody could approach the town from this direction without his seeing them. Granny had awakened him at four that morning and sent him out in the darkness with orders to bring word of anyone heading their way. It was a lonely but necessary watch according to Granny.

The only living thing he had seen beside the flies that were constantly pestering him was the moccasin making its way toward the swamp. It passed under his tree not long after daylight and the very sight had sent a shiver up his spine. He hated snakes, all snakes. Someone told him once that some snakes were harmless and to let them live. To him it didn't matter what kind they were. He gave them all a wide berth. An hour had passed since the snake disappeared and the sun was two hours high now. He yawned and patted at his mouth. The night had not been long enough. But the day was likely to be very long. He hoped Granny would remember and send someone to take his place. His belly was beginning to growl and he felt the first pangs of hunger. The small piece of bread he managed to find before Granny sent him on his way would have to hold him until his watch was over. The old woman was scary but he respected her. Everyone did.

Rufus settled back against one of the limbs and felt a sharp pain in his right shoulder. When he felt the pain, he remembered the sharp broken branch that protruded about an inch in his direction and why he hadn't settled against that limb before. He raised his shoulder and quickly froze as he did. About a half mile to the north he saw movement. It was slight but it caught his attention. Rufus shaded his eyes, half-closing his right one to the glare of the sun. At first, as he stared into the distance, he thought he must have imagined the movement. Then he saw them. Five riders just breaking through the trees, their horses moving steadily toward him. Rufus slid from the tree quickly and began running hard toward the shantytown. The riders had not seen him. He was sure of that. It took him less than two minutes to cover the nearly quarter mile back to the town. Big John Andrews was the first he saw and he started waving his arms wildly.

John saw young Rufus coming the last hundred yards and stopped to watch. He knew Granny had sent the boy out, and now as he covered the last few yards John anticipated the worst. The old woman said Carter would come and the way the boy was running, John figured she was right.

Rufus was panting hard and clutching his side as he stopped in front of John. "They's comin'. They.... Five. They comin'."

"Five?" John questioned.

All Rufus could do was nod his head violently and point back in the direction he had come.

John turned and sprinted up the path between the shacks. As he went, he shouted the word and several men moved quickly. There had been no work in the fields this morning. Granny had more important things for them to do on this day. Now, as John ran up the path toward her cabin, she stopped rocking and tapped the old corn cob pipe on the chair arm. The old woman had been expecting this and she didn't wait for John to speak.

"I heerd. Now git them youngun's out of sight. You got our men set about?"

"They's ready," John said. There was a certainty about the way he spoke the words and that concerned Granny.

She measured him as she spoke. "You don't do nothin' without I tell you. You hear?"

"We doin' it your way for now, Granny. But them whites ain't gonna push us down." An old rusty pitchfork with one prong broken off was leaning against Granny's porch. John had put it there earlier in the morning, and he picked it up now and held it menacingly in both hands. "They ain't grindin us under their heels no more."

"Shet yer mouth, John. This ain't no time fer boastin' or threatenin'." The old woman turned her attention away from John for a moment. She stepped off the porch and stared down the path. The riders were visible now through the trees. They had stopped and were surveying the shantytown from a safe distance. Granny grunted in satisfaction as she studied the scene around her. The children and most of the women were out of sight. A few of the older women, the ones who had lived through the last years of slavery, were still visible in front of some of the shacks. They were not afraid but she imagined they would make themselves scarce soon. John was standing beside her, the pitchfork prongs pointed down and resting on the hard ground.

~ ~ ~

"I don't like the look." It was Pete Billings who spoke. The five had pulled up several hundred feet from the first cabin and were studying the layout.

Amos grunted and lifted his huge frame off the saddle until he was supported by his feet in the stirrups. He could see very little from here.

"Let's go in. We ain't gettin' nothin' done out here," Floyd growled. He patted the rope draped over his saddle horn. "The sooner we ride in, the sooner that no good house-burnin' nigger'll be swingin from the end of this here hemp."

Alf's eyes were gleaming. "Yeah, I say let's git on with it."

Amos brought his arm around and caught Alf hard in his stomach. The wild-eyed gleam disappeared from Alf's face and his breath whooshed out of his mouth leaving him gasping.

After a moment, he sputtered. "You didn't have no call to do that. I was...."

"Shut up, idiot," Amos growled. "I'll decide when you talk and I'll decide when we go in."

Alf dropped in his saddle and began to pout.

"Jim, you got the eyes. You see anything in there?" Amos asked.

Jim spat a stream of tobacco, half of it landing on Alf's boot, and pointed toward the town. "Old woman, the one they call Granny and a big nigger. Few other old Mammys scattered about. Don't see none other." He was standing up in his stirrups with his right hand shading his eyes. "Yep. 'Bout it," he said relaxing back down on his saddle. Then he added. "Don't see the big nigger, the one they call Jesse."

"All right," Amos said finally, "let's go in. Spread out and keep your traps shut.

I'll do the talkin'. And be rememberin' they got themselves some guns."

"'Bout time," Floyd growled and kneed his horse until it moved up between Amos and Alf. As he did, he spit his own stream of tobacco off to the right. As Jim's had a moment before, it splashed on Alf's boot and the crazy man came upright on his horse. But before he could protest, the other four were moving toward the shantytown, leaving him sputtering.

~ ~ ~

"They comin in," John said under his breath.

"Who it be?" Granny asked.

John studied the riders for several seconds before answering.

"Floyd Carter, he be one." John continued to study the riders. "The other four be them brothers from t'other side of the swamp."

"Billings," Granny muttered. "That's what I reckoned. They is bad medicine."

"Bad medicine or no, they ain't scarin' me none," John grunted.

"Keep yer wits," Granny ordered. "Don't do nothin' stupid." Her eyes were moving back and forth to the cabins on each side. If the men were in place as John said, there would be one in the nearest cabin on the right and one positioned in the nearest cabin on the left. Two more were in the next two cabins on each side of the path. All the men were out of sight and all knew how to use the old civil war repeating rifles that Holland had given them several years before. The rifles were meant for hunting. Now it might be necessary to use them to protect the hunted.

Amos, Floyd and Jim came first with Amos in the middle, his horse slightly ahead of the other two. Pete and Alf, still growling about the double dose of tobacco juice on his boots, had dropped back about twenty feet. The three in front had their rifles resting crossways in front of them. Each had a finger resting on the trigger. Pete and Alf had their weapons propped on their right shoulders, barrels pointing skyward. Their fingers were wrapped around their triggers. They moved in slowly, past several shacks. As they did, the women that were on the porches disappeared inside until only Granny and John were still visible at the far end of the dirt path.

"I don't like it," Pete grunted.

"He don't like it," Alf gloated and his finger instinctively tightened on the trigger.

"Shut up, the both of you," Amos spat.

When they were thirty feet away Granny raised her wrinkled hand. "You done come fur enough. State yer business and git."

John moved up close to Granny's shoulder, towering over the little woman.

Amos looked from side to side. The hairs were standing on the back of his neck the same as when the bear had come up suddenly on him ten years earlier in the swamp. He felt the eyes from the cabins on both sides of the path. They were there. How many he could only guess. But they were there, probably with guns pointed at them. This was not the time for a challenge. Amos knew he had to bide his time. He shook off the feeling of danger and focused on the two standing in front of him.

"We ain't come to trouble you none old woman. You got a boy here name of Jesse. We done come for him. He burnt down Floyd Carter's house with women folk inside."

Granny cleared her throat. "You ain't the law and you ain't got no business with him. Now git."

"Ain't got no business," Floyd screamed. "Why you old...." He didn't finish the sentence when he saw John take a step toward him. His eyes left Granny and focused on the big black man until he was sure the threat had passed. When he looked back at Granny, he was a bit calmer. "He burned down my house. Near killed my little gal." He patted the rope and leered at Granny and John with renewed anger. "We gonna hang him for a lesson."

It was Amos taking the lead again. "Where you got him hid, old mammy?" Amos grunted. His voice had an edge to it as he raised the gun muzzle straight up and let the butt rest on his right leg.

Granny held Billing's gaze without speaking. Confrontation was the last thing she wanted. Guns were a last resort.

It was just then that the worst happened. The small girl appeared from behind the near cabin on Granny's right. Somehow, she had been overlooked and now she came running directly toward the riders, stopping just beside Alf's horse. The wild man stared down at the five-year-old in astonishment. For an instant he was unsure how to react.

"Ethel, you git inside that house! Right now, youngun! Go!" Granny shouted at the girl. She was standing less than a foot from Alf's tobacco stained boot, grinning up at the crazed man. When Granny yelled the child turned to go but she didn't move fast enough.

Amos had turned in his saddle and was staring back at the child. "The brat, Alf. Grab the brat before she skedaddles."

Alf grunted, reached down, grasped the girl under her right arm pit and swept her up and onto the saddle in front of him. "I got her, Amos. I got the little nigger gal." Alf laughed that crazy wild laugh of one who is unbalanced and held little Ethel tight against him. He pulled a long knife from his belt and held it next to the girl's throat. "You want I should cut her up some?"

It was Granny weaving her way through the front three horses until she was next to Alf's. "Let that child be." She raised her arms up toward Ethel but Alf held tight. Just then a young black man in the shack on the right came out on the porch and leveled his rifle at Alf's back.

"No, Ezra! Don't do no shootin'! You might hit Ethel!" It had gone terribly wrong, and Granny turned to make sure John did nothing foolish. It was a good thing. The pitchfork was off the ground and pointed in the direction of Floyd's chest. Carter had turned his attention to what was going on to his rear and didn't realize the threat that was approaching him.

"John," she shouted and the big black man halted, stared at her a moment, then lowered the fork to the ground.

"That's better, old woman. Now you, boy, with the gun. Lay it nice and easy like on the ground or I'll have my brother cut this youngun's gizzard out. And he's just crazy enough to do it, too." Amos glanced back at Alf, who smiled wickedly at the prospect. Ezra hesitated only a moment, then placed the gun on the porch and stepped back.

"Smart boy," Amos said. He looked at the shacks on either side of the path. "How many more you got in there? You git all them guns out here." He hesitated a moment. "Now," he yelled.

Granny looked toward Ethel. Alf's grip was tight and the child was whimpering. "Sam, George, Willie. Come out slow. Don't do nothin' dumb."

There was a sound on each side of the road, and Sam and Willie came out, their hands up with the guns sliding through the door in front of them. George still hadn't appeared.

"George Hamilton, you hear what I say?" Granny turned and

was shouting toward the near cabin on the left. "You hear me good. Git that rifle and yerself out onto that there porch!" The brown saliva from her chewing tobacco had streaked the left corner of Granny's mouth, and she flicked out with her tongue and it disappeared.

Still no sign from the cabin. It was Amos who yelled toward the cabin now. "Boy, you got to the count of five and then I'm gonna turn Alf loose on this little gal."

It was then that the rifle slid out onto the porch and a tall slim boy with his hands held high followed. He was still in his teens, shirtless and shoeless. A dark scowl creased his lips as he stared toward the horsemen. Ethel was his sister. It was his responsibility to have someone watch her, but in the haste and anxiety of the moment he had forgotten. Now, he cursed himself under his breath.

Amos shifted in his saddle and faced Granny again. "That all, old woman?"

Granny nodded. "That be all."

"It better be." He stared down at Granny. "You best be talkin' true. Alf still got that one," he said pointing at Ethel. "Right handy with a knife, he is. Ain't got no sense. But I never seen no one skin a critter better. Never seen him skin a person though. Might be right interestin'." He glanced at Alf and smiled. Alf moved the knife from the girl's throat to her stomach and grinned broadly.

The little girl started crying and wiggling. The movement made Alf grasp the girl even tighter and make a cutting motion in the direction of the girl's midsection.

"Amos Billings. Control that brother of your'n." Granny wasn't giving orders. She was halfway pleading and it worked.

Amos turned to Alf. "Put that knife to rest." Alf frowned but reluctantly complied.

"Pete, collect them guns," Amos ordered.

Amos looked from the young black men who had been hidden just a few minutes before, then back to John. The man still held the pitchfork in his right hand with the point pressing into the ground. John felt the anger and hatred boil up in his gut. Granny had been wrong, he thought. His hand tightened on the fork and he felt the muscles in his shoulder go taut.

"You, I don't like your look," Amos said and pointed his rifle toward John. The barrel was pointing over Granny's left shoulder and directly at John's chest. "Now, you jist let that there fork drop or I'm a gonna make you a new bellybutton a mite above the other un."

John didn't move.

"Do it, boy. I ain't sayin' it no more."

After another moment, John released the handle of the pitchfork and it dropped in front of him. Satisfied, Amos dropped the barrel of his gun until it pointed toward the ground again. Then he shifted his attention back to Granny.

"Git on with it, Billings. Find out where that house-burnin nigger is," Floyd ordered.

"How 'bout it, Mammy? You ready to talk?"

Granny rubbed the back of her hand across her mouth and transferred the tobacco juice to the side of her dress.

"Let the child down. She ain't done you no hurt."

Amos shook his head. "The boy first. Where you got him hid?"

Granny looked toward Ethel and the leering giant of a man who was holding her as if she were no more than a rag doll. She was treading on dangerous ground. These men were just as likely to kill Ethel as they were a snake. Still she lied.

"Don't none of us know. He lit out when he heerd Carter was after him."

Billings glanced at Floyd and the storekeeper shook his head. "Ain't likely. His woman just bore him a new brat. Naw," Floyd continued. "He ain't far. These people protect their own. They got him hid somewhere close and I aim to find out where. I say slit the brat open if they don't tell us."

"Hear that" Amos growled down at Granny. "We ain't buyin' yer story. Let's hear a different tune if'n you care about that one." Amos pointed his thumb back over his shoulder to where Ethel had gone still in Alf's strong grip.

Granny spit again, wiped the saliva with the back of her hand

and continued to stare up at Amos. When it was evident that Granny wasn't going to speak, Amos turned to Alf.

"Draw some blood out of the brat's finger, just a bit to let the old woman know we mean business."

There was movement from the porch on the left and John reached down for the pitchfork. Amos raised his gun toward John, and Jim, sitting to his left, leveled his on George before the slender boy could jump from the porch. It was Granny that intervened before shots were fired.

"Wait!" She yelled and held up both hands toward Amos. "Wait!" Don't do that child no hurt. John, you and George stand still. We ain't got no choice but to tell these," she paused in mid-sentence and put extra emphasis on her next words, "fine white men what they wants to know." She spit again but this time she didn't nod her head toward the ground. Her gaze was fastened on Carter and the stream of tobacco juice landed on his horse's hooves causing the black animal to stomp the ground and shake his head violently. The quick movement threw Floyd off balance. For just a moment the storekeeper thought of raising his gun and blowing the old woman away. But it was just a moment and he regained his composure. It wasn't her that Floyd wanted. It was Jesse. Still, he thought, he had no conscience about coming back after this thing was over and wiping out the whole lot of these people.

Amos had held up his hand to stop Alf before he could hurt Ethel. Now, he looked down at Granny. "Go on, woman. We all waitin'."

"First off, you gotta promise no hurt will come to that girl." Granny was pleading again but she felt she held at least some leverage over the man.

"We ain't gonna hurt her if'n you tell us what we want to know, but I'm growin' weary and Alf is jist a pantin' fer some action. Don't try our patience no longer. You hear what I say?"

Granny looked from one to the other of the five men before she answered. They had won for the time being and she knew it. "He done took to the swamp, done lit out yestidy. He know that swamp like the back of his hand. Ain't none of us can find him in there if'n he don't want us to."

"Granny!" It was John and there was pain in the big man's voice.

"Hush, boy. Ain't nothin' more we'uns could do less'n we wanted to see little Ethel hurt." The fire was gone out of Granny now. If they caught Jesse it would be her responsibility. No matter what had caused it. She was responsible. For the first time she felt unsure of herself. She also knew that when this was over she was finished as leader of her people.

"You believe the old woman?" Pete asked.

Amos nodded. "You see how that big un jumped when she told. He weren't actin'. Pure pain is what he felt." Amos nodded again. "She was tellin' it straight all right." He paused again. "Anyways, if she wuz lyin' we'll come back and clean out the whole lot of them and she done knows that." Amos paused and let that sink in but Granny didn't budge.

"Put Ethel down." It was John standing shoulder to shoulder with Granny now. For the first time he seemed to be taking charge.

"Settle back, boy," Amos said and motioned John to keep his distance. He raised his gun and wiggled it toward him. "We'll be ridin' out soon now. The girl goes with us a ways." He pointed at George. "That one can follow if he's a mind to and bring her back." Amos looked over his shoulder at Alf and motioned back toward the direction they had entered the little shantytown.

"You go first, Alf."

"Can I cut her just a mite, Amos?"

"Git, boy, afore I do some cuttin' of my own."

The smile on Alf's face disappeared and he turned his horse and moved back down the path. Pete followed, then Floyd, Amos and Jim. When they cleared the trees, Amos took the lead and headed his horse north at a gallop. Half a mile from the shantytown, he reined the animal to a stop.

"Let the brat down, Alf."

"Aw, Amos. I ain't had no fun yet. Can't I...."

"Do what I say, you crazy idjit."

Alf obeyed, but he didn't let Ethel down gently but dropped her roughly to the ground. The little girl squealed, got to her feet and raced down the path toward the shantytown and her brother who was running toward them.

They watched for several seconds; then Amos kneed his animal and the five men rode on toward the swamp. Floyd looked up toward the sun off his right shoulder and guessed it to be just two hours short of noon. He shivered at the thought of the swamp and the trouble that lay ahead. Still, he was determined. Before another twenty-four hours passed, they would catch that house-burning nigger and string him up. That thought made him shiver, this time with anticipation.

# CHAPTER 17

IT WAS THE MIDDLE of the morning before I was able to slip away to look for Eddie. I knew he would be afraid to come back to the house. He certainly wouldn't look too kindly on me when I found him. I betrayed him and, I was sure in his eyes, we were no longer friends, much less best friends. At that moment, with what had happened, I wasn't too sure I cared. Still, I was concerned about his well-being.

When I didn't find him anywhere around the ruins of his house, my next thought was the swimming hole. But it didn't seem likely that he would go there. Not today. Not with our secret out. I'm not quite sure what turned me in the direction of the swamp. But that's where I found myself headed.

Mama's voice and the look she gave Papa kept coming back as I hurried through the woods. "The truth could save Jesse's life," she had said. When she looked up at Papa there was pain in her eyes and I knew whom she meant when she added. "It might save someone else's life." The thought of what could happen to Papa and the other men made me move even faster though I wasn't sure what I could do now.

~ ~ ~

Papa and the other men were reining up in front of Mr. Holland's house about the time I began my search for Eddie. Papa stiffened his legs and stood straight up in the stirrups. As he did, the leather saddle creaked under the strain of his weight.

"Hello, the house. Holland, it's Reverend Peterson and some friends," Papa called.

There was an immediate chorus of barking from somewhere in the back. It sounded far off and lasted close to a minute. Then as suddenly as it started it stopped.

Papa took in the porch, the swing on the far side, a straight chair next to the door and on the near side, nothing at first. Then he saw the stick lying in front of the screen door.

"He may be out back with the dogs," Meecham offered.

Papa stepped down from Satan and started up the path between the high grass to the porch. He noticed the broken step and stepped over it to the next. The stick he saw next to the door took a different dimension now. Papa recognized it as the cane the old man used. He called out Mr. Holland's name again. Still, no answer came back. When he bent over to pick up the cane, he saw the dry, red splotch next to the handle. His first thought was correct. It was blood.

A low growl just inside the screen caused him to glance up quickly toward the door. For the first time he saw the ragged wire and the hole that had been forced in the lower right hand corner. Several strands of brown hair were visible where something had gained entrance to the house. The growl came again and he stood up with the cane in his right hand.

"What's the trouble, Preacher?" The question came from Joe Garvey, one of the men in the wagon.

Papa only raised his hand as he moved toward the screen door, cupped his hands and peered into the darkened hallway. He could see him now. Holland was lying face down at the foot of the staircase with his arms stretched to either side and his head and upper torso resting on the bottom two steps of the stairs.

Next to Holland, lying on his stomach facing the door with his paws resting on the old man's legs, was the dog, his head held erect as he measured Papa with his eyes. His top lip was curled up and away, showing a mouth full of teeth. The low throaty growl was evidence that he meant for no one to disturb his master.

Papa stepped back and motioned to the others. "Come quick!"

Meecham came first and halfway to the porch he recognized the stick in Papa's hand.

"That's Holland's cane."

Papa nodded and pointed to the steps. "Watch that broken step."

Meecham leaped to the second step, followed closely by the others. Papa peered in the screen door again as Meecham came up beside him. He moved aside and motioned for Meecham and the others to look inside.

"Don't open the screen door yet," Papa warned.

Garvey swore under his breath, then remembering who Papa was, he gulped and shook his head.

"Is he dead?"

"Most likely," Papa said and nodded.

"Maybe he ain't. Leastwise, we gotta see about him," Meecham stated. He reached for the door handle but Papa grabbed his arm.

"Wait. That dog'll attack anyone who steps inside." Papa squinted through the door again. The hall ran from the front past the stairs and Holland's body to a door about thirty feet toward the back of the house.

"You men keep the dog's attention. I'll go around back and see if I can get in. Maybe I can get the dog away from Holland and into that back room. I might trap him there until we can see about Holland."

One last time, Papa looked through the screen. The dog was crouched next to the motionless body, his head now low to the floor as he stared up at the men. His mouth was still curled showing a generous portion of his teeth. The animal was not about to let anyone near Holland.

With that, Papa slipped around to the back of the house. The bottom of the back door was two feet above ground level. Rot had taken these steps years ago, and Holland had piled several cypress logs on top of each other to form a step between the ground and the door. There was no screen on the back, but the main door was shut. Two other dogs, smaller than the one guarding the old man, were some distance behind the house. They were eyeing Papa closely but not threatening to attack.

Papa turned his attention back to the house and tried the knob. It turned and he stepped inside. The door on the far wall was closed, the one that probably led to the hall where Holland and the dog were. When he shut the outside door, the room became dark and for the first time he realized there were no windows, no way to let light in except by the door.

Remembering the direction to the door on the far wall, he slipped across the small room and felt for the doorknob. After a moment, he found it and turned it quietly. As he thought, it opened into the hall. Some twenty feet away the dog lay motionless. It was still hovering next to Holland's body and watching the men on the other side of the front screen door. Papa's presence still had not been detected but now, without the screen door separating him from the dog, the situation became even more serious. It also looked as if the animal had scooted a few steps closer to the screen door, while remaining in its attack crouch. Now was as good a time as any, Papa decided, and he looked back across the darkened room to make sure he had secured the outside door. Then he took a deep breath, opened the door wide and stepped into the hall.

In full view of the animal, Papa whistled and began waving his arms. It turned its head and glared first at Papa, then back to the screen door. The angry mongrel was unsure about what it should do next. It looked from the men glaring at him through the front screen and then back to Papa. It seemed to be weighing its options about who to attack first? Papa was highly visible and accessible and the dog finally settled on him. It came out of its crouch and turned full toward Papa and the open doorway. As it continued to stare toward him, Papa stepped back into the shadows, partially closed the door just enough so the animal lost sight of him. Through the crack at the back of the door, Papa watched as it glanced back at the men on the porch and then to the inviting open doorway where Papa disappeared. Probably afraid it was losing its prey, the dog bounded quickly in Papa's direction. The momentum of its charge carried it several feet into the darkened room. Papa stepped quickly around the door into the hall and closed it behind him. A split second later the dog crashed into the closed door and the angry barking and clawing began as the animal struggled to regain entrance to the hallway.

By the time Papa turned back toward Holland's body, Meecham was already bending over the man. It was only a moment before he looked up at Papa and shook his head.

"Been dead awhile, I reckon," Meecham muttered.

Papa knelt beside Holland and examined the pool of dry blood next to his head, then glanced at the marks leading from the body to the front door.

"Coulda fell down them stairs, I suppose," Sam Adams offered.

"Maybe," was all Papa said. Then after a moment he repeated. "Maybe."

Meecham stood up and shook his head violently. "Naw. Somebody done knocked him on the head, I'm a guessin'." He looked toward Papa, who was still examining the scuff marks on the floor. "You a thinkin' the same, Preacher?"

"We can't be sure how he received the blow to the head. He could have fallen, then crawled out onto the porch. Possibly, someone found him there and pulled him back in here." Papa motioned toward the marks on the dusty floor. They led from Holland's boots to the front door.

"But," Papa continued thoughtfully then paused, "but if someone found him, why didn't they come forward and report it?"

Papa pointed to Holland's cane that Meecham was now leaning heavily on. "If he fell and crawled out to the porch, his cane would have been in here." Finally, Papa shook his head. "No," he said firmly. "He wasn't hurt in here. Whatever happened, happened outside. And whether he died from a fall or whatever, someone dragged him in here and left his cane out on the porch where the injury occurred." Papa felt the body. Like Mr. Meecham said, Holland had been dead for some time.

"Happened a good while ago, probably yesterday. Plenty of time for somebody to put out the word." Papa said.

"You think somebody done kilt him?" The question came from Mr. Garvey. He was one of Papa's most reliable church members, a married man with six children, all girls.

"I'm not saying that for certain, Brother Garvey," Papa answered shaking his head. "I pray to heaven that wasn't the case. But, someone put the poor man in here and whoever did made no effort to report it. Whatever," Papa said, "we have come here for a purpose and we must not get sidetracked. Brother Garvey, I hope that you will see to Mr. Holland's body." Papa motioned to Sam Adams. "Mr. Adams, would you assist Brother Garvey in caring for the body. The rest of us will push on with the business that brought us here. We'll leave you the wagon. If the two of you will be so kind as to transport the body to the church and report this sad event to Doctor Smith." With that Papa turned and, with the rest of the men following, left the house. Adams and Garvey stayed behind to tend to Mr. Holland's body.

~ ~ ~

I'm not sure what was causing me to hurry toward the swamp, whether fear, shame or instinct. But, there I was half running, half stumbling, tears streaming down my face and scratches from the thorn bristles all over my arms. It had been half an hour since I slipped out of the house, and I was beginning to wonder if I was going in the right direction. Maybe Eddie was at the swimming hole after all. Maybe he was hiding somewhere that even I didn't know about. That thought caused me to slow up for a moment. But it was only a moment. The swamp wasn't far now. I could go at least that far before I turned back. I needed to find Eddie and persuade him to tell the truth before someone got hurt or, even worse, killed. The thought of death, maybe Papa's, scared me and spurred me on. I felt more guilty than ever now; and if I had known about Mr. Holland at the time, I'm not sure how I would have reacted or what I would have done. But I didn't know and at that moment I was hoping that the entire mess could be stopped without someone dying. If Eddie would confess to his pa maybe we could stop this before anyone got hurt. It was a thought and deep down I prayed I could make it happen. But first I had to find Eddie.

~ ~ ~

John watched the four brothers and Carter ride out of the shantytown. When they were out of sight, he rushed into his shack and pulled a long knife out from under his mattress. Granny was waiting outside his door when he came out.

"What you plannin', John?"

"Helpin' Jesse," he snapped.

"How you gonna help him? You gonna git him caught," she said.

John glared down at Granny. "Twernt me that done told them where he was. Now I gonna find him afore they does."

"How you gonna be able to git to the swamp before they do? You ain't gonna be able to slip by them without they seein' you," she protested.

"They's more than one way into them swamps." He looked over Granny's shoulder at Ezra and several more of the young men that were listening. "Jesse done took me in another way once. It ain't the best. More dangerous, but it's a way and it's faster."

He pushed past Granny and the young men parted, all but Ezra.

"I'm a mind to go with you."

"I ain't got time fer you, Ezra." Realizing the harshness of his voice, he reached out and squeezed the younger man's arm. "I appreciates the offer but I can travel a mite faster alone."

It was Granny who spoke again. "Then, if you're of a mind to go, take in some vittles and fresh water." She motioned toward one of the younger women. "She done got vittles and water ready." Granny reached out and touched John's arm. "Don't you go and git yerself kilt John Andrews. You a good man. You take care, now, you hear."

John nodded and gathered the food and water from the younger woman. Ezra was still standing in the path when John was ready to go. They stood facing one another; then Ezra moved to the side and they all watched John disappear behind one of the shacks, moving north toward the swamp.

~ ~ ~

I had been searching along the boundary of the swamp for some time and was just about to turn back toward home when I saw him. Eddie was sitting near the edge of the woods, his back propped against a large oak tree. He was half-hidden from me and facing toward the swamp. In the distance I could see several flat bottom boats tied at the edge of the water. I was just a short distance from him before he knew I was there. When my foot broke a dry twig, he jumped and turned and saw me. His eyes were as big as saucers and his mouth wide open until he realized it was me and that I was alone. The look he gave me sent a shiver down my back. For a moment we held each other's gaze. Then, he turned away from me and looked back toward the swamp. I watched as he picked up a small stone and pitched it toward a tree a few feet away.

"You told on me," he snapped. Already, he was trying to gain control of me and the situation we were both in. I could see that he had been crying from the streaks of dirt that ran down his cheeks just below his red eyes.

I dropped down beside him, determined not to let him intimidate me, and leaned back against the tree. For several seconds neither of us spoke. Finally, I got up the courage.

"We done wrong, Eddie. We done wrong in smokin' and we done wrong about not tellin' about it until it was too late. Now we gotta do right. You gotta tell it wasn't Jesse that done set the fire. We gotta do it together."

When I looked at him again, the tears were welling up in his eyes and beginning to follow the same path the earlier ones had traced. It was the first time I actually saw him cry, the first time he showed any weakness in front of me.

"He done it. I seen him," Eddie shouted and rubbed a dirty forearm across his face.

"You gotta tell what's true, Eddie. You know it was us. It weren't Jesse."

"No!"

He got up quickly, turned his back on me and the swamp and started back through the woods in the direction I had come from. I hurried after him and caught up near a creek that fed into the swamp.

"Eddie, wait. Listen."

He kept going at a fast pace. I reached to take his arm but he only shook my hand off and continued through the dense wood. It was the sound of hoof beats off to our right and back in the direction of the swamp that slowed him down. We were hidden by trees when the sound of the horses' hooves died. As if they could hear us, we both held our breath and dropped to the ground. Whoever it was, neither of us were ready to be found. As we peered through the underbrush, we could make out the shape of several riders. They had stopped and were sitting motionless near where I had found Eddie. I recognized them immediately—the four Billings brothers and Eddie's pa. The sight made me freeze even more. Papa had told me a long time ago that the Billings were bad and to stay away from them. Still, I wanted Eddie to tell his father. I reached out and touched his arm and he shook my hand off violently. I nodded toward the men and mouthed that he should tell the truth. This time it was his head that he shook violently. I wasn't about to confront this bunch by myself so I just shrugged my shoulders and knelt down further into the underbrush.

~ ~ ~

Amos had been mulling a thought over in his mind ever since they dropped the child outside the shantytown. If Jesse was in the swamp and heard them coming, he might try to escape out the other side. Amos was familiar with two ways into the swamp and there could very easily be more. They needed to cover both of those two ways. It was at least an hour ride on horseback to the other side of the swamp. By the time they reined up where the boats were tied, Amos had made up his mind.

"Jim, you recollect the time me and you done come into the swamp by way of that old creek up to the north?"

Jim nodded.

"You remember that place where them willows grows next to that creek bout half way in? Jim nodded again.

"I'm a thinkin' that nigger might try to sneak out of the swamp on that side if'n he hears us comin'. We need to cover that direction, too. You and Carter git yerselves round there. Start straight in and meet us at that clearing where the willows be.

"It's nigh onto an hour's hard ridin' to there. I ain't hankerin to spend me no night in them swamps," Jim growled.

Amos turned his head in Jim's direction and glared at his younger brother.

"I ain't askin' you what you want to do. I'm a tellin' you to git and take Carter with you. If'n you know what's good fer you. If'n you don't, you ain't gonna be hankerin' fer nothin' no more." He spit a stream of tobacco without batting an eye. Jim knew better than to argue any more. He turned his horse toward the northeast and was moving slowly in that direction when Floyd shook his head.

"I ain't missin' out on no hangin', Billings. I done paid you good money for the satisfaction of bein' in on the kill. How am I goin' to know if you done caught him and strung him up if I ain't there to see fer myself?"

"Storekeeper, I'm a goin' to say this just one more time. You git yerself along with Jim afore I decide to cut yer gizzard out." Amos looked toward Alf. "You wantin' my idjit brother turned loose on you?"

Floyd started to say something, thought better of it, then kneed his own mount and rode off after Jim. He was beginning to realize his mistake. When he made this deal with the four brothers, he assumed his money would allow him to be in charge. He had no more illusions about that. Amos was the man and he knew better than to cross him. He had made his deal with the devil and it looked like the devil had him.

~ ~ ~

Eddie and I sneaked closer so that we could hear what was being said. We were still a good ways off when we saw one of the brothers break off and ride in the opposite direction from where we were hiding. A few minutes later we saw Eddie's father follow. The two disappeared through the trees leaving the other three sitting astride their horses beside the boats. They were saying something I couldn't hear and I bent forward hoping to hear some of their conversation. That was a mistake. I lost my balance and fell heavily against a low hanging dead limb. It cracked under my weight and the sound echoed across the clearing. I dropped back into the brush, but it was too late. One of the brothers shifted his eyes in our direction just as I tried to right myself.

~ ~ ~

It was Alf who raised his arm and pointed in our direction. "Amos, they is someone out in them woods."

Amos spun around in his saddle and stared across the clearing toward us. "Go git um," he snapped and pointed in our direction.

Eddie responded quickly. "Them Billings done seen us," he stammered. "Let's git."

I didn't need a push. What Papa told me about the four brothers screamed in my head. So when they started our way, I turned and started running into the thicker underbrush. I ran fast and behind me I could hear Eddie panting hard. Under the thick canopy of trees it was beginning to become harder and harder to see. As I ran, I glanced back over my shoulder every few seconds to check on Eddie and the two horses that were pursuing us. A rotten log lay across our paths and I nearly saw it too late. I jumped it but caught my right foot on a snag. Still, I was able to regain my balance by catching my body with both hands. I was about to yell over my shoulder to Eddie about the log when I heard him squeal. He tripped on the same snag that I had caught my foot on. But Eddie was not so lucky and he fell heavily to the ground behind me.

"Jamie," he cried. "Jamie, help me!"

I caught a small pine and spun myself to a stop. Eddie was lying face down, his arms reaching out toward me. The two riders were bearing down on us. I looked quickly away from Eddie and toward what might be freedom in the distance. Maybe I could still get away. My first thought was run and keep on running. Let Eddie face the brothers. All this was his fault, not mine. As soon as I had the thought, I knew I couldn't. Eddie couldn't face the Billings alone. Besides, they were on us now. I couldn't get away. So, I just stood there watching the men coming toward both of us. We were destined to face the Billings together. Even though I wasn't trying to get away any longer, Eddie still wasn't sure about me.

"Don't leave me, Jamie, please! Don't leave me!"

I wasn't leaving him. I couldn't. One of the horses jumped the log, his hooves just missing Eddie. His eyes were fixed on me. The other rider slipped out of his saddle and grabbed Eddie. Dropping my head, I slumped against the tree gasping for breath. I barely felt the rough hands jerk me away from the tree and lift me into the saddle.

"This un's the Carter brat," I heard the smaller of the two men say as he wrapped his arm around Eddie's waist and effortlessly stepped back up into his saddle. "Don't know the other."

They took us back through the woods and across the clearing to where Amos waited, leaning on his saddle horn. The one who had me gave a push and I went sprawling at the feet of Amos's horse. A moment later Eddie came flying off the other horse and landed next to me.

"Ain't that Carter's brat?" Amos growled.

"At's him," Alf chuckled.

Amos stared at me and scowled. 'What's yer name, boy?"

My lips seemed to be stuck together. When I was able to pry

them apart, nothing came out.

"I'm speakin' to you, boy! What's yer name?"

"James," I managed. "Ja... James Peterson." I was shivering all over.

Amos eyed me suspiciously. The look on his face made me shiver all the more. He spit a stream of tobacco my way and I felt part of it splatter on my pants leg. But I didn't look down to see. I was transfixed by his eyes. They were evil and I could imagine all sorts of terrible things.

"Soul saver's brat," he finally grunted. "What you two doin' out here?"

I was shaking so badly I couldn't answer.

"Answer me, boy," Amos snarled. "You out here spyin'? You heerd what me and my brothers been sayin'?"

"No," I managed. "We didn't hear nothin'. We just been playin'," My voice sounded hollow and far away and I stuffed my hands in my overall pockets to stop them from shaking.

"What we gonna do with them?" Pete asked.

Amos looked from Pete to Alf, then toward the boats. "Chuck um in one of them dugouts. They done heerd us talkin'. I ain't wantin' them to sic no law on us."

"We didn't hear nothin'," I stammered. "Honest. We ain't gonna tell nobody nothin'."

"Shet yer trap, boy," Amos snapped.

"But, we didn't do nothin'. We didn't hear what you said," Eddie managed. "That was my pa who just left."

Amos ignored Eddie and looked toward his two brothers, focusing on Alf. "Well, what you waitin' fer, stupid? I said put um in a dugout. Do it now."

Alf slipped out of the saddle, grabbed both of us by the arms and shoved us roughly toward the boats.

"Git in and sit still," he ordered. The evil grin that stretched across his face terrified me. When I looked at Eddie, I realized the man had the same impression on him. I looked back over my shoulder and saw the other two brothers whispering to each other. Their backs were to us and I could hear only bits and pieces of what they were saying. I imagined that they were planning something bad for us. The hair stood out on the back of my neck when I heard the word "quicksand." I knew for certain then what they had in mind.

It was Alf who spoke first. I had taken my eyes off of him and was watching the other two intently. When I looked back at Alf, he had a long knife in his hand.

"Can I slit their throats, Amos?"

Amos turned and glared at his brother. "Put that knife away." Then he glanced up toward the sun. "We're burnin' daylight. Hide them horses yonder in the brush and lets git on with our business."

# CHAPTER 18

THE PLACE WAS CALLED Alligator Hole. It was five acres
of kidney-shaped land in the middle of the swamp, surrounded on
all sides by water. The only way to reach the island was a narrow
dirt bridge that at one time was more than fifteen feet wide. Over
the years with erosion and the rising water, the bridge had narrowed
significantly. The island itself was overrun with thick underbrush
around the shoreline. In most places the growth was as high as ten
feet. Because of that, someone on the main bank would have a very
difficult, if not impossible, task of seeing anyone in the interior of
the island. The vegetation and trees also meant that the gators and
moccasins that inhabited the island shoreline had perfect cover.

In the middle of the island was a large clearing that covered
at least half the total size of the island. And in the middle of the
clearing a small grassy knoll rose maybe fifteen feet above the surrounding water. Although gators occasionally strayed into the
clearing, they very rarely climbed to the pinnacle of the knoll. It
was where Jesse was heading. He felt he would be relatively safe
there. Several years had passed since he had been to Alligator Hole.
He was probably the last person to visit the island. It was not a
place one ventured for a Sunday picnic.

Ten years earlier Jesse and John had stumbled on the place by
accident. Young enough to still feel invincible and much more
foolish than they should have been, the swamp and the island was
an adventure for both of them. They realized very quickly that
the swamp was serious business and though they did venture back
occasionally, they did so with great care and respect. Now Jesse

stood on the main bank and considered the narrow bridge. It was perhaps a hundred or more feet across to the island and while the bridge was barren of vegetation, he noticed that in places it narrowed to no more than six or seven feet. Many years ago the island had been a part of the main body of land. Now the water and swamp were taking over and one day the bridge would be gone. In ten years, maybe less, Alligator Hole would be cut off completely from the mainland except by boat. And while Jesse could tell that the water was no more than four or five feet deep in some spots, no man in his right mind would attempt to wade across. The gators would be on them before they were halfway to the other side.

Jesse stood now at the point where the bridge crossed to the island. As had been the case every time he had been to Alligator Hole, he could see a dozen or more alligators sunning along the edge of the island. Half of their bodies were covered by the heavy vegetation that came within a foot or so of the murky water. Now, as he stood watching them, it seemed that they all had their snouts pointed directly toward him. They were well aware of his presence. One was dangerously close to the spot where the bridge connected to the island. The big gator's body was pointed toward a spot on the bridge about twenty feet from the other side. It was ready to move and the look in its eyes said it was hungry. Jesse hesitated now and measured his chances. If the gator did decide to meet him halfway or even more than halfway, he could retrace his steps to the mainland. But if he made it across he should find safety on the knoll in the interior. A thought flashed through his mind. What if the gators had multiplied to such a degree that all of Alligator Hole was infested with them. If that were the case, he would be trapped on the island. And if he was trapped on the island... Jesse shuddered at the thought. But just as quickly he put it out of his mind.

His first concern was to get across the bridge without the gators catching him. If that happened, it would be over in a matter of seconds. He felt an icy feeling run through his body. He wasn't afraid of many things but he did have a great deal of respect for gators and snakes. As he contemplated his next move, he thought if he could get at least halfway across before there was any movement from the gators, he could outrun them to the other side. None of the reptiles were moving toward the dirt bridge. It was now or never, he thought. Quickly, he searched the far bank one more time, then glanced to his left along the near bank. Nothing. But the near bank to his right was a different story. A ten foot gator lay just twenty feet away. It was facing the opposite direction, half-hidden in the undergrowth and mud of the main bank. As yet the gator gave no indication that it knew he was there. He watched it for a moment. Once on the bridge there might be no turning back. The gator on this side would most certainly see him and cut him off if he turned back. But Jesse had no choice.

Cautiously he stepped onto the bridge, his eyes riveted on the closest gator on the far side. It seemed to be the only one close enough to intercept him. He moved slowly, ten then twenty steps out onto the bridge. He was about forty feet out when the gator lifted his head and opened its menacing jaws. For perhaps ten seconds the jaws remained open; then with a loud clack they slammed shut. Still, it did not move. Jesse hesitated and watched it for a moment then glanced back over his right shoulder at the one he left behind on the main body of land. As he suspected, it was watching him but had moved no closer to the bridge. He could still retreat if he had to. The gator behind him was giving no indication that it was going to move any closer. It seemed to be biding its time. Jesse was close to the point of no return. If he went much farther it could quickly cut him off. His hands were clammy and he wiped them on his overalls and moved forward slowly, hoping slow movements would not cause either of the reptiles to react. The gator on the far bank was watching, his body poised at the edge of the water. The one behind him still wasn't moving.

Jesse was nearly halfway across when the gator on the island moved. In several short quick steps it was in the water, the snout aimed at the narrow part of the bridge some thirty or forty feet in front of Jesse. It meant to cut him off from the island and catch him at the narrowest part of the bridge. Jesse looked hurriedly behind him. The big gator on the mainland made his move also. The time for caution was behind. Jesse broke into a run. It was already evident the gator from the island would arrive at the narrowest part of the bridge before he would. All of a sudden the water was swarming with half a dozen reptiles. They were all pointed toward the bridge. But the only one that could cut him off was the one that made the first move. It was now only a few feet away and moving fast. When Jesse was still several steps away, the reptile pushed its snout onto the bridge. Its feet were searching for a solid grip on the muddy ground, the yawning mouth already poised to welcome its prey. Five feet from the open jaws, Jesse jumped. He felt something brush his right leg. Momentarily he lost his balance but only for an instant. He landed with his right foot on the bridge and the other sliding down into the water away from the gator. Both hands found the solid dirt of the bridge, and he was able to pull his left foot out of the water and onto the bridge, righting himself as he did. It was then that he heard the powerful jaws snap shut with a sickening crunch. Glancing down quickly, he saw that a large rip had appeared in the right leg of his overalls.

Jesse moved fast now and didn't stop until he was on the island. To his rear he could hear the gators thrashing about in the water. But they wouldn't catch him now. If he remembered correctly, only twenty or thirty feet of underbrush lay between him and the clearing. He would be safe then. He would be safe, he thought, if no gators lay hidden in the thick vegetation that separated the bank of the island with the interior. Panic wove through his body again, the same he had experienced earlier. What if there was no clearing anymore? Years had passed since he had been here. His survival depended on whether the island remained as he remembered it. Still, he plunged ahead. Whatever lay in front of him, he had no choice now. It seemed the undergrowth was thicker and deeper than he remembered. Was there a clearing? After what seemed an eternity, he broke into the open. And as he did, relief flooded through him. The clearing was still there, much the same as it was the last time he was here. The knoll in the middle was not quite as grassy as he remembered. For that he was grateful. It would be easier to watch for unwanted guests.

Jesse was in the middle of the clearing and up on the knoll before he stopped moving. From here he could view several hundred feet in every direction. He was spent now, more from the tension of the moment than the short run across the bridge and through the narrow strip of undergrowth and trees. Sinking to his knees, he fell forward balancing himself on his stiffened arms. His breath was coming in gulps as he surveyed the clearing in every direction. No gators were in sight. As he noticed when he first broke into the clearing and viewed the knoll, the grass was lower here than he remembered. No chance for man or varmint to happen up on him as long as he remained vigilant. Jesse closed his eyes and after a moment he relaxed his arms and rolled over on his back. The sunlight flooded down on his face and he realized the day was at its midpoint.

Several minutes passed before he grabbed his ankles and pulled himself into an upright position. The place had plenty of space on all sides. In here his main concern was no longer the alligators, but snakes. Even in the short grass they could be right beside him before he knew it. They were as deadly as the gators and much more subtle. He was not totally safe. He would never be totally safe here. Great care would need to be taken. His eyes fell on an old dead tree that had fallen sometime in the past. Wood for a fire, he thought. He would not survive without a fire. It would be his first line of defense should predators invade his space while he was here.

~ ~ ~

The boat that Alf shoved us into had enough water in it to come up over our shoe tops. When the three men finished their whispering and got into the boat, we were more than ready to use the bailing cans they threw our way. I had never been in the swamp before and was terrified at the thought. But more than that, I was terrified by what the brothers were planning for us. Whatever it was, it was going to happen in the swamp. I could hardly breathe from the fear.

With Eddie and me bailing at full speed, it took the better part of a half hour to remove most of the water from the boat. All the while, the brothers were moving us further into the depths of the swamp. I didn't dare look up until the water was nearly out of the dugout. But when I did stop and look around, I thought we had been bailing all day and the sun was setting. I wasn't sure just how far into the swamp we had come. Overhanging branches were hiding the sun's light, and that made it look even more bleak and scary than I ever imagined. My knees were getting stiff from lack of movement, and without thinking I stood to stretch. A hand caught me and slammed me roughly back onto my seat.

"Sit still, brat, or I'll feed you to the gators," Amos growled.

I froze in my seat. Eddie, sitting beside me, did the same. I could tell he was just as scared as I was, maybe even more. It was several minutes before I found the courage to even glance sideways. As I did, an alligator slid soundlessly into the water about fifty feet to our left. It disappeared under the water and I expected to see it rise any moment and try to take my left arm off. Instinctively, I moved even closer to Eddie as if just the nearness to another human being could help me. I hunched my shoulders and buried my hands between my knees, pulling my arms closer to my body. Eddie saw the gator and moved against my right side. He was trembling to such a degree that I thought he might be having a rigor.

"You okay?" I whispered.

All he did was nod and continue to tremble. I felt sorry for him even though I blamed him for our being here in the first place.

The boat was gliding along smoothly between the cypress trees. Pete was on his knees in the front, paddling on both sides. Once, when I found the courage to glance over my shoulder, I saw that Alf was riding the back seat with Amos on the seat just in front of him.

I'm not sure how long we had been traveling when Pete stopped paddling and pointed to a spot several hundred feet ahead. The bank was free from underbrush for perhaps a twenty-foot stretch. A large cypress stood fifteen feet out into the murky water, its branches rising far above all the others.

Pete was looking back toward Amos and I heard him grunt. The boat turned sharply to the left and made for the spot where Pete was pointing. It landed with a thud, and Pete jumped out and pulled the bow up on solid ground.

Amos grabbed both Eddie and me by the back of our overalls and lifted us from our seats.

"Out," he ordered.

He gave both of us a shove, and as I scrambled to keep my balance, I tripped over the side of the boat and sprawled face down on the ground. Eddie landed in Pete's arms and was quickly thrown to the ground next to me.

"Pull the boat into them weeds and tie it down," Amos ordered. He stood with hands on hips, turning slowly around as he made the full circle twice with his eyes.

"Which way we go now, Amos? Huh?" Alf questioned.

Amos rubbed a hand through his thick beard without answering.

"Huh?" The crazy brother persisted.

"Shut up, fool, and let me think."

"Ain't no call to talk that way," Alf whined.

Amos took a couple of steps in Alf's direction, grabbed him by the shirt and waved a big fist in the man's face. "I said shut it up. I ain't goin' to say it no more. I ain't wantin' to hear nothin' from you less'n I ask. You hear, boy?" He gave Alf a shove and the man fell back against a small cypress tree near the edge of the water.

Silence reigned now. Amos studied the surrounding area again and turned toward Pete. "Best I can remember, they's several places I'd hide in the swamp if'n I was on the run. That nigger probably knows them all."

Pete cleared his throat and nodded toward Eddie and me. "What about them?"

"They's plenty of time. They ain't goin' nowheres." The sound of

Amos' voice when he spoke about us sent a shiver up and down my spine. I knew if Eddie and I survived, we'd have to do something soon. But I feared if we ran and did get away, we might never survive the swamp. Quicksand, alligators, snakes. One of them would surely get us. But, I knew that the Billings were going to kill us. Stay with them too long and be killed for certain or take a chance on the swamp. I had already come to the conclusion that the swamp was our only chance. There would be no mercy from the three brothers. We had to take the first opportunity we had to escape.

Amos grunted toward us. "Keep an eye on them brats." He leered at us for several seconds then looked toward Alf. "One of them tries to skedaddle and..." He put his finger to his throat and made a cutting motion from one side to the other. Then he looked at us and grinned. "You whelps get the message?"

I nodded. I'm not sure how Eddie responded.

Finally, Amos turned to Pete. "Let's go."

It was all he said as he moved off through the underbrush. Two rough hands lifted me and tossed me half running in the direction Amos was taking. Eddie was right behind me and I could hear him breathing hard and swearing softly at my back. I was close behind Amos now and looking from side to side for a possible escape route. Our time was growing shorter with each step. Soon these three would probably meet up with Eddie's father and the other Billings. They would have to kill us before that. I was watching now, watching and waiting for our chance, and I hoped Eddie was up to it when the opportunity came. We needed to find a moment to talk.

Only a fool, I thought, would not be aware of what lay ahead for us. Eddie knew. We both knew that we had to find a way to escape. It was our only chance.

# CHAPTER 19

THE SUN WAS STRAIGHT up in the sky when Papa and the other five riders reined their horses in. They were still hidden by the woods, but they could see through the underbrush to the shantytown more than a quarter mile away.

"Looks quiet," Meecham said.

"Umm." Papa answered. He studied the path into town, carefully considering what the people there were prepared to do to protect one of their own.

"You want we should ride straight in?"

Papa shook his head. "No, you stay here. I'll ride in. We don't want to rile them. With luck we've gotten here before the trouble but it isn't likely."

In his own mind Papa knew that trouble had already been there. The shantytown would be the first place Floyd would look for Jesse. Still, if he could convince Granny that they were only there to help, they might be able to get to Jesse first.

"You men make yourself seen but stay well away from the town. Understood?"

Meecham nodded and all five moved out of the trees and into the clearing. Papa was the only one that continued slowly toward the trail that led into the little community.

~ ~ ~

Ezra saw him first and ran up the path to Granny Ruby's. She was sitting on her porch half asleep, her eyes closed, rocking slowly back and forth. The corncob pipe had long since gone cold and was drooping lazily out of her mouth and resting sideways on her chest. Some of the unlit tobacco had spilled and scattered down the front of her dress all the way to her waist. But even in her semi-conscious state, her ears were still attuned to what was going on around her.

She heard Ezra's quick step from the path and opened her eyes. He was moving swiftly, a concerned look etched on his face.

"Granny, that preacher's a comin' back in. They's more a them out a ways. He comin' in by hisself."

Granny stirred slightly and stared into the distance. Papa was still too far away for her to see clearly, but she got to her feet and came down the steps. She was leaning heavily on her walking stick. The events of the morning had taken a lot out of Granny and she was feeling her age even more than usual.

When she could finally make Papa out at the far end of the town, she started down the path to meet him. As they moved toward each other, more men and women came out of the shacks and began to congregate along the path, giving Papa a narrow lane to maneuver Satan.

They met halfway.

"Granny Ruby," Papa said and nodded.

"Preacher."

Papa could sense the weariness in her voice.

"Granny, Mr. Holland is dead. It's possible someone killed him. Could've been accidental but I fear it wasn't."

She didn't answer at first, but Papa could see the impact the words had on her. She was probably closer to Holland than any white person. With this new information, the people began to move in closer to Granny and Papa. The sudden hostility was evident.

"What we care if some white done died?" It was a young woman that had moved close to Satan's right flank. Murmurs of agreement spread through the crowd.

Papa ignored the woman and addressed Granny. "He was a fair man to you and your people, Granny. We'll bury him tomorrow. I'm hoping you and all your friends here will come."

"We ain't doin' no such, white man. We ain't comin' to no white man's buryin'." Ezra blurted this last bit out.

Granny reacted now. Ezra barely had the words out when Granny turned and brought her walking stick down hard on the young man's shoulder. His knees buckled and he slumped nearly to the ground before he regained his balance.

"Shet that mouth, boy. And the rest of you. Don't you know who give us this land? Don't you know who bought us seed? Mr. Holland, he done treated us like kin. Even before we was freed. They's a bunch of you here that 'member when you was slaves. He done took care of you like you was kin. His woman was good. He was a good man. He was special good to me, special good."

Tears had welled up in her eyes as she looked up at Papa.

"If the good Lord allows, we'll be there for the buryin', Preacher. Least wise most of us will."

Papa nodded.

"Granny, you know that Mr. Holland isn't the only reason I came. You know why I'm here."

"I knows." She nodded and Papa paused to glance at the crowd that surrounded both of them. Then he turned his attention back to Granny.

"Has Carter been here, Granny?"

The old woman nodded. "Him and them Billings done come early on. They lookin' to kill them a black man."

As if the black horse Papa was astride understood Granny's words, it snorted and shook its' head back and forth.

Papa reached down and stroked it gently on the side of its neck. "Easy, Satan. Easy now." Satan settled slowly and Papa again turned his attention back to the little woman.

"Granny, do they know where to find Jesse?"

The woman looked sheepish and was quiet for a moment. Finally, she nodded slowly. "They know he done took to the swamp."

"Where Granny? Where in the swamp?"

Granny looked from Papa to the people who had moved even closer to horse and rider. She was about to answer when Ezra spoke again.

"We ain't trustin' no white man be he preacher or no."

Papa pointed back over his shoulder as he spoke. Seemingly, he was ignoring Ezra. "I have some good men here and they came to help Jesse. We think we know how the fire started and if we're right, Jesse has nothing to worry about." Papa leaned forward on his saddle horn as he continued. "Unless we can find him before Carter does, we can't help him. Granny, you must tell us where Jesse is. It's his only chance."

"We ain't trustin no white man," Ezra shouted again.

"You best shut that trap or I be shuttin' it fer you."

As she spoke, Granny turned and raised her stick. This time Ezra stepped back away from her and closed his mouth. His hands dug deep into his overall pockets and his chin drooped to his chest. Satisfied, Granny turned back to face Papa.

"Why does you want to help us, Preacher?"

Papa straightened in the saddle and looked down at Granny. He knew she wanted to believe him.

"What's right in God's eyes for a white man is right in God's eyes for a black man. The color of a person's skin does not alter the moral obligation one human being has for another. It's our duty to help Jesse. Guilty or not, we must not let Carter find him first. I think you know what will happen if he does."

The woman was studying Papa's face. She liked what she saw but didn't speak.

"Do you understand what I'm saying, Granny?" Papa knew she did but he needed some confirmation from her. He could feel the people around him murmuring softly to each other. They were trying to decide if this white man was telling the truth or lying like some of them felt all white men did. "If Carter and the Billings get to him first, they'll kill him. You have to trust me, Granny."

Finally, she nodded. "I trusts you, Preacher."

An immediate murmur rose from the crowd of people. It was nothing audible that either Papa or Granny could make out. Papa was not going to wait to find out their sentiments but pressed

Granny further.

"Then help me put an end to this."

Granny took her eyes off Papa and measured the crowd that was pressing close around Papa's legs. If she was still the unspoken leader, it was now that she had to take advantage of her position. She raised the stick over her head and motioned to the people.

"All you, hush your mouths and give this good man breathin' room afore that black animal done gets het up." She waved the stick back and forth again. "Hears what I'm sayin' now. Move back away from that animal and be quick about it."

It took a few seconds for her orders to sink in but then slowly all the people moved back several feet from Papa and Satan. When she was satisfied, she turned her attention back to Papa.

"I afeard you's too late, Preacher. When Floyd Carter and them Billings come a ridin' in here a while back, they caught one of the younguns. Swore they'd cut her bad if'n we didn't tell where Jesse be. I didn't have no choice but to tell them."

Papa shuddered at the thought of the Billings out there somewhere on Jesse's trail. A dangerous bunch like Amos and his brothers, now with Carter pushing, wouldn't hesitate to kill Jesse. And with the swamp just a short ways off, a body could be hidden and never found. Nobody would ever be able to prove otherwise.

"Where is he, Granny? You know we're his best chance to survive."

She hesitated and looked around at her people. She was about to tell another white man where he could find Jesse. Some of the people would consider her a traitor. But when she thought about it, she knew this preacher was right. It was Jesse's best chance to survive. Her mind made up, she looked back to Papa.

"He done took to the swamp. He be hidin' at a place called Alligator Hole. I told them Jesse was in the swamp, but I didn't tells them about Alligator Hole." She hesitated before continuing. "Preacher, they gots a half mornin' start on you."

"Much obliged, Granny. We'll do everything we can to get to Jesse first." Papa started to turn Satan, but Granny reached up and caught the reins at the side of Satan's head.

"I'm feered there ain't nothin you can do, Preacher. Big John, he done took off to find Jesse after them five left. Said he was goin' to find Jesse first. If he do, then maybe they'll be comin out on their own. We got some of our people watchin' where Jesse went in and where the Billings likely goin' in."

Papa shook his head. "But if they catch Jesse and John in the swamp..."

Granny raised her hand and Papa hesitated. "They's regular swamp rats, them two. They ain't likely to catch either one, leastwise not in them swamps. It's out here in the open them white trash can run our boys down. It's out here that they gonna need your help. Preacher, I'm sayin' to let them two work it out in the swamps. If'n them Billings run them out, that's the time fer you to step in. You understandin' what for I'm sayin'?"

Papa nodded but he wished he could be as sure as Granny seemed to be.

"All right, Granny. We'll do it your way. I have good men with me, men who want to do what's right. We'll give Jesse and John a chance to escape the swamp on their own. You said John went in by another entrance. If you'll send one of your men with a couple of mine we'll be able to warn them if they should come out that way. In the meantime, some of us will go to where the swamp boats are tied and wait with some more of your people there. Carter and his bunch will go in by boat." Papa hesitated before continuing. "If they went in at all."

Granny motioned to Ezra and George. "Them two will go with you." She looked hard at Ezra and George. "You two do zactly like this here preacher say. You hear? I don't want no arguin'. You hear me good, now. You give them a mite of trouble and you gonna answer to me." Her eyes were focused on Ezra.

Neither man responded.

Granny grabbed Ezra by the arm and shook him hard. "You hearin' me, boy?"

"I hears you, Granny. I hears you."

"You best hear me.  How 'bout you, George?"

The other man grunted and nodded.

Granny eyed them for a moment then turned back to Papa. "They good boys. They gonna do whatever you says or they gonna answer to me."

Papa nodded, well aware that what Granny said was gospel to these folks. "Good. We'll do it like you say for right now, Granny. But if Jesse and John aren't out of the swamp by noon tomorrow, some of us will go in."

"Agreed, Preacher."  Granny nodded and Papa turned Satan back along the path. With George and Ezra following close on the stallion's heels, they made their way through the crowd of people to where the other riders waited.

# CHAPTER 20

AMOS BORED HIS WAY through the underbrush with the power and recklessness of a wild pig. I stayed close behind. It became evident that the safest place for the time being was on his heels. We must have covered half a mile when we came to a small clearing where he held up his hand for us to stop.

It was a needed relief and I slumped to the ground. Eddie collapsed next to me. It was the first time since the boat that we were close enough and had an opportunity to talk. Eddie was gulping deep breaths with his arms draped over his knees. His face was ash white now, and he knew as well as me what was about to happen to us.

"They're goin' to kill us," he whispered before I could say anything.

I nodded and stared into his wide eyes. His body was trembling and he was grasping one hand with the other trying to keep them from shaking.

"They're goin' to pitch us in quicksand," he stammered. "What we gonna do, Jamie?"

Without answering, I glanced around at the three men. Amos was standing straight, his head raised to the sky as if sniffing for direction. Pete was leaning against a tree chewing on a weed while Alf was snickering and whispering something in Pete's ear. Every few seconds he would glance our way and a wicked grin would spread across his face. Pete seemed to be ignoring his brother, not looking our way. We had very little time and we both knew it.

"Did you hear them say that?" I was surprised that I found my voice was uncommonly calm under the circumstances. Eddie had only acknowledged what I already feared. I just wasn't sure how the Billings were planning to do away with us, but I knew that quicksand was a probability.

"I heerd Alf whisperin' to Pete. They thought I was too far ahead to hear them. They said soon as Amos comes on a quicksand bog, they gonna chuck us in and ferget they ever seen us."

All of a sudden I was trembling again; and when I looked his way, I noticed that Amos was eyeing us. Unlike Alf, Amos seemed to be all business. Evil was shining in his eyes and I wondered if, like his brother Alf, he didn't find just a twinge of excitement at the thought of seeing the two of us slide silently down under the muck. We didn't have long for this world if we didn't act soon. A thousand thoughts raced through my mind at one time. But it kept coming back to one thing. We could find a quicksand bog on the other side of the next patch of undergrowth. And when we did... I didn't want to think about that.

Amos turned away and began whispering to his brothers and nodding in our direction. When his eyes were diverted from us, I grabbed Eddie's arm.

"We got to get away. As soon as we start out again, you watch me. Stay real close. When I run, you run too." I searched his eyes for a reaction but I could only see fear.

"They catch us, they gonna kill us fer sure."

"They're gonna do that anyway," I whispered.

Finally, Eddie swallowed and I watched the lump in his throat roll around and then disappear. He was finding it hard to swallow just as I was. But he finally nodded. He knew what we had to do and knew it was now or never.

In my desire to get my message over to Eddie, I took my eyes off the brothers. I wasn't aware of Amos until he was towering over us. His massive hands grasped the back of our shirts and jerked us roughly to our feet.

"Git up," Amos growled.

He didn't need to say it for he had already deposited us on our feet. He glared down at us for perhaps half a minute, then started out through the brush again. I knew what was expected of us and ran to catch up. I hoped Eddie remembered what I said and was staying close. Fear kept me from glancing back to be sure Eddie was there, but then I heard him padding along behind me and knew his own fear would keep him at my heels.

We had been moving for about five minutes when we broke into another clearing and Amos came to an abrupt halt. He stopped so suddenly that I nearly ran into him. He glanced from one side of the clearing to the other, then stooped over and picked up a rock about the size of an apple. He tossed it up twice, catching it in his massive hand, then tossed it toward the center of the clearing where there was no grass. It landed with a dull sickening thud and lay there for perhaps five seconds, then slowly disappeared into the muck. Amos had found his quicksand. It was evident where the deadly bog began and ended. The absence of any living vegetation spelled the boundary. It was about twenty feet across and looked for all the world like just another dusty patch of ground in the midst of the swamp. But it wasn't. And as I stood there staring after the rock that had just been eaten by the slime, I realized this was to be our burial plot. I looked at Eddie and he had turned completely white. We were both thinking the same thing.

Pete and Alf moved past us and paused on either side of Amos. Alf knew what was about to happen and was chuckling and glancing over his shoulder in our direction. His giggle was like that of a child as he punched Amos with his elbow. Then as if he was trying to see down into the muddy slime to the rock Amos had just sent to its last resting place, he leaned out over the bog. I'm not sure why, but it came to me all of a sudden. Alf, who so wanted to see us pitched bodily into the quicksand, was giving us the only chance we might have. I moved forward quickly, much as Eddie and I would do when we were roughhousing in our yard, and put my shoulder into Alf's backside. I hit him hard and without any thought or concern that my actions might cause his death. It was the only time I ever wanted to hurt someone. The crazy man screamed an obscenity and landed several feet out into the bog on his stomach. He began flailing in the mud. I was already moving away from the quicksand by the time I heard that eerie sucking sound. I didn't stay to see what happened because I was running and yelling over my shoulder to Eddie.

"Run, Eddie," I shouted. "Run."

I was thirty feet away and bursting through underbrush that we had passed through just a few minutes before. I started to shout at Eddie again but there was no reason to. He was at my right elbow trying to pass me. Somewhere behind us, I could hear Alf screaming for help and Amos cursing for all he was worth. The amusement I had felt for a moment faded quickly. I could hear Alf and Amos and could tell their voices were a good ways off. From Pete, the quietest of the brothers, there was no sound. He might be close behind us, maybe with his hands reaching out to grab us right then. I looked over my shoulder quickly. No one was in sight. I slowed my pace and when I did, Eddie did the same.

"Listen," I whispered. There was no sound of anyone in pursuit. We started running again, this time not quite as fast and after about five minutes of constant movement, we broke into another clearing and collapsed against the trunk of a huge magnolia tree. I touched Eddie's arm and we both held our breath and listened. Still silence, no more screaming, no loud thrashing in the brush from the direction we had come. We were safe for a moment.

~ ~ ~

John had been working his way through the swamp for the last hour. The going was slower and harder than he remembered. Half the time he was knee deep in water, always watching for gators and snakes. So far, as luck would have it, he had seen neither. He really wasn't sure what he would do if he encountered one or the other. It was dangerous but he owed Jesse. He owed him his life.

His friend had pulled him out of quicksand with an alligator no more than fifteen feet away. He owed Jesse big time.

He was moving slowly through the underbrush when he saw Amos. The man was off to his right about a hundred feet away. Just as Amos had, John stopped dead in his tracks. Thankfully, Billings had not seen him yet. Amos had his arm poised above his head and was just about to pitch what looked like a large rock at something. A moment later, when the rock left Billings' hand, John suspected why. Amos was testing for quicksand. By now he was able to see the two young boys, no more than ten or twelve years of age, and two more of the Billings brothers. He knew them, knew what they were like, knew that everyone gave them a wide berth. He searched the surrounding area. Carter and the other Billings, the one named Jim, were nowhere in sight. Not knowing where the other two were gave John an eerie sensation. Still, he kept the three in sight. If they saw him, it would be bad. He probably wouldn't be able to escape all three.

John watched as the two younger brothers moved up beside Amos. He recognized the two kids now. One was the preacher's kid and the other was the Carter boy. Then he stared in disbelief as the preacher's kid rammed the crazy brother in the rear end. He saw the big man fly out several feet and heard the splat as Alf's body dug into the bog. He almost shouted with joy as he watched the two boys take off through the high weeds. John knew he would enjoy what happened next but instead, he took note of the boy's direction and followed a parallel path to intercept them. Not able to see them in the high underbrush, he followed them with his ears. Because of their noisy thrashing, John never had to get close enough for them to see him. Early on he realized that the other two brothers must have been trying to rescue their brother. The boys had a good head start on the Billings. Perhaps five minutes later the noise subsided and John moved toward their last sounds. He slipped quietly through the brush until he saw them. They were resting against a magnolia tree whispering quietly. From his hiding place he could see them clearly. It would be easy for him to slip around and come in from behind them.

~ ~ ~

My first thought when I heard the twig snap behind me was that Amos and the other brothers had found us. But I had no time to react. A strong arm wrapped around my waist and lifted me off the ground. I looked toward Eddie and saw him in the other arm, his feet flailing the air.

"Make noise and I'll cut you ear to ear and cry fer you tomorrow."

I didn't recognize the voice. But the arms that held us were black. At first I thought it might be Jesse, but it wasn't his voice. Whoever it was, was strong and gave no evidence that they were about to free us. After a moment, I stopped struggling and as I did, Eddie followed suit. I turned my head as far as I could to see the face of the black man who held us and caught a glimpse out of the corner of my eyes. I recognized him as the one they called John. He had passed through our little community on a number of occasions with Jesse. But, unlike Jesse, I had never made contact with him. I had no idea what kind of man he was. I could only hope we had not escaped the brothers only to fall into the hands of someone who was just as ruthless. I feared the worst. Had we escaped the lion's den only to stumble into the bear's trap? Did this black man know that we were responsible for what was happening to Jesse? If he did, we were surely dead. Tears were streaming down Eddie's face. He must have been thinking the same as me.

Then we heard it—the sounds of men running through the thick vegetation, coming in our direction. I knew who that was and the realization made me freeze. The black man, John, the one I thought might slit our throat any second, dropped us gently to the ground and put a finger to his lips.

"Shush," he whispered. "Follow me quietly if'n you don't want them to give you no quicksand bath." Without waiting for us to speak, John moved off in a ninety-degree direction from where he heard the men coming. I didn't argue and neither did Eddie.

We knew what was waiting if the Billings caught us. Maybe this man, John, wouldn't kill us after all. We followed without a word.

# CHAPTER 21

WHEN ALF LANDED ON his stomach in the quicksand, Amos' first reaction was to forget Alf and run down the two boys. If he had thought there was any way the boys could escape the swamp alone, he would have left Pete to pull Alf out of the mire. It was not brotherly love that affected his decision.

"I oughta let you rot in that bog," Amos growled at the desperate man.

Luckily for Alf, his legs sank first and his upper body, from his hips up, was free of the sucking sand. He reached toward his brothers and solid ground, his eyes large and round and his mouth open. Only gasps escaped his mouth as he looked pleadingly toward the other two men. Pete was down on his knees, reaching as far out toward his brother as he dared. But the two men's hands were still a foot apart.

"Fetch me that limb yonder," Amos snapped, pointing as he did toward a fallen limb by the side of the quicksand.

When Pete took his hand away, Alf tried to paddle himself out of the muck. His movements only caused him to sink further until only his chest and arms were still clear.

"Amos, pull me out, please!" The words came out of his mouth like a gargle. Fear had rendered him senseless. He was only minutes from death and he knew it.

"Quit whinin' and squirmin'," Amos ordered. "If we ain't got trouble a plenty, you go and let a wet-nosed twerp toss you in there. I still got a good mind to let the bog have you."

"Please, Amos," Alf pleaded. "I'm sinkin'. Uh, uh," he grunted and began to flail again.

As he did, Amos took the branch from Pete and shoved it out toward Alf. He grabbed it and held on tightly as Pete and Amos began to pull. Slowly, Alf came up until his stomach was again showing, then his waist. Finally, after about a minute of cursing and pulling, Alf turned loose with one hand and dug his fingers into solid ground. Pete and Amos dropped the branch, grabbed Alf under each armpit and pulled him clear. Totally exhausted, Alf lay there on his stomach for several minutes, groaning and gasping for breath.

When he was finally able to talk he rolled over on his side and began pulling himself to his feet. "I want to kill them myself," he muttered. "They're mine, Amos. I'm gonna tear both those little brats to pieces." He looked up toward Amos almost pleadingly. "Can I, Amos?"

Amos, back on his feet now, hovered over his younger brother. All of a sudden he pulled back his foot and kicked his mud-caked brother roughly in the ribs. Alf let out a yell and nearly rolled back into the quicksand.

"I shoulda left you to sink you worthless hunk of humanity. You see what you done. Them brats is way out ahead. You done let them git away. If'n we don't catch up to them, I'm goin' to chuck you back in the sand and hold yer head under myself."

Alf forgot his threat toward Eddie and me as he tried to escape his brother's wrath. "Ain't no call to badmouth me that way," Alf moaned and rolled on his side away from the quicksand. His eyes were round and afraid again. "Twernt my fault. It was them brats that done it. I didn't take no notice of them about to boost me that away." He paused now and thought about what Amos said to him. "You wouldn't, Amos. You wouldn't toss me back in there."

Pete finally came to Alf's defense. "Leave him be, Amos. He's had enough scare for one day. We gotta catch up to them younguns. Ain't no time to fight amongst ourselves."

Amos took another look at Alf, grunted and started off in the direction where we had last been seen. Pete helped Alf to his feet and the two of them fell in close behind Amos.

~ ~ ~

Now, as we heard the noise from the three brothers' approach, John went scurrying off through the underbrush with Eddie and me trying to keep up. We followed him due east for a quarter mile, stumbling over fallen tree limbs and fighting our way through clinging briar bushes that tore and pulled at us until our clothes and arms were crimson with our own blood. I wanted to stop and rest, but this was no time or place to be concerned about comfort. This was about survival and all three of us knew that Amos and his brothers would dog our trail until they caught us or we escaped the swamp. We had one advantage. They thought we were two frightened boys running wild through the swamp. And frightened we were. But they didn't know about John and that was to our advantage.

After several minutes, John came to an abrupt stop. He shaded his eyes and looked up through the trees for the sun. It was slightly behind us. He stared at it for a moment then dropped his head and studied the trees and underbrush around us. It all looked the same to me, dense and unfriendly.

"This way," he finally said and took off ninety degrees to the left of our original path. We were traveling north and what little we could see of the sun through the canopy of trees showed it to be at our left shoulder. After several hundred feet John stopped abruptly again. I was following too close and ran into him. He reached back and put a hand on my shoulder and, as one, all three of us crouched low.

"I'm tired," Eddie moaned just a little too loudly.

John jerked around and eyed Eddie furiously. "Hush, boy, or we'll all rest permanent like. I needs to listen. You hear?"

Eddie cowered down even lower and we crouched there peering through the underbrush for several minutes. I was convinced the brothers were nowhere near and was beginning to relax when I saw Alf. John hadn't seen him and I touched his arm and pointed.

He was standing fifty feet away, his knife unsheathed, facing ninety degrees to our position with his right side visible to us. If not for the seriousness of our situation I think I would have burst out laughing. He was caked with mud nearly to his shoulders and, because of the extreme heat, it looked as if the mud was already drying and beginning to crack. The normally silly look that usually spread across Alf's face had been replaced with a sinister scowl that caused my whole body to tremble. This hulk of a man was out to kill us any way he could. He would not wait for quicksand the next time he got his hands on us. I'm sure Alf felt the knife would do just fine.

John grabbed Eddie and me by the arm and motioned with his head in the opposite direction of Alf. We dropped flat on our bellies as John motioned us to do and crawled slowly away. After several minutes, we broke out into a small clearing. Just a few feet away there was what appeared to be a shallow pool of murky water about thirty feet across. A few feet out into the pool the trunk of a fallen oak rested just above the surface of the water, held that way by a series of branches that protruded below the surface of the water. The branches had sunk into the soft bottom and were keeping the body of the tree resting at water level. John stopped and put his finger to his lips. It wasn't necessary. We were both too scared to let out a sound.

He listened for a few seconds, then turned and motioned us to follow him into the pool. We slipped silently into the water and waded out to the trunk. John hoisted himself over to the other side of the massive tree until it was between him and where we had last seen Alf. Eddie and I pulled ourselves up and over the trunk, one on either side of John. Our bodies sank slowly into the grass and weeds growing waist deep around us. After a minute or so our legs began to slowly rise to the surface where they lay visible at water level. Still, with the thickness of the grass and the height of the fallen oak it would be hard for anyone to see any part of us from a distance. John found a spot where the oak formed a canopy of branches and leaves that provided cover from the bank. It was evident the tree had not been down long. The few leaves that were visible were still green and it was evident the limbs had not grown brittle to the touch. We were well hidden and from here we could see anyone approach for more than fifty feet. Now all we had to do was wait and watch.

Only seconds passed before John let go of the tree, put his hand on Eddie's back and mine and gently shoved us down out of sight. Just before he did, I saw Pete slip through the underbrush. He was looking off to his right and away from us. But as my head moved below the tree trunk, he turned and looked directly toward me. I couldn't see him now so all I could do was hold my breath and hope he didn't see me.

There was silence for what seemed a lifetime before I heard Pete. "They ain't nowheres about." He was at the edge of the pool, no more than fifteen feet away.

"I still ought to blow that half-wit apart and leave him for the gators," Amos snarled.

"Aw, let Alf be, Amos. He can't help it if he ain't got no smarts," Pete said.

"I'm goin' to cut them brats in little pieces and feed them to the gators when I find them," Alf swore. "You hear what I say, Amos. When we find them, you gotta let me have them. Promise you'll let me finish them. Promise." Alf pleaded.

"Suppose they get away, maybe even find a way out of the swamp. They could stumble onto Jim and Carter coming in from the north," Pete said. "Carter ain't gonna take too kindly to us wantin' to kill his kid."

I heard someone spit and the splash of his saliva landed not far on the other side of the tree trunk.

"Ain't likely to ever know," Amos said.

"Yeah, but what if?" Pete insisted.

This time it wasn't spit that I heard splashing from the edge of the pool.

"He could make trouble fer us," Pete went on.

"If'n that happens, we might jist be forced to walk out of the swamp without Carter," Amos answered.

"You mean kill Carter. What about the rest of the money? He done hid it somewhere we'll never find."

"Man'll spit out a lot of information if you're danglin him upside down above a quicksand bog," Amos answered in a calm, quiet voice.

I looked past John at Eddie and saw him stiffen at the words. John just put his finger to his mouth and shook his head. As we lay there in the weeds and water, the voices began to fade as the brothers moved away from the pool. I could tell they were still in sight so we continued to lie as quietly as possible. A few more seconds passed before the voices faded completely.

I felt it first as it slapped the bottom of my shoe. When I glanced over my shoulder I saw the snake and froze. The Cottonmouth moved past my feet and slithered up onto the back of John's half submerged legs. He recognized what the sudden weight was and froze just as I did. His eyes were huge and I could see the fear when he glanced my way. I was in such a position that I could see the reptile clearly. It was enormous, nearly as long as my body and as big around as my upper arm. The blackish gray snake stopped momentarily, draping its body across John's legs just below his knees. It was resting, seemingly trying to decide where to go next. Then, as suddenly as it stopped, it turned its snout to the left and began moving up John's right leg toward his lower back.

I couldn't move as I watched the snake slide up just below his waist and pause again. John's shirt was loose at the waist and the snake found an opening where the bottom edge was floating in the water. The moccasin slid its head under the shirt and started to move up John's back. I watched the shirt lift as it moved toward John's right shoulder. About halfway up it stopped again and lay motionless for maybe a minute. I glanced quickly at John. His eyes were closed and his teeth were clenched. When I glanced at John's back the snake was moving again. As quickly as it had slithered up his back, the head turned and slid down and out of his shirt. It paused again for several seconds before sliding on down his left leg. The reptile slipped off his leg and glided effortlessly across the murky water. The last I saw of the moccasin, it was disappearing into the foliage on the bank some twenty feet away.

The Billings were gone by this time, their voices lost in the distance. John came up quickly as I did. Eddie, who was unaware of what had just happened, got to his feet slowly, his thoughts still on the brothers. John and I looked toward where we last saw the snake. Finally, John looked down at me and just shook his head. It was the only acknowledgement either of us made about the reptile. But we both knew how close we all came to what could have been a sure death.

John's voice was clear and strong as he lifted us over the fallen tree. "Move young'uns'. We still gots a piece to go."

We put the sun behind us and made our way east. Somewhere to our right and south Amos and his two brothers were still searching. Earlier I heard Amos mention something about some willows. I didn't know where that was but I hoped it was far away from where we were headed. I could only hope they would continue to move in a different direction from us.

~ ~ ~

Papa, Sam Griffin, and Walter Frazier, along with Ezra from the shantytown, rode to the spot where we had entered the swamp as prisoners of the Billings brothers. George took the other two men to the spot where John had entered the swamp.

Papa felt uncomfortable about being unable to do anything but wait until morning. Jesse was in the swamp, possibly in trouble already, and John could be walking into a trap.

Ezra was riding the back of Satan with Papa. When they entered the clearing where the boats were tied, he pointed over Papa's shoulder toward a stand of trees some distance away.

"We got people in them trees," Ezra said.

Papa kneed Satan and the big stallion galloped toward the

woods. Once there, Ezra slipped off Satan and lifted his hand. It was then that the four men emerged from their hiding place.

"Granny Ruby sent us," Ezra said.

The four men eyed Papa and the other men suspiciously, at first wary of them and why they were here.

Ezra sensed their feelings. He wasn't sure about these white men either but he nodded to his friends. "They okay. They here to help. Granny done puts trust in um."

The four men from the shantytown seemed to relax, but they moved away and turned their backs on Papa and the rest of the white men and began whispering something to Ezra. After a minute, Ezra nodded and came back to where Papa sat.

"They done found three horses back in them woods," Ezra said pointing off toward a stand of trees several hundred feet away. "Probably belongs to them Billings."

"Show me," Papa said.

With Papa following astride Satan, Ezra strode off toward a thicket of heavy underbrush. Several hundred feet away they came upon the three horses.

"Only three," Papa said.

"They's three of the ones that come lookin' fer Jesse," Ezra said. "They the same animals I done seen early on."

"But there should be five of them," Papa answered.

"But there is three of um," Ezra insisted.

"And two are missing," Papa continued. "Where are they?"

Papa slipped off Satan and examined each of the horses' hind quarters. No brands were visible. Mr. Holland's horses all carried his brand, Papa thought. If Floyd was riding a Holland horse, then he had moved on elsewhere with one of the brothers.

"Ezra, do you remember who was riding these three horses?"

Ezra stroked his chin for a moment and his brow wrinkled from thought.

"The meanest of the bunch, the one they calls Amos, was sittin' on the big gray horse. He done most all the talkin'. I took note of him real good." He looked at the other two horses and shook his head. "I ain't sure bout the others."

Papa looked again at the three horses then to Ezra. "Do you remember if Carter was riding one of these?"

Ezra shook his head quickly. "He was ridin' a right handsome one. His'n had a fancy saddle with sparkly things all over. Ain't none of these."

Papa knew the saddle well. Holland had brought it home from Memphis two years earlier. He was especially proud of it and kept it in his house, not in the barn. The saddle had probably not been used more than a dozen times in those two years. It was certainly not something he would have let Floyd borrow.

He was sure now. Floyd had been to the Holland place. But that still didn't prove he had killed him. But right now Papa would have bet his life on it if he had been a gambling man.

Papa patted the horse Amos had been riding on the flank and moved back beside Satan. "Let's leave these horses as we found them, Ezra. If the Billings come back we'll know right where they'll be heading." With that, Papa turned Satan and moved back toward the clearing where the other men waited. It was still early afternoon.

# CHAPTER 22

MOVEMENT THROUGH THE SWAMP was slow and painful. More than once we waded through shallow pools of water because the undergrowth was so dense. Because of our encounter with the snake, I was terrified every time we did. It wasn't just the snakes that I feared but the alligators that inhabited some of these small pools that spread all through the swamp. Once, when we were wading a pool that seemed innocent enough, I failed to stay right behind John. That was a mistake and I stepped into a hole under the water and sank to my shoulders. The suddenness of my misstep caused my head to slip under the murky slime and I came up sputtering. John was only a few feet ahead and, when he heard me, he came back to lift me out. I tasted the rank, foul-tasting water for the next hour. Eddie was quiet during this time. He followed John without a word. I'm sure that his mind was on his father, and for the first time I really believe he was grieving for what we had set in motion. Even he knew that no good would come from any of this, and I think he was aware now of what eventually lay in store for him if we came out alive.

John continued to press on toward the east. Sometime after mid-afternoon he came to a small clearing and stopped to get his bearings. Eddie and I were both thankful for the rest but before we could be comfortable with the surroundings we both searched for grass in the clearing. No grass could mean quicksand. When we were satisfied that the ground was firm, we dropped down and just lay there on our backs looking up at the umbrella of trees that covered most of the sky.

"We ain't doin' no good," Eddie whispered. It was the first time he had spoken in more than an hour.

I looked at him and he must have realized I didn't know what he was trying to say.

"We ain't never goin' to git outa here." He nodded toward John. "Him and Jesse are goin' to see to that. They goin' to kill us sure cause we done blamed Jesse for the fire."

I shook my head violently and reached over and grabbed his arm. But he shook my hand loose and sat upright with his arms draped across his knees.

"They gonna kill us, Jamie" Eddie insisted.

Again I shook my head and glanced toward John. I didn't think he had heard Eddie. I bent close to his right ear and whispered. "He coulda done us in a hundred times already." I saw Eddie's eyes get bigger all of a sudden and his face turn white.

"You right, boy. I coulda done ya in a bunch a times. Without you whelps I coulda already found Jesse. They's quicksand, snakes, gators, all them things. I could still do you in."

John had come up behind me without my knowing and towered over us. His hands were planted firmly on his hips, and as I looked up at him what little sun was visible through the trees was framed between his body and the crook of his left elbow. Staring into the sun's glow like that, I could barely make out the scowl on his face. Still, I could not imagine him doing anything violent.

"Maybe I wants Jesse to do it. If I done heerd you right, he got the most right, ain't he?"

I swallowed and nodded. John knew the truth now. And maybe he was capable of doing more to us than I thought. At that moment I imagine my face must have been as white as Eddie's.

"Now, you younguns git to yer feet before I make a peace offering with Mr. Gator over there."

He motioned back over my left shoulder, and I turned my head to where John was looking. The alligator was lying motionless about thirty feet away. Though he wasn't as big as some I had seen, maybe eight or nine feet, he was still as deadly. I'm not sure how long he had been there, but I am sure he wasn't there when we arrived in the clearing. His eyes seemed to be boring right into mine as if he was imagining how my tender body would taste. I scrambled to my feet quickly and planted myself behind John. As much as Eddie had always hated black people, I found him trying to root his way in between John and me. When I peered around John toward the alligator, I'm sure I saw disappointment in the reptile's eyes. He was probably thinking about another meal missed. I was thankful he was going to miss this one.

John chuckled at our plight and led out toward the east again. We passed about twenty feet from the gator and Eddie and I both put John between the killer and us. As we disappeared through the brush, I glanced back. The gator did not move but only turned his head to follow our flight.

~ ~ ~

Amos was kneeling beside the cold remains of the fire Jesse had built the night before. He took a stick and poked down in the ashes. They were cold all the way through. But, they were fresh remains. He knew someone had spent the night here. And he knew it had to be Jesse. Footprints were in the soft dirt leading off toward the northeast. Pete was studying the tracks that disappeared into the brush. Amos looked up when the rank odor suddenly invaded his nostrils.

"He ain't here no more is he, Amos?"

Alf was bent over him, the mud from his adventure in the quicksand caked over his clothes and arms. The sight made him look more like the mummified remains of some long dead Egyptian king. His face seemed to be the only part of his body not covered with the gray muck.

"You stink worser'n ever," Amos spat as he got to his feet. "I smelt skunks that ain't near so rank." He spun his brother around and grabbed him by the back of his collar with one hand and the seat of his pants with the other. Before Alf could react, Amos guided him across the clearing to the shallow pool and pitched him about ten feet out into the water. Then he turned and gazed around to the willow trees that surrounded the clearing. The place was much the same as he remembered. A moment later he turned his attention back to Alf.

"You come outa there afore that stink's off, and I'll pitch you back in and scrub it off myself with an oak limb." He pointed his finger at the man and stood staring at him until Alf dropped his head and began scrubbing at the caked mess that covered his body all the way up to his neck.

"Amos, take a look at this," Pete said from the far side of clearing.

Amos watched Alf for several more seconds then turned and walked over to where Pete was examining the bushes.

"He lit out this way, I reckon."

Pete was pointing to a bush with a half broken branch hanging limply about waist high.

"They's more sign of him through there. I followed a ways. It's clear and easy trackin'."

"Ain't no use worryin bout trackin' him. I reckon I done figured where 'bouts he's headed."

"Where?" Pete asked.

"No worser spot outside Hell."

Pete stared at Amos, his eyes questioning his older brother.

"The niggers call it Alligator Hole. Heerd some call it Alligator Island. Been there twice. Ain't never been out on the island. Ain't in no all fired hurry to go there neither." Amos paused and peered off in the distance for several seconds. "Figured the boy wouldn't have the stomach to go there."

Pete whistled. "I heerd you tell about it. I wouldn't think he would have no mind for it either. Not from what you done said about it."

Amos glanced over his shoulder at Alf whose eyes were fixed

on Amos as he splashed water over his body and mumbled under his breath. When Amos returned Alf's stare, his brother dropped his eyes and began scrubbing even harder. Amos grunted in disgust and looked up toward the sun. They had only an hour or two before sundown. It would be hard to reach Alligator Hole before nightfall. Morning would be better even though he didn't like the idea of spending the night in the swamp. They could get there in the morning, do what they had come to do and be out of the swamp by early afternoon. His main concern now was the two boys. If they didn't catch them in the swamp and they found their way out... Amos knew that could be big trouble. If that happened they might have to deal with more than the boys. But Amos knew it would be difficult for them to find their way out alone. He nodded his head and smiled. They would not survive a night in the swamp. Either the quicksand would get them or a gator or moccasin. They would be no problem. With that, he dismissed them from his mind and concentrated on what must be done next to trap the one called Jesse. He turned to Pete.

"We'll bed down here and start early...."

The scream stopped Amos in mid-sentence. He turned just in time to see Alf beating a path through the water toward shore. The alligator was some fifteen feet behind him, gliding gracefully through the water. Its powerful jaws were beginning to open, in anticipation of clamping down on Alf before he could get to solid ground.

Pete dropped his rifle barrel and sighted in on the gator.

Before he could pull off a shot, Amos grabbed the barrel and raised it skyward. "No." It was all he said.

Both men watched as Alf reached the bank and pulled himself out of the water just in time. The big gator snapped his jaws shut, catching a portion of Alf's pants leg that had slipped down below his right foot. The gator ripped it savagely from his leg almost pulling him back into the water. For a moment it slowed Alf down, but as the gator was preparing to snap down again, Alf rolled over and scrambled away quickly from the powerful jaws. For a moment it seemed the gator was going to pursue his prey. Then, as quickly as it had appeared, it slid slowly back into the pond. The remnants of Alf's pants leg were still visible in the reptile's mouth as it slipped back under the dirty water.

"Shoot it," Alf yelled.

He rolled over on his stomach and jumped to his feet, grabbing for Pete's gun as he did.

"Shoot the varmint," he yelled again as Pete pulled the gun back.

"Shut up, fool," Amos said and moved across the clearing toward where the gator had disappeared into the water. Any sign of the reptile was gone, and the pond was just large enough and deep enough so that they would not be able to see it unless it wanted them to.

"You was gonna let it git me," Alf cried. "You was gonna let it eat me." Then, just as quickly, he turned and walked to the middle of the clearing and dropped heavily to the ground.

"Gonna let it eat me," he said one more time and, with both arms draped over his knees, he dropped his head and began whimpering.

"We shoulda shot the thing," Pete said.

"You as dumb as him," Amos answered and motioned toward Alf. "You want the nigger knowin' we're about? And them brats. You wantin' them knowin' where we are? He done made enough noise to tell anyone we're about."

Amos continued to stare at Pete for several seconds then turned toward Alf, sitting forlornly in the middle of the clearing, still whimpering.

"You still ain't got all the mud off."

Alf looked up and his eyes got as big as saucers. "I ain't goin back in there. You ain't gittin me back in there."

He was already on his feet before he finished the sentence. His fists were clenched and he was ready to do whatever it took to assure that the pond would not be his final resting place.

Amos started to advance on his younger brother, then thought better of it. He eyed Alf for several seconds, then gave a short grunt and turned away, throwing back over his shoulder as he did. "Jist keep yer stinkin' self clear of me."

~ ~ ~

John seemed to be tireless. After what seemed like hours, but had to be much less, he stopped motionless in his tracks and caught hold of my arm. Eddie came up on his other side and John wrapped his arm around him and held him steady.

"Hush, the both of you."

He knelt and pulled us down beside him. I could tell he was listening because he tilted his head and turned it first to the right, then after a few seconds, turned it back to the left.

It took a minute but then I heard them.

We flattened ourselves there on the warm ground, staring toward the sound of voices. As they moved closer one became increasingly familiar.

"It's Pa," Eddie whispered.

I don't know where it came from, but suddenly there was an old rusty knife pressing against Eddie's throat.

"Either of you boys yell out and all they gonna hear is a gurgle cause I'm gonna slit this here boy ear to ear." John was whispering but Eddie got the message. It wasn't necessary for me because I knew what Mr. Carter was about and who he was with him. The other man had to be Jim Billings and I knew he was just as dangerous as his three brothers. And I didn't trust Eddie's father at all. He was mean. John was looking at me, and I could tell he was measuring me to see if there would be any danger of me shouting out. I nodded and instinctively put a hand across my mouth to let him know my feelings.

Floyd and Jim finally came into sight and, as they did, I glanced over and saw John press the knife even more firmly to Eddie's throat. My friend's eyes were closed and it seemed to me that he had stopped breathing. I prayed that he had taken John seriously. Even though John threatened us more than once, I knew that he was our best way out of the swamp. He was probably our only way out of the swamp. Now, as I watched, I saw that Carter and Billings were working their way in the opposite direction of where we were heading. They were most likely, I decided, heading someplace to meet up with the other three.

We hid there for several minutes after the sound of their voices died in the distance. When we did get up, I felt a sharp pain in my left rib cage and looked down where we had been lying. There was a sharp pointed rock about the size of a lemon where my left side had been resting. John had been pressing me down hard but in my fear and excitement, I never felt it until now. I rubbed the tender spot and slowly the pain subsided. With all that we had in front of us there was no time to worry about minor discomforts.

Eddie was staring off in the direction where his father and Jim had disappeared moments before. I wondered if he thought about running after them. John must have been thinking the same thing. He had Eddie's left arm firmly in his grasp.

"Boy, you ain't thinkin' nothin' dumb, I hopes." John held up the rusty knife. "I can stick this twixt yer shoulder blades afore you can make five steps."

Eddie shook his head violently. "I ain't. I ain't goin' nowheres."

"You best not try."

John turned and started in the same direction we had been traveling before. This time Eddie surprised me and jumped in front of me, up close behind John. He must, I thought, have decided the same as me, that John was now our best and only way out.

Perhaps after an hour, maybe longer, John came to another abrupt stop. Ahead was a large area of water. There must have been several hundred cypress, tupelos, magnolias, and red gum trees rising through the surface of the water. Off to the left, I saw what looked to be an island. From where we stood it looked as if water surrounded it on all sides. It seemed calm and peaceful until I saw them. Alligators were everywhere along the bank. It seemed like there must have been a hundred but, in reality, twenty or thirty was closer to the truth. My skin crawled at the sight and I found myself searching the ground all around to be sure one was not sneaking up on me.

When John tapped me on the shoulder, I jumped straight up. He grinned I think for the first time and, without saying a word, pointed toward the island. Eddie nodded and swallowed hard. He had seen the gators too. "That where Jesse be."

"Out there," I mumbled and pointed, "with them gators?"

John nodded and cupped his hands to his mouth. A sound came out like nothing I had ever heard. He waited and watched the island for perhaps half a minute. Then he cupped his hands again and repeated the sound. Again, we waited. This time what must have been an answer wafted its way back to us. It didn't sound exactly the same as John's call, but it must have been what John was listening for.

A grin spread over his face and a moment later we saw Jesse work his way out to the far edge of a long narrow dirt bridge that led from the island to the main shore. John raised his hand and Jesse returned the greeting. It was short lived for now Jesse turned his attention back to the alligators. Several were only a short distance from the bridge. We watched as he seemed to search the main bank where we were. None of the alligators were on the passage so it gave Jesse a free run across to the main shore and he started that way. As he did, a half dozen or more of the alligators slid into the water and headed for the bridge. They planned to cut Jesse off before he could cross the hundred or so feet. They were beaten before they got halfway to the bridge. In only moments, Jesse had leaped off the bridge and was beside us, breathing hard.

"You okay, brother?" John asked.

"I'm fit." Jesse muttered. "Done glad to see somthin' sides those varmints."

"I brung you somethin'," John said and motioned toward Eddie and me.

Jesse was puzzled. "What them two doin' here?"

There was a rustling in the brush and an alligator appeared about twenty or thirty feet away. The reptile stopped and stared at the four of us.

Jesse spoke first. "Let's move away from here. They ain't used to seein' so much good food goin' to waste without they do some-thin' bout it."

We moved inland, away from the lake for several minutes until we came to a small clearing. Jesse stopped and crouched down. John did the same and pulled us down with him.

Jesse pointed toward Eddie and me. "Now, why they here?"

"They was back yonder a ways. They was about to git pitched into quicksand by that oldest Billings brother, the one called Amos."

A look of puzzlement spread across Jesse's face.

John shook his head and continued. "Them Billings done hooked up with Floyd Carter. They's out here lookin' fer you. And they ain't goin' back till they find you."

"That boy," Jesse said, pointing toward Eddie. "He's Carter's kid. Carter ain't gonna do away with his own."

"Carter and one of the Billings weren't with them when they latched onto these two. They was gonna do away with them afore they met up again here in the swamp. Carter would've been no more the wiser. Nobody woulda ever known what happened to these youngun's. We seen Carter and the other Billings brother a ways back. They was headin' to where we last saw the other three. I'm a thinkin' they is joinin' up somewhere back there. Then they'll be comin' fer you."

Jesse looked from Eddie to me.

"You boys done got yourself into a heap of trouble."

"Yes sir," I mumbled. My eyes were glued to Jesse. In the years that I had known him, I had found him gentle and friendly and had tried to return the kindness. But this wasn't normal circumstances. He was being hunted now and we were in the way. Another thing that must have been weighing on his mind was the possibility that we were responsible for his predicament.

Suddenly, he focused on Eddie. "You tell your Pa that I done set fire to your house, boy?"

The sudden question caused Eddie to shrivel into himself. It seemed his eyes had grown even larger than I had seen them earlier. His hands were shaking uncontrollably and he stuffed them into his overall pockets. It didn't help. I could see that they were still shaking. I wouldn't have been surprised if he had jumped up and begun running. But, the only way he could run without passing by the two men was back toward the water and the alligators. Eddie had more sense than to do that.

"You best answer me, boy."

John rested his hand on the old Bowie knife in his belt. It was an intimidating gesture and all of us, including Jesse, saw it. Eddie's whole body stiffened, and I wondered myself if they were about to do away with him and then me.

Jesse reached out and touched John's arm lightly.

"Don't be scarin' the boy none," he said calmly. Then he looked back at Eddie. "You goin' to tell me the straight of it ain't you, boy?"

It was like opening a door and a torrent of rain pouring in. The words rushed uncontrollably out of Eddie's mouth.

"I never meant no harm. Me and Jamie," he looked at me, "me and Jamie we was under my house smokin'. His ma called and he started home. I stayed, just to finish my smoke. I weren't there but a few minutes after you left, Jamie." He was looking at me and his eyes were pleading for understanding. But it wasn't me he needed understanding from. "I didn't want to waste the rest of my smoke, so I leaned back against the post. I put the cigarette on an old piece of wood and closed my eyes." He hesitated and glanced up at Jesse for just a second. Tears were welling up in his eyes and beginning to roll slowly down his dirty face. He dabbed at them with the back of his hand and the dirt and grime streaked across his cheeks. "I didn't mean to do nobody no harm but when Ma called, I plumb forgot my smoke there on that dry wood. I was scairt she'd catch me under there so I just started crawling out. I remembered the smoke when I was out from under the house, but I thought it would go out by itself." Eddie took a deep breath. He was looking at me again, as if I was the one he had to account to. "I seen you go by," he said sheepishly and glanced at Jesse. "When the fire started, I never thought to blame nobody. It just come to me."

Eddie looked at me again and for the first time I could see the shame in his face. The next was aimed at me. "I was scairt you'd tell somebody about our smokin' and Pa'd find out and skin me alive fer doin' it. Then he'd figure how the fire started and beat me dead, maybe."

For the first time but not the last I felt sorry for Eddie, squatting there in the little clearing. His chin was resting on his chest and large tears were streaming down his filthy cheeks.

I'm sure right then he felt like it might be his last day on earth and the next words out of John's mouth didn't help anything.

"We oughta feed him to them gators," he said.

Jesse shook his head. "The boy done told what's true. He gonna tell truth to his Pa. Then this'll be done." He paused and looked Eddie squarely in his eyes. "You gonna tell your Pa ain't you, boy." It wasn't a question and I'm sure Eddie thought his life depended on his reply.

He looked from me to John and then to Jesse. "I will."

Jesse looked at me now. "How 'bout you, boy. You gonna tell what's true?"

I nodded. "I already told my Ma and Pa what I thought happened. They know it weren't you."

Jesse seemed to be satisfied. He glanced up at the sky and searched for the sun. "If'n we push hard, we can be outa here afore too late."

"You ain't goin' to kill me?" Eddie asked.

"No, boy. I ain't meanin' to do you no harm. I'm goin' to leave that up to your Pa. I spect he'll figure out somethin' fittin'."

Then Jesse looked sternly at Eddie. "You best tell all, boy. If'n you don't." He stopped and looked toward John. "If'n you don't." He stopped again but this time put his forefinger to his throat and made a cutting motion across it. "Ain't no tellin' what John might just do."

Eddie seemed to draw inside himself again. "I'll tell true," he whispered.

Jesse eyed Eddie for several more seconds before turning his attention back to John.

"We best be movin' fast. I ain't wantin' to spend no more nights in here," Jesse said.

Eddie moved out of the way and was scooting back toward an old log. He pushed himself off his rear and sat down hard on the log. I moved over and was about to sit down beside him when I saw the snake. It was lying slightly hidden in some foliage under the log, only a foot from Eddie's ankle. I tried to form the words but before I could it struck. Its fangs dug into the meaty part of my friend's right leg, just inches above his ankle. Eddie gave out a shriek, lost his balance and fell away from the snake. I started toward him but a rough hand caught me by the arm and shoved me to the side. I saw John leap toward my terrified friend, his knife out. He grabbed the snake's body with his left hand, jerked it loose from Eddie's leg and, with one slash, cut the serpent's head off before the thing could react.

Jesse was kneeling beside Eddie within seconds, examining the wound. His own knife, much cleaner than John's, was in his right hand. Eddie was writhing on the ground, his face a mask of pain and terror. His wild eyes were fixed on the still writhing body of the snake at the far side of the clearing. His mouth was open but no sounds were coming out. Saliva was running profusely down his chin. In his terror, he was trying to draw away from Jesse. The knife in Jesse's hand, the snake. He was out of his head with fear.

"Be still, boy," Jesse ordered quietly.

But Eddie continued to squirm on the ground, all the while trying to move away from Jesse.

Jesse motioned to John. "Hold the youngun' down."

John knelt and wrapped his strong arms around Eddie. I could tell my friend was trying to scream but only a hollow sound came out of his throat.

Jesse looked at me. "You, boy. Hold his leg still."

I was frozen in place. I heard Jesse speak but I couldn't move. All I could do was watch.

"You, boy. I sayed to hold down thisun's leg. Do it now." Jesse's tone was firm and decisive now as he glared at me.

I focused now on what Jesse was saying and came slowly around to the other side of Eddie, dropped to my knees and caught hold of Eddie's right foot. Jesse had his knee dug into Eddie's left leg. With his left hand he was trying to help me hold Eddie's leg. As small as he was, his fear had made him too strong for the three of us to hold him still. Finally, Jesse nodded to John.

"Make the boy sleep awhile."

John knelt beside Eddie and looked toward Jesse. Clearly, he didn't want to hurt Eddie but Jesse nodded toward my frightened friend. That's when John finally brought his big fist down across Eddie's jaw. Eddie's body collapsed and his eyes closed. The kicking and fighting stopped and Jesse went to work. He cut a notch out of Eddie's leg, bent over and began sucking. After a moment he lifted his head and spit. He repeated the process several more times. Finally, he straightened and tore a strip off the bottom of Eddie's shirt and tied it tight just above the knee.

"We gots to hurry. John, you lead out. Boy, you next. I'll carry this one and follow. We gots to git him to a healer."

John pointed north but Jesse shook his head.

"It's the safest but takes too long. This boy needs outa here quick. That's west."

A frown spread across John's face, but Jesse ignored it and lifted Eddie into his arms.

"West," Jesse repeated. "Towards the sun."

"May not any of us gits out that way. Them Billings be there," John said pointing toward the west.

"We gots to go that way. He ain't got no chance less'n we do." Jesse said quietly and nodded toward the setting sun and Twin Willows where we had last seen the three brothers.

# CHAPTER 23

PAPA WAS SITTING ON a log at the edge of the clearing. From his vantage point he had a clear view of the water access to the swamp and the boats tied along the shore. Anyone trying to leave the swamp by boat would likely tie up here. If they chose to exit somewhere else, he and the men with him would not know it until morning. The damage could all be done by then. Papa didn't like the idea of the brothers and Carter in the swamp with no one to help Jesse and John. If they caught those two, no one would ever find them. Carter and the four brothers would see to that.

There was movement beside him and he glanced up to see Frazier who had been squatting against an old oak. Walt stretched, spit a wad of tobacco juice in the direction of the swamp, then turned his back and wandered off into the thicket. Papa watched him go, saw him step over a downed log in the distance, then turned his attention back to the swamp. His gaze had just settled on the boats when he heard Walt's voice.

When he turned, Walt was down on one knee. Papa's first thought was that he had stumbled onto a snake. He jumped up and started in that direction but before he was halfway to the man he realized it was something else. Frazier was bent over studying something on the ground. The man reached down and picked up an object and held it close up to his face. When Papa arrived, he offered it to him.

"A knife. Looks almost new," Frazier said

Papa was already studying the area closely, paying little attention to what Walt held out toward him. The tracks of several horses were evident and it looked as if there had been a scuffle. Some of the taller, more brittle weeds were broken and the grass was bent over. Papa took notice now of the small knife Frazier placed in his hand.

"Found it here. Looks like maybe someone was rollin' on the ground and it fell out of their pocket."

Papa stared down with disbelieving eyes at the knife. It looked just like the one he bought at Carter's store just a few weeks earlier. He stared at it for several seconds then turned it over in his hand. The letters JEP, scratched into the black handle, leaped out at him. He opened the large blade, then the small one. No rust. The blades were still as shiny as the day he had bought it for James.

"You know this knife, Preacher?"

Papa dropped to one knee and studied the tracks carefully. When he was satisfied they were fresh, he got to his feet and stared toward the swamp, dropping the knife into his pocket as he did.

"It's my boy's knife."

Walt whistled low. "What you figger happened?" Walt stopped a moment then whistled again. "You ain't thinkin' your James done come afoul of them Billings?"

Papa didn't answer. He was striding toward the swamp, his long legs eating up the ground in great gulps.

By the time Frazier caught up to him, he was untying his bedroll from Satan's rear flanks, causing the big horse to stir.

"Whoa, boy. Stand easy." Papa patted Satan on his rump and flipped the bedroll on the ground.

"I'll be needin' your shotgun and a box of shells, Walt."

"You ain't aimin' to take off into them swamps this time of day," Walt protested.

Papa turned to Sam and Ezra. "I'd be much obliged if you men would help me dip out one of these boats."

"Now, be reasonable, Preacher," Frazier argued. Out of the corner of his eye he saw Ezra and Sam start across the clearing to where the boats were tied. "Ain't nothin' you can do this late. You said yourself that you ain't never been in the swamp. They's gators and all manners of wild critters out there. You ain't likely to come out if'n you go in there alone."

Papa turned and looked at the man. "You think they'll let James live after he sees what they've done?" He picked up the bedroll and looked at Walt. "Do I get the gun?"

"Your boy may be to home," Walt persisted.

"And if he isn't, then it may be too late. I'll lose the daylight. Do I get the gun, Walt?"

There was a pause while the two men stared at each other. Finally, Walt sighed and handed the gun to Papa. "I got some shells in my saddle bags. Ain't many." He lifted the flap on the brown leather bags and fished around for a moment. He brought out a handful of shells, reached in again and brought out two more. "All I got, Preacher."

"That'll do. I'm much obliged."

Sam touched Papa on the shoulder. He had left Ezra to finish dipping out the boat. "I'll be goin' in with you, Preacher."

He had broken his own double barrel shotgun in two and was inserting shells into the chamber as he talked.

"I'm thankin' you for the gesture, Sam. But, I'm sayin' no. You got a wife and four kids and I'll not be responsible for makin' a widow out of your Martha."

The three men were moving across the clearing toward the boats. Walt had picked up Papa's bedroll and it was draped across his right shoulder.

"You ain't got no chance against all them alone," Sam argued.

"I won't be alone. Jesse and John are out there. And then there's the Lord. He'll be with me all the way."

Walt and Sam could only look at each other and shake their heads. Papa glanced at them and smiled as he stopped next to the boat where Ezra had just finished dipping out the water. He stuck his hand toward Ezra, and the man stared at Papa for several seconds before grasping it. "I thank you, Ezra."

Papa stepped into the boat, took the bedroll from Walt, and laid it on the back seat. Then he picked up the bedroll and tossed it to Walt. "I'm thinking I won't need this after all. If you'll be so good brother Frazier to strap it back on Satan, I'd appreciate it." With that he propped the shotgun against the front boat seat and sat down on the middle seat.

"Ain't no way we can change your mind, Preacher?"

Papa shook his head in Sam's direction. "If you men will kindly give me a shove."

They watched him for some time as he moved smoothly across the water until he finally disappeared among the shadows of the cypress thicket on the far side of the narrow stretch of water.

~ ~ ~

John knew we would arrive at Twin Willows before dark. Soon after we started, he told Jesse that it was his guess that Billings and his bunch would probably set up camp at the clearing. It was one of only a few places that a person would feel halfway safe in the swamp at night. He argued that we should swing out and go well around the clearing, but Jesse only grunted and nodded straight ahead. He knew that Eddie's best chance to live was to get out of the swamp as fast as possible. Twin Willows was the straightest and fastest way out. They would decide what to do if and when they came upon Carter and the brothers. John didn't like it but he reluctantly consented. He was still leading the way through the thick underbrush, making a trail for the rest of us as he went. For all his tough talk, I was slowly learning what kind of man John was. Several times he glanced over his shoulder to inquire about Eddie and I heard the concern in his voice. I was following close behind John but not so close that I would cause him to stumble. Once, when he got careless and a limb sprang back in my face, he glanced back and grunted an apology.

We had been moving at a steady pace for about an hour when I heard Jesse clear his throat. I looked back in time to see him spit out a mouthful of blood.

"Rotten tooth. Been botherin' me fer a time."

That was all he said and I never thought about it again.

~ ~ ~

Amos heard the two men coming when they were still several hundred yards away. Carter's high-pitched voice carried through the swamp like the wail of a bobcat. Amos let out a low curse under his breath and strained his eyes toward the sounds. By the time they broke into the clearing, he was boiling mad.

"You have any luck?" Carter growled when he saw Amos moving toward them. The storekeeper was unprepared for the heavy hand that suddenly smashed into his cheek. He stumbled backward into a surprised Jim, his rifle falling harmlessly to the ground beside him. A warm taste of blood flowed down the inside of his mouth and nausea swept over him as he tried to right himself and pull his unsteady legs together under him. He glanced at the gun but quickly thought better of it. Instead, he wiped at the blood that was beginning to flow out of the left corner of his mouth. His expression changed from one of bewilderment and anger to hurt.

"What'd you do that for, Amos?" Floyd howled.

"You ain't got the brains of a ninny, storekeeper." Amos looked to Jim now. "You ain't got no smarts either, boy. How you think you and this...." For lack of words, Amos waved his arm wildly toward Floyd. "How you think we're gonna find that nigger if'n you go prancin' through the swamp announcin' you're a comin'?"

Jim started to speak but Amos cut him off.

"Keep shut. I ain't anxious to hear none of your smart back talk. I got me enough misery with yer idgit brother."

With that Amos turned and stalked away toward the small pond.

"How I ever got borned into a family of idjits. Ain't got sense enough," and he looked toward Alf now. He was sitting on the ground grinning and taking in the whole episode, happy that Amos was taking out his anger on someone besides him. Mud was still caked to his upper body. Amos continued his tirade now in Alf's direction. "Ain't got sense enough to change their long johns when they mess them up." The smile disappeared from Alf's face as Amos continued his tirade. "One's a half wit and the other two is just plain stupid." He was muttering something about stupid storekeepers as he began unbuttoning the straps of his overalls. A moment later he dropped the shoulder straps and disappeared into the underbrush, pulling his overalls down as he went.

~ ~ ~

Papa was pulling hard on the single oar. The little boat glided soundlessly between the cypress trees as he moved deeper into the gathering darkness. Since entering the swamp he felt as if he was entering another world, one so peaceful and quiet that he wanted to hold his breath to keep from disturbing nature's handiwork. It seemed his very breathing might upset a delicate balance, a balance God had set on a knife's thin edge. And, yet, as he viewed the beauty around him, his common sense told him that the place was filled with death, his own if he was not careful. And, he thought, his son's if he could not find him. Maybe it was too late already. And maybe, he thought, James wasn't even in here. Maybe what he had read into the finding of the knife wasn't what he feared at all. And yet his instinct told him James was too protective of his prized possession to lose it in a playful scuffle. His son had somehow found himself in this swamp. And he was still alive. Of that he was sure. James was alive and he would find him.

The sight of the snake draped from an overhanging limb some twenty feet to his right caused reality to set in quickly. The hair on the back of his neck seemed to be standing erect and the palms of his hands were uncommonly damp. Still, he focused on what had brought him here and pulled deeper into the swamp, not quite sure where he was going, only that he had to get there as soon as possible. He knew that finding the Billings clan before they did something to James was remote. Even finding Jesse or John would be a problem. And, he thought, once he found his son, finding his way out of the swamp would be a challenge.

Half an hour after he lost sight of Walt and Sam, he noticed the cypress trees were getting thicker. The water here was only a couple of feet deep; and more than once he was forced to get out of the boat and lift it over the shallow parts into deeper water. For several minutes something had been bothering him, something he should remember. But he couldn't put his finger on it. Something was wrong. He shaded his eyes as the late evening sun slipped between some branches and touched the left side of his face. It was then it hit him. Swampers had told him years before that the main body of land was due east when you entered the swamp from where he had. He lifted his hand and looked to his left. He was moving north. How long had he been moving north?

Papa turned his head and his eyes searched to the right, toward the east. Water, cypress and low hanging branches were all he could see. No land, nothing but water was visible.

He dipped the paddle into the water on the left side and the boat slid around until he knew the sun was behind him. He couldn't have come too far to the north. This time he would keep the sun behind him. At least he would until he could no longer see it. If he didn't find the big island, as the swampers called it.... Well, he would just have to wait and see. And do a lot of praying, he decided.

# CHAPTER 24

WE COULD HEAR THEM arguing and yelling between themselves at least ten minutes before we could see them or smell their campfire. Through the brush, perhaps three hundred feet away, we squatted and watched until we were sure all five men were accounted for.

"Best we move north a ways and slip around them," Jesse whispered. Eddie was on the ground in front of Jesse, and when I looked down at my friend I could see the fever in his glazed eyes. But there was something else. Fear. Eddie was convinced he was dying. And I think he knew right then that Jesse was his only chance to live.

Jesse lifted Eddie again and nodded to John.

"You want I should tote him a mite?" John offered.

Jesse shook his head. He seemed determined to carry my friend until either Eddie died or he collapsed.

I saw John shake his head in a gesture that I took to mean that we would never make it in time. Jesse interpreted it the same.

"He ain't gonna die," Jesse said firmly but quietly. "Now move, John. Times a wastin'."

And move we did. We went north for maybe ten minutes circling the Billings camp. All the while darkness was beginning to set in. After that first few minutes we turned west again, the camp of Amos Billings and his pack out of sight to our left. It wasn't long before their voices began to fade just as the light was doing. John was still leading, and I was following just a few feet behind when we came to a dead tree that had fallen months, maybe years before. John stopped for a moment, put his hands on the top and vaulted over. The top of the trunk struck me just about head high, but there was a small crawl space underneath. I was about to crawl under when the vision of the snake that struck Eddie came vividly back into my mind. I decided to go over the top as John had. A branch shoulder high to my left and another protruding out on top of the fallen tree seemed ideal to pull up on. I grabbed one then the other and jerked myself upward. The darkness was on us now, and I could just barely see John's face over the trunk as I strained to gain the top. There was a crack and all of a sudden the branch in my right hand broke. My left hand was no longer firmly grasping the other branch and I found myself falling. Even though my instinct told me I shouldn't, I yelled.

When Jesse's hand reached down and touched my shoulder, I drew back in fear and would have yelled again if not for the strong hand that moved quickly over my mouth.

"Hush, boy. You hear. I say hush."

John had vaulted back to my side of the log and was kneeling beside me. Jesse took his hand from my mouth and held it up in the gathering darkness and we listened. A moment before there had been no sound of talking. Still we heard nothing, only the sounds of the swamp. Then we heard a voice from a long way off.

"You hear that, Amos. It was one of them brats." The unmistakable voice of Alf made a chill run the length of my spine. But it wasn't Amos that answered Alf.

"One of who? Ain't nobody out here but that black house burner." Again the voice was unmistakable. It was the slightly northern twang of Eddie's father that reverberated back across the swamp.

I looked down at Eddie; but if he recognized his father's voice, he gave no indication. The poison had him in a daze. His body was trembling and his eyes were glazed and unseeing. I thought right then that he would never make it out of the swamp alive.

"Shut up, the both of you. Keep shut and listen."

My whole body trembled as Amos' voice cut across the swamp. For some reason the older Billings scared me more than Alf. Maybe he was crazy too. Maybe all of them were.

For several minutes we knelt there beside the old tree. The longer we listened to the silence, the calmer I became. Maybe they had settled back down in their camp and decided that what they heard was some wild animal. I hoped so. We were about to start moving again when we saw the glow from their torches.

"They comin'," John whispered. "We gots to go."

Jesse reached across and grabbed John's arm.

"Ain't no way I can keep up and tote the boy. They'll catch us sure." Jesse was shaking his head; and as I looked into his eyes, they seemed to have the same glazed look that I could see in Eddie's eyes. I attributed it to the semi-darkness.

The silence seemed to last forever between the two men who had our lives in their hands. Then John spoke.

"I'll lead them a chase and give you time to make for your boat. You get these two younguns outa here."

I'm not sure why to this day, but my hand reached out and touched John's arm. "I'm going with you. I can help lead them away."

John's mouth started to open but I shook my head. "Ain't no use arguin'. Ain't no way you can keep me from followin' after you," I said firmly.

"Be dangerous, boy," Jesse said quietly.

I could barely see Eddie's face now but I knew he wasn't long for this world if he didn't get help soon and I figured Jesse could move faster without me trailing along behind him.

"If it'll help you and Eddie get away, I want to do it."

Jesse looked at John and nodded. "Ain't no time for discussin'. We best go while there's still time. Two of you can move fast. You knows the way out, John?"

John only nodded. Then without another word, he got to his feet, put his strong hands on my waist and lifted me onto the tree trunk. I dropped to the other side and in a moment John was over and by my side.

He took a last look at Jesse. "Be careful, brother." They clasped hands across the tree and nodded to each other.

Then John touched my shoulder. "We best go, James. Stays close behind me and don't talk. We'll go a ways and make a racket to draw them away from Jesse and the boy."

It was the first time he had called me by name. I wasn't even sure he knew it until now. John took one last look at his friend kneeling across the downed tree. "Best you wait till we gets a ways off. When you hear our racket, make for the boat." With that, John turned and we moved off away from Jesse and Eddie.

~ ~ ~

When he was satisfied we were well on our way, Jesse picked Eddie up and slipped quietly back into a thicket where he placed his hand over Eddie's mouth. There he crouched and listened.

It was only minutes before he saw the first one. In the light from the torch he recognized Carter, then one of the Billings. From the glow of their torches he could make out where all five men were. Carefully and gently, he pressed his hand to Eddie's mouth and held it firmly.

The boy was burning up with fever. He didn't have long and even if he got him to a doctor he might not make it. The five men were moving straight toward him, not more than fifty feet away.

It was then that he heard the sounds. To the men stalking him, it must have sounded like some large animal crashing through the underbrush. But Jesse knew what it was. John had found a limber sapling among a group of larger trees, and had pulled it over and let it spring back and forth. It did the trick. The torches, which had been moving directly toward Jesse and Eddie, started moving at a right angle to them now. All five were following the sounds, sure that they were hot on Jesse's trail.

~ ~ ~

John started moving west again with me close on his heels. Every few minutes we would stop and make sure the torches were visible in the distance. Then John would make some noise to keep them on our trail.

About half an hour after we left Jesse, we stopped for the third time. The glow of the torches was farther away now, and they seemed to be motionless. John put his hand on my shoulder and pulled me to the ground beside him.

"Let's rest a spell and listen."

~ ~ ~

Amos had stopped in a small clearing a few moments before. He was holding the torch high above his head and straining his eyes in the darkness. Something was wrong. The hairs on the back of his neck were stiff and his senses told him something was amiss.

Pete had come up beside him and, like Amos, was peering into the darkness as if he expected to see Jesse or one of the boys go running by. "What's wrong, Amos?"

"I got me a bad feelin." Amos glanced across the clearing to where Floyd was squatting out of earshot. "What if them boys done latched on to that nigger, Jesse? They could be outa the swamp while we out here chasin' shadows. If that be the case we could find law waitin' fer us when we leave the swamp." Amos paused. "You take Alf and backtrack to where we done left the boat. If'n you catch them slit their throat and dump them in the quicksand. All of them including that big nigger. You understand? We ain't playin' around no more. You hear what I say?"

Pete nodded and glanced toward Floyd. "What about him?"

"Don't you worry none. I'll take care of him if need be."

"Suppose we don't catch up to nobody?"

"Then meet us back at that place where the willows be come mornin'."

Pete nodded and turned to Alf. "Alf, we gonna backtrack and be sure that Jesse feller ain't got behind us.

"Aw, Pete, I...."

Alf stopped in mid-sentence when Amos's head shot around

toward him. He knew better than to say anymore so he just nodded and dropped his gaze.

"Be gone, the both of you," Amos growled.

# CHAPTER 25

JESSE WASN'T SURE HOW long it had been since he had last seen the glow from the torches. He estimated that he was still at least an hour from getting the boy out of the swamp. For some reason he was having a difficult time with his eyes adjusting to the darkness. Normally that wasn't a problem but tonight it was and he had to pick his way slowly through the swamp. Luck had been with him so far and his instinct had allowed him to make the right moves. But there was still a good distance to go. He knew the boat couldn't be more than a half-mile ahead. The quicksand trap he passed only a few minutes earlier was the same one he had encountered the day before and it was close to where he left the boat. He was feeling somewhat better even though the dry tightness in his throat was beginning to bother him more. In a short time he was confident they would be safe in the boat. His confidence was short-lived with the first sound of voices somewhere behind him.

~ ~ ~

Pete and Alf were making good time, cutting south across the swamp to where they estimated the boat to be. Alf had been grumbling most of the way. He was unhappy about being left out of what he was sure would be the hanging of Jesse. It angered him that Amos treated him so badly and he had been bending Pete's ear ever since they had gotten out of Amos' earshot. It was this grumbling that Jesse heard as he paused in the clearing not far from where the boat was hidden. From the sounds they were only a short distance behind him, close to the quicksand he had just passed a few minutes before.

The two brothers were moving across what at first seemed in the semi-darkness to be a large grassy area. Alf's confused mind told him they were on a fruitless chase. Jesse was somewhere behind them. Possibly Amos had caught up to him by now and he was swinging from some tree limb. With all of Alf's raving, Pete was just a little disappointed himself at the prospect of missing the hanging. But what they were about was more important.

In the swamp a man's mind is allowed only a moment of wandering and in some cases that moment could be one too many. This turned out to be that moment. As they broke into the small clearing they took no notice of its nature. If they had studied it properly it would have looked like a large area of firm, dry land. It was neither firm nor dry and neither man noticed it. Pete was five feet out and up to his knees in the quicksand before he could react. The torch he had been holding was now laying flat on the surface of the bog several feet in front of him. The dampness of the quicksand had quickly extinguished the flame. Only Alf's torch shed light on the predicament Pete had blundered into.

"Alf," Pete sputtered as he began to flail about. "Quick, take my hand! Pull me out!"

Pete was thrashing wildly in the bog reaching toward Alf while his brother looked on with a half smile on his face. It was a sight, Alf thought. It was his turn to enjoy the panic of someone besides himself. Still, it was Pete. After a moment of enjoying his brother's plight he reached as far as he could. But in his hesitation, Pete had slipped a little farther down into the slimy mess. Their hands wouldn't reach. For a second their fingertips touched but Alf almost lost his balance. He dropped to his knees, then flat on his stomach and tested the ground before he reached for Pete again. The smaller man was almost waist deep. But he seemed to be sinking more slowly now.

"Hold on, Pete. Hold on." Alf's eyes searched as far as his torch would let him and they finally fell on a limb on the other side of the quicksand. "There's a limb over there. I'll fetch it and pull you out."

"Hurry, Alf! I'm sinkin' fast! Hurry!" Pete was breathless now and his eyes were filled with terror in the light of Alf's torch.

The limb was about three feet long and, in testing it, Alf found that it was strong enough. By the time he got back to Pete, the little man was up to his chest in the muck and his voice was gone. All he could do was gasp and wave his arms wildly toward his brother.

Alf pushed the stick out to Pete and he grabbed hold and held on for dear life. For a moment it seemed the quicksand would not let go its hold. Then, slowly, Pete's body began to rise out of the slime. He came up to his waist; then slowly his legs began to appear. The terror-stricken eyes of a few moments before began to change and a silly grin appeared on his face. In another foot or so he would be able to reach solid ground and pull himself out. Then all of a sudden the grin on Pete's face disappeared as his eyes focused on something that had suddenly appeared behind his brother. Alf was unaware of the monster that had moved silently up behind him. But Pete saw him. He saw his only hope about to disappear and he jerked hard on the limb. But he still couldn't reach solid ground.

"Pull, Alf! Pull!" He shouted.

At that moment Alf heard it. The roar was unmistakable and when Alf turned and looked up into the eyes of the bear no more than an arm's length away it paralyzed him. Standing on its hind legs, the animal stood nearly two feet taller than Alf. Its front paws were raised and reaching out to embrace him. He was no longer concerned with Pete. Alf let go of the limb. His only thought now was escape. But there was no escape. The powerful, hairy arms of the bear engulfed the big man and pulled him against his chest. As it did the strong jaws crunched into Alf's neck. It brought an agonizing scream that echoed across the night sky.

Pete could only watch in horror as the bear began dragging a screaming, thrashing Alf back away from the bog. Even with blood gushing from the wound in his neck, Alf was still clawing for anything to save him from the inevitable. In less than a minute the sounds of Alf's painful death wails were silenced.

Pete had his own problems now. His hands were groping again for the bank only inches out of his reach. He was sinking again, back to his waist, to his armpits. Saliva was flowing freely down his chin, and his eyes were bugged out in terror as he clawed for a hold. In his subconscious he thought he heard the last crunch from the bear as it continued to tear Alf's lifeless body apart. The quicksand was up to his chin now, getting in his mouth as he tried to cry for help. It was up to his nose, clogging his nostrils, already beginning to suffocate him. The last thing Pete saw was the small frog sitting next to Alf's dying torch. Then he sank out of sight and into his final resting place.

~ ~ ~

Jesse was pulling the boat out of the weeds when he heard the first yell from the direction of the light. A moment later, as he watched, the light got dimmer but didn't go out completely. Less than half a minute later he heard the first scream. Just before the scream he thought he heard that same roar he had heard all those years before with his father. Then came more yelling and screaming and then a scream that sent shivers racing up and down his spine. After that there was nothing but silence and then a few moments later, darkness in the distance. He could only guess at what happened and knew that it couldn't be good for someone.

Eddie was in the boat now. The boy's fever was dangerously high and his leg was swollen twice its size. Mercifully, he was unconscious. Jesse pushed the little boat into the water and climbed in the back. As he did, nausea and dizziness hit him again. It was all he could do to keep his balance. For the last hour it had been getting worse and now he was beginning to feel very weak. He put his problem to the rotten tooth and began pulling as hard as he could on the paddle, aiming the little craft back along the trail of cypress that would take them out of the swamp. As he did, Eddie turned on his side, let out a groan, and fell silent again.

# CHAPTER 26

WE SEEMED TO BE traveling in a circle. Once, when I looked up at the moon through an open patch in the umbrella of trees, it was directly behind us. Fifteen minutes later I discovered it off my right shoulder and then a little later, when we paused to catch our breath, it was in front. I wondered if we were lost. I think John was concerned too because he kept looking up and checking as I did. Still, we were keeping ahead of the Billings and giving Jesse time to get Eddie out of the swamp and to the doctor. John hadn't seemed concerned when we heard Amos order two of his brothers to head back to the boat thinking Jesse might be behind them. He was definitely behind them. But, according to John, the two were too ignorant to catch an old swamp rat like Jesse. I found comfort in John's confidence in Jesse and managed to concern myself with only John's and my safety. That was beginning to become a great concern. If we were lost, how would we ever get away from Amos and his brothers? How would we find our way out of the swamp?

We were slipping through the brush with the moon to our back. It was good that I couldn't see myself. I could only imagine the way I must look, scratched from head to toe, my clothes half-ripped off, and mud caked up past my ankles from the mire we had been forced to wade through. My legs were aching, and more than once I regretted my decision to stay with John. By now, I thought, Jesse and Eddie must be out of the swamp and safe. I could be too if I hadn't gone with John. But when I thought of John, my guilt for the whole episode made me realize my place was here trying to help undo the tragedy Eddie and I had created. My concern returned to

Eddie and whether Jesse would get him out in time to save his life.

"Dear, Jesus," I whispered half out loud. "Protect Eddie and Jesse." As an afterthought I continued. "And please help me and John."

John turned his head and looked down at me, his feet still moving. "What's that, boy?"

Before I could answer it happened. One moment John was moving smoothly along in the darkness, the next the right side of his body seemed to crumple under him. The sharp crack that followed and his cry of anguish sickened me. His body fell backwards, knocking me over like a twig in the path of a giant oak. By the time I regained my balance and crawled over to him, he had pulled his right leg out of a hole and was bent forward with his head pressed against the inside of his right knee. His hands were gripping his ankle as he rocked back and forth moaning quietly.

"What is it, John? What happened?" It was more of a plea than a question. I hoped he would leap to his feet and tell me it was nothing to be worried about. But he didn't. Instead, he continued to rock and moan. He was still holding tightly to the ankle that I now knew must be broken.

Over my left shoulder, I could see the flames from the torches growing closer by the second. Had they heard John's cry?

John was still moaning as he lifted his head and glanced in the direction of our pursuers. He searched the darkness around us. The underbrush was sparse. Not many places to hide.

"Boy," John whispered, "help me to that big cypress." He pointed off to our left about a hundred feet.

"Can you walk?"

"I think I done broke my ankle."

I was shaking as I provided a crutch for John and we hobbled toward the huge tree. The pain must have been unbearable, but John never let out another moan. His concern now was for the torches and the men carrying them. They were drawing nearer by the second. For several minutes we remained motionless and watched. I even found myself holding my breath, afraid that even the sound of my breathing might give us away. After a minute I felt John's grip.

"James, they comin' right at us. They goin' to see us fer sure." He paused a moment to gather his thoughts. "I can't move no more. You ain't strong enough to help me." Again, he paused and I realized the pain was sapping his strength.

"I can lead them away." The sound of my voice and the words coming out of my mouth seemed foreign. Had I really said that?

"No boy, it's too dangerous. They catch you and...." He didn't finish.

"We ain't got no choice, John." I took a deep breath and continued before I lost my nerve. "I can do it," I said quickly. I knew it was now or never. They couldn't be more than three or four minutes away.

"You sure, James?"

"I'm sure, John. I got to. It's our only chance."

John squeezed my arm and with his head he motioned to the big tree he was sitting against. "Come back to this tree as soon as you can get rid of them. Remember, James, the big Cypress tree. When you done gone a ways, call out Jesse's name like he done left you behind. It'll pull them away from here. And you take care. You hear me? Don't take no chances."

"How will I find my way back?"

John studied for a few seconds. "Light out that aways. Keep the moon off your left shoulder. Hide out there somewhere and let them pass you by. When you starts back, keep the moon to your right and watch for this big tree. Now, go." John gripped my arm harder. "You good, James. You knows that. You good."

He released his grip and I stood up. Then, I turned and, crouching low, moved off with the moon off my left shoulder.

~ ~ ~

Jesse was just a hundred feet from the shore. Somewhere in the distance, it seemed miles away, he could hear voices. With his blurred vision, he could make out lights. But he couldn't concentrate. It seemed as if his head was about to explode. His entire body ached like he had not known since pneumonia had nearly taken his life ten years ago. If not for his strength he would have died then. The boat was barely moving now. Every dip of the paddle was painful. Somewhere, he imagined that he heard Granny Ruby shout his name. That couldn't be. Then he felt the boat scrape bottom. Hands were pulling at him, trying to lift him from the boat. But he fought them. The boy needed a doctor. Why couldn't they just leave him alone and let him get the boy to a doctor? Through his swimming eyes he saw more hands and arms, strange shapes lift Eddie from the boat.

"Snake. Bit him on the leg. Got to get the boy to a healer," Jesse managed to get out.

He struggled to get to Eddie but all the hands were too much for him.

"We got the doctor here, Jesse. That boy's gonna get all the help he needs. But what got you all fevered up?"

Jesse felt a hand pressing against his forehead and recognized Granny's voice. For the first time in hours he let his body go limp, but as he did the nausea and weakness overwhelmed him. Everything was swimming.

"Don't know," he managed. "Been ailin' fer an hour or so."

Doc Smith took Granny's place beside Jesse now and pressed his large leathery hand against the black man's forehead. "What got hold of you, Jesse?" The old doctor paused and rubbed his hand gently over Jesse's feverish brow. The blood caked on Jesse's lips and chin told their own story. He knew then. "I think he's been poisoned. Jesse, did you suck the venom out of Eddie's leg?"

Jesse could hardly hold his head up now. It was waving like grass in a strong wind.

"Jesse, did you suck out the poison?" The doctor asked again.

He could barely open his mouth. "Reckon I did."

Doctor Smith took hold of Jesse's chin, forced his mouth open and turned his head to the light from a torch.

"There's blood in his mouth too."

"He done been fussin' bout a bad tooth fer a long time," Granny Ruby offered.

"Merciful heavens," the doctor said. "Some of the venom must have gotten into his blood stream."

The doctor stood up solemnly.

"Load both of them into the wagon. We must get them to my office as soon as possible."

As he turned, his eyes caught Mama's. She had been there since shortly after dark. Mr. Frazier had left soon after Papa to report that Papa had gone into the swamp looking for me. Mama, Mrs. Carter, and Doctor Smith had returned with Walt to wait out the vigil. Granny Ruby and most of the shantytown were there by the time Walt got back with the other three.

The doctor rested his hand on Mama's shoulder. "There's no time to question him now. Likely, he wouldn't be able to tell us anything in his condition."

Mama nodded.

"Will you come back with me? There's nothing you can do here right now and I'll be needing help with these two," he said, pointing toward the wagon where Jesse and Eddie were now resting.

Mama nodded toward Mrs. Carter. "What about Sarah?"

Doctor Smith shook his head. "She'll not be able to help, not the state she's in. I know you're concerned about your family, but I do need your help. Will you come with me?"

Mama nodded, took one last look toward the swamp and followed the doctor to the wagon. Mrs. Carter and Granny Ruby were already in the back with Jesse and Eddie.

~ ~ ~

I had been slipping quietly through the underbrush for several minutes, careful to keep the moon riveted to my left shoulder. Several times I stopped and searched the darkness for the tree where John was. The last time I hadn't been able to distinguish it from the others and it scared me. Still, I knew our only chance was to lead them off in another direction. I might have gone further if it hadn't been for the roar. Somewhere, not too far away, some animal had let out a tremendous cry. The sound could have been from an alligator but I wasn't sure. I froze in my tracks, not moving for perhaps half a minute. The thing was somewhere in front of me and I wasn't anxious to get any closer. I took a deep breath and decided it was here that I had to do what needed to be done. I opened my mouth, hoping there was still strength in my voice. I had to make it convincing.

"Jesse, Jesse, don't leave me! I don't know how to get back to the boat." The sound of my shouts over the sounds of the swamp terrified me. I hoped my voice was strong enough to carry to the brothers and Mr. Carter and turn them away from John.

Now, I waited straining to hear and see through the dense swamp. If they had discovered John, there would have been a commotion. So far the only thing I could hear were the normal night sounds around me. The loud roar of a few minutes earlier had not been repeated.

I settled in the brush straining to hear and see the torches I expected to be heading my way. The hand that came from nowhere and closed on my mouth and the arm that wrapped around my chest caused my entire body to convulse. I wanted to scream but the strong hand that clamped over my mouth wouldn't allow it. For a moment I think my heart stopped completely and I went limp. I was caught. I was about to die.

"Be quiet, James." My heart skipped a beat. I couldn't believe my own ears. It was Papa.

~ ~ ~

"That was a kid," Carter said. The three men had been sighting in on a big cypress and were nearly there when they heard the shout.

"Sure sounded like it," Jim agreed.

Amos didn't answer. If they found those kids alive, he might just have to do away with the storekeeper along with both kids. He hated to lose the extra money. But some was better than none.

"What's a kid doin' out here?" Floyd asked.

"Ain't no never mind to me what he's about out here. The yell came from over that direction." Amos was pointing to the right of their path, away from the huge cypress they were closing in on.

"I'm wantin' to know what some darn fool youngun is doin' out here in the swamp this time of night," Floyd insisted as he stared into the darkness.

"So shut the yappin', and lead out. We'll soon know." Amos growled and gave Floyd a shove.

Floyd moved off in the lead this time. Amos wanted to keep the storekeeper in front of him now. Whatever might happen when they caught up with the kids, he wanted to be sure he had the drop on Carter. Floyd had made only a few steps when he tripped and went sprawling on his stomach, his torch flying one way and the rifle the other. He came up cursing.

"What's the matter with you, fool?" Amos spat.

"Hole," Floyd grunted. "Hole big enough to swallow a man." He had regained his feet, picked up his torch and was holding it over the two-foot deep hole.

Amos spit a mouthful of juice toward the hole and glared at Floyd.

"You aimin to catch that dirty nigger?" Amos grunted.

"I'm goin' to catch up to him and hang him."

"From the sound of that brat, the nigger done started back for the boat."

Floyd looked from Amos to Jim and back to Amos. He still wanted to know why some kid was out here in the swamp. But it wasn't his business so he nodded and pointed away from where they had been heading.

"Then we best be headin' back to the boat."

Amos pointed with his rifle. "Them boats is this way." He started out without waiting for Floyd or Jim.

"What about the kid?" Jim asked.

"Let the gators have him." Amos threw back over his shoulder as he turned away from the tree John had crawled behind only moments earlier.

~ ~ ~

Papa unclamped his hand from my mouth when he was sure I would not cry out. When he did, I turned and buried my head in his chest, sobbing quietly in the darkness. For the first time in hours I felt safe. Even here in the swamp with Papa, I felt safe. As my self-control returned, I turned and through my tear-blurred eyes, I watched with Papa as the glow from the torches slowly began to move away from us until it finally, along with the boisterous talk, disappeared.

With his strong arm, Papa turned me and started leading me through the swamp. But I knew that we were not moving toward John and I pulled him to a stop.

"No, Papa. No. We can't leave John. He's hurt. He can't walk." I hoped my voice hadn't carried too far and aroused the Billings bunch.

Papa stopped, dropped to one knee and took my shoulders firmly in both hands.

"Where is John?"

I looked over my right shoulder, then my left, then to the moon. I turned and put it on my right shoulder and pointed.

"He's back there. Next to a big cypress. He stepped in a hole and, maybe, broke his leg."

"Show me, James," Papa said quietly. "And keep your voice low."

I nodded and started off with the moon to my right shoulder. It seemed like we walked forever before I finally recognized the tree framed in the moonlight. I was beginning to wonder if I had gotten myself turned around when I finally saw it looming above the rest of the trees. Throwing caution to the wind, I broke in front of Papa and sprinted toward it. I prayed that John was still hidden under it.

"John," I called quietly, straining my eyes to pick out the man in the darkness.

"I'm here, James. I'm here."

I'm not sure why but when I finally made him out still resting against the tree, I dropped to my knees and threw my arms around him. John wrapped his arms around me and we shared a moment that I will never forget. In so short a time we had developed a bond that would never die.

"John, I've brought help. I've brought my papa."

"You did right good, James. You done saved my life. You a brave boy."

A moment later Papa took my shoulders and lifted me up. Then he knelt beside John.

"James said your leg might be broken."

"I done think it is. It hurts powerful bad."

"Can you walk at all if I support you?"

"I'm thinkin' I can."

"I can help, too, Papa," I offered.

"That's all right, James. I think John and I can make it all right. You'll have to lead the way. John can help us with the direction." Papa looked at John and received a nod in return.

"I knows the way, Preacher. You lead out, James. That way," John said, pointing to where the Billings torches had disappeared a few minutes earlier.

Papa took hold of John's right arm and helped him to his feet. In the light of the moon, I could see the pain in John's eyes as he made the effort to rise. I waited until both of them had their balance and they nodded to me. For the first time this night, I thought we would make it.

# CHAPTER 27

AMOS HAD BEEN LEADING for the last half hour. The three men were working their way through the dense underbrush, across several shallow streams and were about to cross a clearing a short distance from where Amos knew the boat would be when he stopped short and held the torch out in front of him. Slowly, he passed it back and forth across his body as his eyes searched the surrounding darkness.

Jim came up next to his brother. "Whatsa matter?"

"Seen this place afore," Amos grunted. After a minute, he turned his head toward Jim.

"You see a stick anywheres?"

"Hunh?"

"A stick, dummy. Don't you know a stick?"

Jim looked agitated at Amos' words, but he retraced his steps and in half a minute was back with a long piece of crooked limb.

Amos was muttering under his breath, something about quicksand swallowing a person when Jim thrust the limb toward him.

"We gonna lollygag around here all night?" Floyd asked. "This place gives me the fright."

Amos glowered at Floyd. "You want to lead. Jist take right on off. They's a bog out there that I ain't anxious to stumble into. If'n you want to, you jaunt right on out. Then I'll know where the quicksand is and be able to chuck this stick."

Amos grabbed a handful of Floyd's shirt and shoved the man several feet out into the clearing. Floyd caught himself and retreated until he was behind Amos.

Amos let out a loud laugh. "I thought not, you little weasel." He continued to stare at Floyd until the man dropped his eyes.

Amos laughed again.

"Now let's git," he said and spit a stream of tobacco juice on the ground at his feet.

For several minutes they groped their way along through the short grass. Amos remembered the place. He had been through here in the daylight at least twice. If he was right, somewhere close by there was a quicksand pit about half the size of his shack. The place even gave him the shivers and he was seldom afraid. He was maneuvering slowly, holding the light in front of him so that everything close would be illuminated. With the long stick, he kept poking at the ground. He could see the outline of trees in the distance and had just about come to the conclusion that this wasn't the place he remembered when the grass stopped and he saw something familiar. He stopped in his tracks again.

"Jim."

"Yeah." Jim said and moved up next to his brother. He had both his and Amos' rifle tucked under his right arm and a torch in his left.

"Take a gander over there."

Amos was shining his torch just slightly to the left of their path. Some fifteen feet away they could make out what looked to be the stock of a rifle half hidden by the grass.

"Looks to be a gun over to them bushes," Amos said.

"Shore does," Jim agreed.

"Fetch it," Amos said.

Jim lay the two rifles down and slipped through the grass toward the gun. He was holding his torch out in front of him and bending to pick up the rifle when something in the shadows caught his eye. He stopped and moved the torch to his right. What he saw caused him to straighten and let out a dreadful moan. Suddenly, his legs felt like jelly and he could only look back over his shoulder and gasp in Amos' direction. No words would come out of his mouth.

"What's wrong? What's got into you?"

Jim's mouth was open but still no sound was coming out. Amos dropped the stick and covered the short distance to where Jim stood gawking into the darkness. He stopped beside Jim and strained in the semi-darkness to make out what his brother was staring at. The grass had been flattened between the grassless area and what he was trying to make out on the ground. Amos thought gator at first, then, as he moved his own torch back and forth, he realized what it was. The sight almost made him gag.

He was staring at what was left of Alf's face, his brother's eyes wide in fear, blood caked on one side. His throat was half chewed up or torn away and his chest and stomach were laid open. Amos was still several feet away, but he could see the place where his right arm had been ripped from his shoulder. Blood was beginning to dry there, also. It was all he could take and he turned away, nausea sweeping up from his stomach and into his throat. He felt that warm sickly feeling in his mouth and then it gushed forth. For nearly a minute he stood with his hands on his knees and his body heaving violently.

Then as quickly as it started, it stopped. He had no more to give. When the heaving was over, he straightened and looked at Jim. His younger brother was staring at him. His own vomit lay at his feet as he wiped the sickening mess from his mouth. Floyd had come up beside the two of them and saw what they were look-ing at. But, for Floyd, the sensation was not as traumatic and he looked away quickly before he took in the whole scene.

"Where's Pete?" Jim finally whispered.

Amos didn't speak but turned and shined his light back and forth across the path they had been about to cross before they discovered Alf.

"Pete," he called, but his voice was subdued, hollow. It seemed a mile away. He moved forward, careful of his footing and called out again. Only the night sounds of the swamp answered him. He took several more cautious steps and waved the light back and forth again.

Amos moved as close to the quicksand pit as he dared and stood staring down at it. For the first time since they had begun their search for Jesse, his voice seemed weak and pleading.

"Pete, you ain't in there are you? Tell me you ain't, boy!"

Jim and Floyd moved up behind Amos and were searching the pit for some sign. Neither knew what they were looking for. Amos was waving his torch wildly over an area where the grass was not growing. What they were all looking at seemed to be no more than a stretch of barren ground with just a trace of water on the surface.

Amos looked up and called out again. "Pete."

He was about to call again when Floyd tapped him on the shoulder and pointed over to the far side of the quicksand. Half hidden in the grass that outlined the bog, was another rifle and laying on the surface of the quicksand, just a few feet from the far side of the pit, was what remained of a torch. For lack of weight, it had not sunk into the mire. A solitary frog sat on the rifle stock.

"That's Pete's rifle," Jim muttered. An expression of anguish spread across his face. "We gonna die out here. We all gonna die." Jim was shaking as he pronounced their impending doom.

"Shut up, fool. We ain't dyin'."

"We gonna die. We ain't...."

Before Jim could finish, Amos turned and brought the back of his hand down across Jim's cheek, sending the smaller man reeling back several feet into the grass.

"You little puke. You always been a coward. Got too much of yer ma in you."

Amos turned his attention back to Floyd, seemingly waiting for the storekeeper to challenge his authority. But it didn't happen. Floyd knew when to keep his mouth shut, and Amos finally turned away and began working his way around to the other side of the quicksand pit.

Jim was back on his feet now. He was only a few feet from Alf's body when he saw Amos making his way around the pit.

"What about Alf? We ain't gonna leave him here are we?"

Amos never looked back, but his voice carried over his shoulder to where Jim still stood.

"Ain't nothin we can do fer him now. Leave him fer the gators. They'll finish him soon enough."

"But he's our kin, our brother. He needs buryin'."

Amos stopped and looked back across the quicksand pit where his brother still stood. "You want to carry him out, go at it. But when I get to the boat, I'm long gone. You ain't there you can swim fer it."

That was all it took. Jim was around the bog and, along with Floyd, they closed up tight on Amos' heels. The man almost chuckled as he glanced over his shoulder and saw both men scooting along close behind him.

"Floyd ain't the only one with a score to settle now. That nigger done caused both our brothers their lives. He won't see the light of another day," Amos swore.

# CHAPTER 28

I'M NOT SURE HOW long it took for us to find Papa's boat. But it seemed like hours. John was in constant pain but he said very little. Papa had to support him and I led the way with both John and Papa's guidance. When we finally did locate the main body of water, Papa paused and searched the waterline in both directions. He wasn't sure whether the boat was to his right or left. When he finally did decide on a direction, we only traveled a short distance before we found it. Papa helped John in and settled him on the middle seat. I took the front and Papa pushed us off and sat in the back with the paddle.

"You know the way out, Preacher?"

"I think so, John." Papa turned the little boat and put the moon on our right. From its position in the sky, I guessed that daylight couldn't be too far away.

When I looked back at John, the moon was beaming down between the cypress trees and I could see the grimace on his face. I wished he could go to sleep and forget the pain but that wasn't possible. Suddenly, I wondered why I wasn't sleepy. I was wide awake. I was tired but there was no sleep in me.

We glided silently through the trees for a long time. I was beginning to wonder if we were going the right way or if we had made a wrong turn and were heading deeper into the swamp. The thought frightened me and I looked back past John at Papa. In the moonlight I thought I could read concern on his face. Maybe he was thinking the same thing. Maybe he thought we were lost too. I glanced at John. While the pain was still evident, he was searching ahead just as I was. Before I could turn around, I saw his expression change and his arm go up.

"Light over yonder." It was all he said.

I turned. It was there all right. A long way yet. But there was a flicker like a fire. And it wasn't moving. It was off to the right of our path, and I felt us begin to turn as Papa slipped the oar down on the left side and began pulling until the little boat was headed directly for the light. As we neared and began to leave the cypress trees behind, I could hear voices. I froze, unable to breathe, wondering if they were friendly or if we had happened up on the Billings and Mr. Carter. I'm sure Papa and John had the same thoughts. As if we all had the same concern, Papa let off the oars for a few moments and let the little boat drift. He was trying to make out the sounds. Then there was a shout. Someone had spotted us. I didn't recognize the voice, but Papa must have for he began to pull again on the oar and before I knew it we were closing in on the shoreline.

"Git the Preacher's missus. She's back from Doc's and over to the fire."

We were still a ways out when someone else shouted.

"She's a comin."

Mama, I thought. I will see her again. I'm not going to die out here after all.

We were just feet from shore now and bodies were splashing out to us, hands grasping and pulling the little boat toward the bank.

"Who's that with you, Preacher?" It was the first voice I had heard several minutes earlier.

"John and he's hurt his leg. Where's Doc Smith?"

"He's tendin' to Jesse and young Eddie Carter. Both got snake poison."

We were on shore now and some of the men from the shantytown were already at John's side, lifting him from the boat. I could only look for Mama. Finally, I saw her running across the clearing toward us.

"Easy with him, men. I think he's got a busted leg. Better get him to Doc Smith's place as soon as possible," Papa said.

Mama and I met halfway across the clearing, and I buried my face in her shoulder and held on for dear life. Tears were streaming down my cheeks and I could feel dampness in my hair as Mama cried silently and held me close. A moment later I felt Papa come up behind me. Mama let go of me with one arm and pulled him to her. She kissed him and I felt his strong hand on my shoulder, squeezing gently.

"Take the boy home. He's had a long, hard day."

"Efren, Jesse and Eddie are both in a bad way."

"How so?" Papa asked.

"Eddie was bitten by a snake and Jesse sucked out the poison. Jesse had a rotten tooth and the doctor thinks some of the poison got into Jesse's blood stream."

"Doc thinks Eddie will be all right. But he isn't sure about Jesse. He said any other man besides Jesse would never have made it out of the swamp. He carried Eddie all the way. He saved Eddie's life."

I had pulled away from Mama and was listening intently. "I gotta go see Jesse and Eddie," I said.

Papa pointed to the wagon without arguing. "I'll be with both of you in a moment. I need to say a word to these people. Then we'll go and see about them."

Mama put her arm around my shoulder and led me toward the wagon while Papa went over to where the people, black and white, were gathered around the fire.

"Men, the Billings should have come out by now. You've seen no trace of them?"

"None," Mr. Frazier answered.

"Well, they can't be far behind," Papa surmised. "Unless they came out another way when they saw the lot of you waiting here."

"Could be, Preacher."

"Keep an eye out," Papa continued. "And be careful. They'll be dangerous."

"Shore will," Ezra put in.

"Don't try to take them. If you do there'll be killing. Good people will be hurt. When I get to the doctors, I'll send for the law. We'll let them handle Floyd and the Billings."

Frazier stared into Papa's eyes for a moment before replying. "Preacher, what Floyd and them Billings boys are a tryin' to do. Well, we just don't none of us hold with it. Maybe we ain't always been what we shoulda been but," Walt paused and looked toward Ezra and the other men and women from the shantytown, "we goin' to be different from here out and I jist think this is the way we mean to start."

"I agree, Walt. But some of these good men may die."

"Anybody that don't want to stay can leave and no hard feelings," Walt said.

No one spoke, black or white, and no one moved.

Papa sighed. "I'll pray for you." He put a hand on Walt's shoulder. "Now, I must go and pray for Jesse and Eddie."

"God speed, Preacher."

"And you too," Papa said and took in the entire group. "One suggestion. Put out the fire and move back into the trees. Out here you're too good a target."

Walt nodded and Papa turned and walked to the wagon where we waited. Satan was tied to the back and he pulled the knot loose and climbed into the saddle. John was stretched out in the back and one of the women from the shantytown was sitting beside him.

Papa looked at Mama. "Drive easy." He kneed Satan and Mama gave a flick of the reins and the wagon moved out slowly.

~ ~ ~

The boat carrying the two remaining brothers and Carter arrived at the edge of the cypress trees several minutes before we did. They were sitting in the darkness trying to decide just how to continue when they heard our boat, a hundred or so yards to their right, as it slid out of the thicket of trees and headed toward the friendly light. They watched as John was loaded onto the wagon and listened to the conversation Papa had with the group before we left in the wagon. By then they had decided to keep to the shadows and make their way several hundred yards to the south of the trap that was waiting for them. There, they beached the boat and made their way back to where they had left their horses. They fully expected their mounts to be gone. But they were still there, along with half a dozen other horses. One lone man guarded them.

In the light from the moon, Floyd recognized Meecham, his neighbor who lived across the road from where his house had been. He was sitting on a boulder with his back to the three of them. A shotgun was propped against his right leg and the horses were tethered nearby.

Amos took in the situation quickly. He could see movement and make out the forms of several men in the darkness. All were facing away from him toward the swamp. He made a swift decision and lifted the knife from his belt. He had crawled only a foot or so toward Meecham when he felt a hand grab his shoulder and hold him steady.

"I ain't wantin' him hurt none," Floyd whispered. "I'll take care of him with my rifle butt." He held his rifle up and began crawling toward the unsuspecting Meecham.

"This ain't no time to show yellow," Amos whispered back as Floyd crawled past him.

But Floyd only shook his head and continued crawling quietly through the weeds toward where Meecham sat some thirty feet away. Halfway there one of the horses stirred and Floyd plastered himself to the ground, holding his breath as best he could. Meecham got up, searched the surrounding area until he was satisfied, and went to the animal to quiet it. He stood patting the horse for a moment, then went back to his rock and sat back down. Floyd began crawling again. The process was slow but he remained careful, moving only a few feet every half minute. He was close, less than five feet away, when Meecham must have sensed that something was wrong. He turned in time to see the butt of Floyd's gun just before it smashed into his left cheekbone. In his haste to knock the old man out before he could yell, Floyd had used more force than he intended. The sickening crunch, as the rifle butt smashed into the old man's cheekbone, left Floyd shaking. He leaned over the fallen man, examined him quickly. He hadn't delivered a death blow. Meecham would recover. In a moment, Amos and Jim were at the horses. The sound of the blow against Meecham's jaw was as much a giveaway as if the man had cried out.

Amos grabbed himself an animal. Jim was in the middle leading one to Floyd before the men at the edge of the tree line knew where the noise had come from. The sound of the skittish horses alerted them to the direction.

Amos pulled his knife out and cut the ropes that held the other horses. Then he raised his rifle and pulled the trigger twice. The remaining animals scattered into the darkness, some half running down the men that were hurrying toward them. Satisfied that the animals would run for some time, Amos reached down and whacked his horse hard on the rump.

"Let's git," he growled.

In the darkness Amos had been able to hear the men talking about Jesse and knew he was at the doctor's house. He hadn't heard why and didn't care. He reasoned it was a good place to hide and took it for granted that's why Jesse had gone there. He knew too that they would have Papa to contend with. They had seen John loaded into the wagon and watched Papa, Mama, and a black woman ride off together. He was prepared to kill anyone who got in their way now. He would have the nigger. He would have both niggers. They were both responsible for his brothers' deaths. And he figured before the night was over he would also have to kill Carter. And anyone else that got in his way.

~ ~ ~

It was an hour before daylight when we reached the doctor's house. John had finally managed to sleep or maybe he just passed out on the ride in. The woman made him as comfortable as possible,

272

laying his head in her lap and singing softly to soothe him. When we arrived, lantern light was showing through a front window.

Papa slipped from the saddle and hurried to the door. A moment later Mrs. Carter appeared. Papa said something to her that I couldn't hear and she nodded and disappeared.

Seconds passed before Doctor Smith came out. He hurried to the wagon, climbed into the back and quickly examined John's leg.

"Let's get him inside."

Papa nodded, reached down and gently gathered John into his arms. I didn't realize how strong my father was until I saw him carry John into the house.

Doctor Smith led the way through the room he used for a waiting room and motioned to a smaller room on the left that I later found out was his own bedroom. "Bring him in here."

John was awake now and, as Papa laid him on the bed, he reached up and grabbed the doctor's arm.

"I heerd them say somethin' bout Jesse bein sick with the snake poison. What's become of him?"

The doctor looked grave as he took John's grip from his arm and knelt to examine his leg again.

"Rest easy, John. I'm doin' all I can for Jesse."

He tested the break just above the right ankle then straightened and looked at Papa.

"Can I talk to you outside, Reverend?"

Then he looked to John. "I'll be right back. We're gonna have to set that break."

Papa followed the doctor out into the waiting room where he closed the door behind them. Mama and the black woman remained with John. There wasn't much in that waiting room; a very worn and outdated couch, two straight chairs, and an old wooden bench that had seen its best years. One picture graced the far wall across from the front door. It was a picture of a young woman, someone I had never seen. Mama later told me it was the doctor's wife. She had been dead for nearly fifteen years.

Doctor Smith sat down on the couch, and as he did I could see his shoulders sag. His white hair was mussed around the edges as he raked a wrinkled hand through it. It seemed that all the energy in his body was released when he sat down.

"Jesse died just before you arrived."

It was all he said, but it felt like a giant fist had just exploded into my stomach and sapped everything out of me. I don't remember moving but I found myself on the wooden bench with tears in my eyes and a hard knot building in my chest. It was pounding like a drum. I could hear Papa's voice but through the tears I couldn't see him.

"Dear Lord, I've been praying all day that we could prevent something like this from happening."

"I know," the doctor answered. "But he saved Eddie. Another hour and I couldn't have helped him either." The doctor shook his head slowly. "I don't see how he did what he did. Any other man would have been dead before he got the boy half way out of the swamp. Most any other man," the doctor continued, "would have let the boy die. But Jesse wouldn't let go until Eddie was safe. Granny Ruby's gone for his wife. There'll be great mourning in the shantytown for a long time. Jesse was not an ordinary man."

"Greater love hath no man...." Papa whispered.

"What's that?" Doctor Smith said looking toward Papa who had sat down on the bench beside me and draped a strong arm around my shoulders. I looked up and saw dampness in my father's eyes.

"John 15:13," was all Papa said.

Mama had come into the room and stood with her hand on Papa's shoulder. She finished the verse. "Greater love hath no man than this, that a man lay down his life for his friends."

"No greater love," Papa said, "especially when a man lays down his life for someone who has meant him harm."

Tears were streaming down my face now, and Mama came around Papa and sat down beside me on the bench. She put her arms around me and I buried my head in her bosom. I'm not sure how long we sat there but it was a long time.

"Jesse was the kind of man all of us would like to think we could be," Papa said. I knew now what Jesse was and what my silence had done to him.

"It's my fault, Papa," I cried. At that moment I wished the Lord had taken me instead of Jesse. What happened in the next few minutes made me think He might take us all.

Amos pushed the door open and strode in like some great beast about to war on its deadliest enemy. The big rifle he carried moved back and forth as he pointed it first at Papa, then the doctor, over to me and then back at Papa's chest. Floyd and Jim stood on each side of Amos, their guns pointed at no one in particular. But by their demeanor, I knew they were ready to do whatever they thought was needed.

"We want both of them niggers," Amos announced. "They done killed two of my brothers."

"No!" I was on my feet before I realized it. Amos' gun rotated in my direction.

"Brat, you done caused me a heap of trouble. It wouldn't bother me none to blow all your guts onto that wall."

Mama was next to me immediately, her defiance of Amos evident in her every move. "You'll lower that gun, Amos Billings, and get out of this house right now." Her voice was steady and her eyes took in the large man without wavering.

"Woman, I ain't got no hesitation bout blowin' you away."

"Billings," Papa called out as he moved in front of both Mama and me. "Nobody in this house has done you any harm."

Amos turned his attention back to Papa. "Hunh, you call two dead brothers no harm," he growled and raised his rifle, pressing it against Papa's chest. "Now git them two out here before I start shootin'."

Now it was Doctor Smith's time. "Billings," he said quietly, almost too quietly, I thought. "I'll not have you come busting into my home like some wild animal gone mad. You take yourself and...." The doctor looked toward Floyd before continuing. "your friends and get out."

"Old man, I'm gonna say this jist one more time. I want them out here or I'll...."

No one had seen the bedroom door open and close quietly. Eddie's mother was taking in the whole scene and now it was her turn to confront the three men. She ignored Amos and looked directly at her husband.

"Floyd Carter," she said, "I never been so ashamed of a human man as I am of you right now."

"Woman, shut up and git back out of the way," Floyd spat. "We come to git Jesse and the other one and we mean to do it."

"Oh, did you now," Sarah exclaimed. "Well let me tell you something about the man you come to kill." She turned and pointed toward the door behind her. "You got a boy lying in the bed in there. He ain't dyin' and Doc here says he ain't a goin' to. But by all rights he shoulda already been dead. And you want to know why he ain't?

"Shut up, woman," Amos shouted. He had retreated a couple of steps so he could keep an eye on everyone, Floyd included.

"Ain't nobody gonna shut me up, Amos Billings, less'n you aim to shoot me down."

She turned back to Floyd. "You want to know why our Eddie ain't dead? Well, want to or no, I'm meanin' to tell you. A snake bit our Eddie out in them swamps today, a bad snake and Jesse Culbreath, that dirty house burnin' nigger that you called him, sucked out the poison and then toted him for hours through that hell hole where you drove him with your craziness." There were tears in Mrs. Carter's eyes. "He coulda let him die out there. Instead," she paused to gather her thoughts and bite her lower lip. "Instead, he's lyin' in there dead from the poison he sucked out of our Eddie. And let me tell you one more thing that our Eddie just told me. It weren't Jesse that done started that fire over to our house. It was your own kin, our Eddie that started it. He was too scared to tell us the truth because he feared you might beat him to death."

This revelation didn't sway Amos. Jesse and John were still responsible for Alf and Pete's deaths. "Dirty, cheatin' dyin' nigger," Amos growled. "They's still one we can settle accounts with."

Amos started toward the bedroom door.

"Wait!" It was Floyd. "Woman, what are you sayin'?"

Amos stopped and glowered over his shoulder toward Floyd.

"I'm sayin' your boy, our Eddie, was out in the swamp today where these good friends of yours done took him. He was bit by a moccasin and Jesse Culbreath carried him out. He done saved our boy, Floyd. And let me tell you one more little thing that Eddie done told me."

"Eddie was in the swamp. You know that certain."

"Yes. And I know somethin' else." She eyed Amos and his brother. "Them two was about to kill our Eddie and James there. They was goin' to drop them in a quicksand pit. That other black man, John, that you want to kill so bad, helped the boys get away."

Amos was fidgeting now as he looked at Jim. Everything was beginning to get out of hand. This new revelation was news to Jim. He had not been with Amos when all that had taken place and he looked to his older brother for an explanation. He was not about to get it right then.

Floyd turned and glared directly at Amos. "My woman tellin' true?"

Amos gripped his rifle but didn't raise it now. "You gonna listen to sob-sister Carter or you goin' to take care of the business we done come for?"

"You was goin' to kill my boy," Floyd shouted.

"The boy done got in our way," Amos growled. Now he raised the rifle in Floyd's direction.

"That's my boy," Floyd shouted back.

"Makes no never mind to me whose brat he be. We still got us a nigger to take care of," Amos said and started toward the bedroom door.

"No!" Floyd shouted. "No more killin'," he said and leaned his rifle against the wall.

"Suit yourself," Amos said. "But, I ain't through. I got two brothers dead in them swamps."

"I said no more," Floyd shouted and grabbed at Amos' arm. Billings wheeled and brought the barrel of his gun down against

Floyd's head. Carter fell hard against Jim, knocking the younger Billings off balance. It gave Papa just enough time. He crossed the few steps between him and Amos and drove his fist hard into Amos' stomach. For all his size, the blow stunned Amos, throwing him off balance and causing his rifle to clatter to the floor beside Floyd's prone body. Papa knelt quickly, picked up Amos' rifle, and brought it up sharply into his stomach. Amos fell back against the wall and slumped to the floor.

Jim had righted himself by the time he saw his brother collapse in a heap at Papa's feet. His rifle was ready and Papa was in his sights. I'm not sure why he didn't shoot Papa right then. But when their eyes met and he saw the look in my father's eyes, he lowered the gun, bent over and let it drop harmlessly to the floor.

"I'm done," he said and raised his hands above his head.

When it was over and Papa had seen to it that the three men were locked up and guarded in Mr. Meecham's tool shed, he came back to Doctor Smith's house where Mama and I waited.

John had heard everything through the closed door and he knew now about Jesse. The two had been friends since childhood and he wept quietly and unashamedly. When we were about to go, he took my hand and pulled me next to the bed.

"James, you done good out there tonight. Real good." He paused and I could see the redness in his eyes and sensed the tears he was holding back. "You come see me. You hear?"

"I will, John," I answered and hugged his neck.

# EPILOGUE

NOW, HERE I SIT staring out the train window these many years later, wondering if it really happened like I remember. Or have the years dulled my memory? Have I forgotten something? I wonder. My thoughts are interrupted as the conductor comes down the aisle and smiles toward me.

"Your stop in fifteen minutes," he says as he looks at the pocket watch in his right hand.

"Thank you."

The surrounding countryside is much the same as I remember. In the distance I can see the beginnings of the swamp where Eddie and I almost lost our lives and where two black men proved to be the greatest heroes, outside of Papa and Mama, I have ever known. Eddie. Thoughts of him drift through my memory. I received a letter two years ago from one of our boyhood friends, Tommy Watson, he of the bad stomach on that hot July day so many years ago. Tommy wrote me that Eddie had died in a fight up in Memphis. He was drunk and in a place he should not have been. A knife had slit his throat. The person responsible was never caught. I had always hoped that our experience in the swamp would change my friend and it did for a bit. But, Eddie soon reverted to the Eddie of old. We remained friends after the incident, but slowly grew apart as our interests went in different directions. Little Sally, Eddie's sister, still lives in the small community in the little house that the men and women built after the incident. One of my first stops will be to see her. Eddie's mother passed away just a year after Papa. I will never forget her courage and how she saved all of us on that night. As for Floyd and the two remaining brothers, years ago I heard that Floyd and Amos had died in prison. Jim, the remaining brother, was out of prison now and living by himself in the old home place. He was much older and I assumed much less of a threat to anyone. Someday, a ways down the road, I will probably go by to see him. He was a lost soul and even though he had meant harm to those I knew and loved, he needed redemption. I knew that I would make the effort to take the Word to him.

The train is slowing and I can see the buildings in the distance. The new train station, built a few years earlier, is coming into view now. As we come closer, I can see Frazier's Hardware just across the dirt road from the station. On down the street a small grocery store has taken the place of the store that Floyd owned. In front of the train station, sitting on the plank walk, two boys with straw hats are doodling in the dirt with their bare toes. It reminds me of a couple of boys I knew those many years ago. One of them even resembles Eddie.

Somewhere in the distance the conductor is chanting the town's name. My one old suitcase slips easily from the rack above my seat. Except for the boy and his mother, the railroad car is empty. As I pass the two of them, the boy looks up and his eyes study me intently. I smile down at him and nod to his mother as I move past them down the aisle. Since there's only the three of us in the car, and I'm the only one getting off, I'm able to negotiate the aisle quickly.

It's hot and humid outside, just like I remember it. The porter, stationed on the platform just outside the car door, reaches to take my bag but I shake my head.

"I'll be getting off on the other side, Porter."

"Ain't nothin' out there, Parson, cept that old graveyard up on the hill."

"I know."

My eyes are already fixed on the cemetery where Papa and Mama rest. I knew long before the train pulled in that it would be the first place I would go. Then, I would go to the other cemetery, the black one where Jesse had been buried those many years ago.

John and Granny were there now. Granny had died just three years after Jesse. John had been dead now for more than a year. He had died of a relatively new illness, a cancer in his stomach. As I learned from a letter that reached me a short time after his death, he had died slowly and painfully. His death saddened me because of the friendship we had enjoyed during those years before I left the old home place, I thought for good. One of my greatest regrets is that I was unable to return home for his funeral. I reached into my pocket and felt the little knife that Papa had given me all those years ago. A single coin lay next to it and I retrieved it, handed it to the porter and thanked him. Then, I descended the steps and started up the hill. The journey had been long and tiring but I was home again. And maybe like Papa and Mama all those years ago, I will be here until the good Lord calls me to my eternal home. I pray it will be so.

*The End*

Bob Smith grew up in Hot Springs, Arkansas. After graduation from high school, he spent two years at Ouachita Baptist University in Arkadelphia, Arkansas, before joining the Navy. During his time in the Navy he met and married his future wife, Barbara Williams. Upon his discharge from the Navy, he went into the aluminum products business with his father in Hot Springs.

In the early 1980s, Bob sold the business and went back to college at Henderson State University in Arkadelphia, where he received a business degree with a major in accounting. Soon after graduation in 1985, Ouachita Technical College, in Malvern, Arkansas, hired him to teach math and accounting. During those years he commuted to Henderson State in the evenings, where he earned a master's degree in business.

Bob retired from teaching in May 2000. His first book, "The Left Side of Reality," was published in 2013. He and Barbara live in Hot Springs Village, Arkansas, where Bob enjoys golf, writing, and being active in his church. They have two children and six grandchildren. Their son, Greg, and his wife, Sue, live in Fredericksburg, Virginia, and their daughter, Sharon, and her husband, Robert, live in Sherbrooke, Quebec, Canada.